NICK SMITH was born in Bristol, Englai
literary award at the age of 15, he has bee
newspapers and anthologies. His previ
Secrets Unleashed and *Milk Treading*.

Nick is founder and director of the ɪ ᴍᴍ ꜱchool Scotland. Somehow, he's also found the time to work as a film producer, bodyguard, landscape gardener, stand-up comic, musician and actor. He has appeared in TV shows, movies and plays, including stage versions of *Breaker Morant* and *Milk Treading*.

He lives in Charleston, South Carolina, where he works with the city paper and the Actors' Theatre of SC.

.

Kitty Killer Cult

NICK SMITH

Luath Press Limited

EDINBURGH

www.luath.co.uk

First Published 2005

The paper used in this book is recyclable. It is made from low
chlorine pulps produced in a low energy, low emission manner
from renewable forests.

Printed and bound by
Scotprint, Haddington

Typeset in Sabon by
S Fairgrieve, Edinburgh 0131 658 1763

Thanks to Mum and Dad

I

THEY WERE KILLERS, all four of them. Cammy was the worst – one jab of his claws and he'd spear his prey. What his brothers lacked in dexterity they made up for in size and strength. They were efficient and complacent. None of them enjoyed death as much as Cammy.

He'd had a wicked glint in his eye since birth. Part of a litter of five, he'd practised murder on ticks and ants before he could see. After suckling at his mother's belly, he'd cock an ear and listen for the scuttling – slap down a paw and flatten his catch. Not because he was hungry; it was in his blood. Killer instinct.

His brothers were made of kinder stuff. Beast, Grass and Skead had never been malicious. They'd always been poor, so when Cammy had suggested going into the execution business they'd agreed fast enough. They'd ploughed every penny into the tools of the trade – traps, spray, electrified grids, powder – and set up shop. It hadn't taken them long to become the best bug bashers on the block.

Pest control was a dirty, thankless task. Cammy kept them motivated with his zeal. He loved to squash little critters, slice them, impale them, munch them up for supper. He'd remind his brothers they had a mortgage to cover, bills to pay, a sister to support.

Beast never let his squeamish side get in the way of a commission. Some cats get excited when they see a termite, smack their lips, dream of eating the little peckers. They know how good they taste. Beast would get a quiver in his belly, a queasy tremor as he watched the shiny bodies and spindled legs. He was no fan of bugs. If he unearthed a colony, he didn't hesitate to destroy it.

Grass was the crew's philosopher. Like Beast he was quick enough to give his prey the chop. Maybe even take some home for supper. Once they were dead his conscience would pay him a call. He'd start moralising, wondering what right he had to snuff out so many lives – no matter how tiny. Eating them wasn't so bad, that was nature. So Grass was the crew's fat philosopher.

He'd share his worries with Skead, the most money-eager of the pack. Skead would tell his twin to stop blethering and buy something nice with his paycheque. Skead had tall hopes for himself; he was going to buy his way out of Skid Row, spend money in the right places, impress the bigwigs and stake a place in the city. He hadn't shared his dreams with his brothers, but he did admonish them for spending so much of their earnings on paint and wallpaper for their sister's place. Keeping her happy seemed to make *them* happy.

The lads would often work late into the night – the critters they caught thrived in darkness. By the time they got home all they wanted to do was collapse in their beds, look forward to breakfast. They all knew what Grass was having.

One particular evening was spent knocking off rats. A cadre of the little terrors had run riot in a chip shop. The lads had stormed Arnie's Emporium, famous for its fishcakes; they'd battered the rats and carried them out by their tails, a crate-load of slick filthy vermine carried to the local butchers. There the rats had been sold for a small amount, which Skead split into four pittances. He already had plans for his share.

At home they found a package waiting for them. Marlax, a poison in powder form and lots of it. None of the brothers could remember ordering the stock. Grass shrugged, promising he'd deal with it in the morning.

Exhausted, they hit the sack. Beast and Grass slept in one room; Cammy and Skead shared another. Come midnight Beast thought he heard a stifled moan. He was about to get up, investigate, when a paw clamped over his nose. He opened his mouth to warn his brothers, but no sound came.

Sinking into oblivion, he wondered if his victims felt the same fear, the same sense of disappointment. Of course not. The pests he killed weren't cats. They were plain dumb animals.

2

DOCTOR SELWYN MOPP was worried, a feeling with which he was not familiar. A veteran veterinarian, he enjoyed the respect of his peers and the general public. Even the gutter press treated him kindly, relying on him for comments on wide ranging medical matters. He hadn't worried in his younger days, pioneering radical forms of medicine. He hadn't panicked while treating his patients as they lay on his operating table, fondly referred to by staff as the slab of doom. Cats clamoured to be carved by him; if they lived they'd be able to tell jealous friends they'd been saved by a surgeon named in all the history books.

Now Mopp was getting long in the claw, elderly pushing on for decrepit. In his late teens, his waning years, his paws had started to tremble. His eyes were muddy with myopia, his hearing shot. He was sure that some of his colleagues at the hospital suspected. The administrator for one: a quiet soul with the power to send him packing, get him struck off. Admiration and a place in history would mean nothing if he lost his monthly paycheque. He had a habit to support.

Mopp left the hospital as the sun reached its zenith. Lunch hour. Most cats stretched the time as far as they could, filling their faces and taking a nap, ready to cope with an afternoon's drudge. For the Doctor it provided an opportunity for him to sate his urges.

The high street was two minutes' trot from A & E, a Mecca of cash and carries, jewel stores, covered markets. He aimed for the large arcade at the far end of the street. His eyes swivelled independently, checking out the bargains in shop windows.

It had always amazed him that anyone would let him loose in an operating theatre – if he couldn't control his eyes, how could he be expected to handle a scalpel? Of course he could do his job, but his pupils liked to roll of their own accord. He didn't like to meet patients before operating on them; the eye thing had the potential to scare them off. He saw them (if he had the time) when the general anaesthetic wore off instead. Surgery successful, thank you Doc, you are a god. Is there something wrong with your eyes?

They didn't work all that well anymore, sightwise. He had good days and bad, often having to press his face against the store windows to see displays. That wasn't what worried him so much as the atmosphere in his place of work.

Friends had stopped talking to him, giving him funny looks. He felt self conscious where he would once have felt important. Certain doctors and nurses made sure not to work with him, especially where delicate transplants were involved. He'd dropped a few fresh organs – a heart, maybe a liver or two – but that was no reason for them to snub him. Once the flecks of dirt were brushed off the organs still did their job. He had rivals, frontstabbers who majored in the mongering of rumours. His reputation was too strong to be eroded by gossip no matter how many boobs he made.

The first shop in the arcade sold dangly things. Mopp was well into these, although he quickly tired of each new purchase. They hung in a closet at home, or ended up gift-wrapped for a relation. It was the act of buying the items that gave him the hots – and would get him into scalding water if he lost his position as Chief Surgeon at Nub City Infirmary. The lecture circuit would be fine for the occasional spree, but he needed a regular pay packet to feed his consumer habit.

Good afternoon, my name is Selwyn Mopp. I'm a shopaholic. By the time he'd bought a dangly piece of merchandise and moved on to the second shop, he was running out of time. He didn't need to buy anything; he had all the useful gizmos, clothes and knick-knacks he could ever want. There was no room left in his four-storey house, chock full of trinkets. Nevertheless a purchase made him feel better, beat the waiting room blues. It cheered him up, gave him a sprightly lift... until he reached his credit limit. Then it was cold turkey till pay-day. The salary went into his account on a monthly basis; those thirty days could seem like nine lifetimes.

The second store, *Feline Groovy*, sold hippy fare – love beads, incense burners, environmentally-friendly kitty litter. The owner raised his forepaws in dismay as Mopp bumped into a lava lamp.

'Watch out, dude! You break it, you pay for it.' The owner was a longhair colourpoint with pink shades and a tie-dye sweatshirt. He smelled fusty, like he hadn't washed himself in weeks.

There was no way any of the stock could appeal to the doctor. A confirmed meatatarian, he'd never attended a demo, never touched nip. He saw enough of the ill effects the drug could cause in the casualty ward. By the smell of things, the owner was burnt out on the substance.

'What can I get for this?' Mopp asked, scattering his remaining change on the counter.

'Not a lot, effendi. Maybe one o' these.' The hippy produced a sachet of Yummy Chunks with extra yeast. The yeast got some cats so excited that it sent them to the heights of ecstasy; it was frowned on in polite society.

'I'll take it.' The item joined the dangly thing in a flash carrier bag. It was time to go back to work before someone spotted him.

The theatre was booked solid for the next six hours, with invalids already prepped. Although Mopp would have plenty of support it was still his shift, the lives of the patients his responsibility. He would have to maintain his wits and stay away from the high street until the next opportunity presented itself. Late night shopping on Thursday, maybe.

First on the slab of doom was a lardy fellow called Churchouse. Arteries hardened, heart in trouble, ugly as seven shades of sin. Mopp split him open with an intern's fervour, a tape playing the latest hit from crooner Doctor Fat. The heart still beat, taking its time to pump its cargo round Mr Caraher's system. Mopp poked at it, jiggled it about a bit, sewed the guy back together.

'I've done my best with this one,' he explained to the nurse who licked his brow. 'Next!'

Case number two was a lad who'd sewn his ears shut. Apparently no one listened to him. Usually a case for A & E, this cloth-eared youth had left his wounds to fester. Delicate skin had grown around the infected areas, making the doc's task a tricky one. He repaired the damage and neatened up the lobes without causing any loss of hearing. With luck and the chance to heal, the patient's aural faculties would be better than they'd been before the self-abusive act.

Miracle number three involved a punctured lung. Some careless tabby on a crowded tram had stabbed the patient with a long, filthy claw. Fortunately the sheath had remained embedded in the chest, preventing any flooding of the lung. As Mopp fixed the mess he grew tired. His paws quaked and he forgot the names of important surgical instruments. Instead of forceps, he asked for chopsticks.

'Getting hungry, doctor?' asked the anaesthetist. He didn't mean anything by it, yet Mopp took it the wrong way, returning the comment with a glower.

What if I make a mistake? It was what he'd been dreading for months. *My paw could slip, I could forget what I'm doing, where I am. What if I have some terrible brain disease? I'll be scuppered for sure then. Ironic. I'd be the only one qualified to operate on myself round here.* Some days he couldn't remember his own name. Knew it sounded like a household object but that left the field wide open. The cleaners would know.

Mopp saved the patient, patching up the lung with help from an intern. By the time the fourth case was wheeled in, the doctor's sight was blurred. A John Doe had been attacked from behind; some ne'er-do-well had bitten a chunk out of his back. Mopp wanted to rest. He thought about the unnecessary items he'd purchased that day.

I'm a silly old cat. Got no business here, threatening innocent people's lives. Got to quit. He would write a letter as soon as he got home, hand in his notice in the morning. The administrator would enjoy that. First he had to finish what he'd started.

Ensuring that the back and caudal bones were straight and secured on the operating table, Mopp removed all infected tissue and checked the siacra bones. Everything seemed in order, nothing severed. Placing gauze over the bite, he protected the wound from further harm. He was flying blind now, relying on instinct rather than his fuzzy sight. He could do this in his sleep, had done it a hundred times before.

'This gentleman mustn't be moved for some time, nurse. Please see that the details go on his chart.'

Mopp's final job was a cosmetic one, an actor called Hairy Bancroft in for routine liposuction. By the time the surgeon was done, sitting panting in a narrow corridor, it had started to rain again. Staff entered the hospital drenched to the skin and unhappy. The wind was too strong for an umbrella to withstand, ready to turn it outside in and wreck it in seconds. Rainfall levels were at a record high; the autumn seemed to be lasting forever.

After forty winks Mopp stumbled to his office, taking care not to slip on the wet puddles left by dripping visitors. It wouldn't do for them to find him flat on his ass, even if it happened by accident. Reaching his sanctum, he found the administrator.

'Attabi. I don't think I heard you knock. Maybe because I wasn't here when you snuck into my room.'

'You know I have the authority to rifle through your things if I'm in a nosy mood,' the administrator replied in a light tone. 'You have something to tell me?'

Mopp felt the weight of the hospital on his shoulders. This was his chance to come clean, express his fears to a guy who could sympathise – or destroy him. It wasn't worth the risk. He bottled out.

'I don't think there's anything I want to discuss.'

Attabi pursed his lips, tail coiling. 'I've let you get away with a lot in this hospital,' he said, 'allowed your reputation to buoy you up, as it were.'

Mopp nodded carefully.

'I've turned a blind eye to your eccentricities, your lengthy lunch breaks, your outmoded opinions.' Attabi drew closer to the surgeon. 'You know why?'

'Because I'm your elder?'

'You are venerated, Doctor. I admire what you've done, the

discoveries you made while I was still clamped to my mother's bosom. That's what makes this so difficult. I can't ignore what's going on in my institution, in this office. I have an obligation, by gum. You see that, don't you?'

'I don't see much these days.' Mopp's eyes rolled about a bit.

'How d'you mean?'

'I mean... I'm too old. Too worn out to carry out my obligations.' The surgeon cleared his throat, trying to look his boss in the eye. It wasn't easy. 'My sight, hearing, balance are all impaired. It's time I retired.'

The administrator sank into a chair, brow furrowed. He lifted a carrier bag from the floor, dumped the contents onto Mopp's desk. 'And you thought this could help?'

The doctor's shoulders drooped. He'd given the game away, spilled the beans and every other vegetable in his metaphorical allotment. Attabi wasn't interested in his age. He was staring at the sachet.

'It's tough enough treating junkies in this place. We can't have staff addicted as well. Plus if what you're telling me about your physical state is true... well, perhaps the yeast extract has affected your health.'

'You're probably right,' Mopp said softly. 'I'll clear out my desk in the morning.'

'You can do it now. I have more competent staff to concern myself with.' Mopp nodded slowly as the administrator left the room. His personal bits and bobs all fit in the carrier. He was surprised to find some loose change in a pencil holder. Wrapping himself in a heavy overcoat, he left the hospital and found himself back on the high street.

By now all the shops were closed and only a few windows were lit. The wind blew the heavy rain sideways, into his face, penetrating his coats. His paws were horribly damp. Attabi would probably sell his story to the papers, make a fast buck at Mopp's expense. It didn't matter any more. Unable to pay his credit card bills and loans, the surgeon would soon receive a visit from the legbreakers.

The hippy was heading the other way, a bobbly hat protecting his ears, squinting against the downpour. Mopp stopped him mid-lope.

'There's nothing open this time of night?' the doctor asked in desperation.

'Nah. I know you! Wrecked anything lately?' the hippy's eyelids were heavy with nip.

'Only my career,' Mopp smiled sadly.

'It's never too late, my friend. My dad's gone back to college. Dropped out when I was born. He's starting a whole new life.'

'What's he studying?'

'Uh... dunno. Something to do with consumerism in contemporary society.'

'A new career, eh?'

'Listen dude, you'll catch pneumonia stopping people in the street and talkin' small. I got to go.'

'Sure, sure.' Mopp watched the retailer turn a corner, disappearing into the gloom of a dripping side street. He followed the soggy moggy and at the other end of the passageway he saw one small gleam of hope. A shop was still open, selling frilly undies. A quick spend would relieve his despair for at least an hour.

There was no shopkeeper inside, no hard sell. He slunk past the lacy lingerie and perused the thongs and see-through boxer shorts. The till was empty, its drawer sticking free like a dry black tongue. No sale. It didn't matter, he had to buy something. Picking a pair of briefs (with a hand-stitched flap at the back for one's tail) he placed his loose change in the till drawer and shoved the pants in his soggy coat pocket.

He was about to leave when he spied a sign pointing towards the rear of the store: MORE BARGAINS THIS WAY. He couldn't resist. He heard distant, high-pitched voices shouting: 'Heave! heave!' as he made his way back past the frillies. A low timber beam bopped his noggin. He let out a low growl – he would have an unsightly lump on his head. This had to be the unluckiest day of his life.

There were no goods out back; whoever had been out there had booby-trapped the area. A long-handled fire axe was suspended from the timber, and as Mopp passed through it swung down to cleave his head in two.

He lay on his back, staring at the ceiling. For once, both pupils were aimed in the same direction, although they were separated by several inches.

It wasn't easy finding a place to live in the overpopulated city. Plenty of folk were moving to the green belt, commuting to work. It made sense: there was more room out there, plenty of field mice, no pollution, no noise. The only snag was the travelling time, wearing workers out before they reached the office. They blamed their bleary heads on the fresh country air.

In the suburbs of Nub City cats lived virtually on top of each other. House prices were high, food was scarce. One in four cubs were born with chronic asthma. Most urbanites had adapted to their tough environment – they were used to the noise, breathed in scum, got on well with their neighbours. They found the country-side too clean or quiet, needed the sounds of trams and rowdy yobs to lull them to sleep every night.

They didn't care about what went on when they hit the sack. When the sun went down the streets turned black and nocturnal cit-izens came out to play, to hunt. Disco kids looked for love; barflies and insomniacs hogged the pubs and bars. Strip joints flared into life, peddling whores and exhibitionists. Females on heat! See the fur fly! Guaranteed six naked, musky mammaries! If you hung around the seedy streets long enough, you'd find drag queens, jailbait kittens, cattle with unnatural appetites. A detective named Tiger Straight spent the night in a diner lapping sour milk from a dirty dish.

As dawn greyed into existence the red lights ebbed. Hookers stopped patrolling the streets. Cops swapped shifts and vulgar stories. Steel shutters tucked adult wares out of sight on all school routes. Bairns would steal anything not nailed down in this burg, from nudie mags to baby buggies.

Drove Loan had once been a country lane. Hedged with green foliage, winding parallel to a bonny brook, it had linked two villages. The city had swallowed up the villages and the quaint little lane had been widened, resurfaced, repaved. Now it was littered with cigarette butts and scattered treats, the pavements polkadotted with chewing gum spat from the mouths of jaywalkers. It was cleaned once a week by a council employee who wasn't famous for taking pride in his work. For the rest of the week Drove Loan, like the suburb it traversed, was left to fester.

An occasional tram would rattle past Tiger Straight's apartment, threatening to loose the windows from their frames. He wasn't fussed. A vase perched on the edge of the sideboard, ready to fall and shatter next time the 2R zipped past. He didn't care about that either. The vase could bleed all over the floor as far as he was concerned. He hadn't been back from the diner for very long and he wasn't allowed to stay – he was having a final clear-out.

The window panes were muggy with dirt. They hadn't been cleaned for three weeks. Tiger had paid the cleaner off on his last visit, explaining that he couldn't afford him any more. Unless the cleaner was willing to work for free, the windows would have to go unbuffed. Tiger had gone without fresh milk for a few days as well. He'd left a note for the dairy, who were quite content to deliver pints to his home as long as he paid off his tab on a monthly basis. The tab had got extremely long that year, and when a couple of heavies had arrived in a milk float to settle the bill, he'd had to explain his financial situation to them. Bottles were no longer delivered to his address. Not that he had one, officially speaking. He was being evicted.

Tiger's apartment was fully furnished. It came complete with a leather sofa, antique standard lamp, king size bed and scratching post. Beautifully crafted religious triptychs and paintings of apes playing pool hung on the walls. The place had central heating, double glazing, a wall screen TV. None of it belonged to him.

One bounced rent cheque, that's all it had taken. It wasn't the fact that he hadn't had the money to pay his landlord. The returned cheque had got him evicted and there was only one possession that he cared to keep. It sat in a long tan case, carefully cushioned to stop it rattling.

Losing your home is a stressful experience, so he aimed to get some relaxation. The best place for that had to be the communal sunbaths. As long as you had a chunk of raw meat for the leopard at the door, he'd give you a sleep rug and beckon you in. Tiger picked a spot where he'd have plenty of space to roll about, flopped his rug down and lay on his back, gazing up at the multiple skylights. They let in rivers of sunlight, raying the cats around him with heat to soothe the most savage aches.

He flexed his paws, warmth suffusing his body. His tail went limp. He panted softly, keeping himself cool. Other cats blinked at him, broad smiles on their faces. Everyone in the baths seemed content.

Tiger was about to drift off when a fat voice aroused him.

'I been looking for you, Mr Straight.'

Tiger gazed up, eyes already beginning to gum with slumber. The voice belonged to a broad bobcat with a towel wrapped round his waist.

'If you're looking for a bathing buddy,' Tiger drawled, 'you picked the wrong cat.'

'Too hot in here for me,' said the bob, licking his paws. 'If I wanted this kinda heat, I'd move to the jungle. I'm from the letting agency, Mr Straight. Your office rent's in arrears. You're hereby instructed to clear your stuff outta there and stay out.'

Tiger closed his eyes, frowned a little. First his apartment, now the office. How was a detective supposed to pay the bills with no clients and no prayer of an overdraft? His brothers didn't have this kind of trouble. They were all engineers, soldiers and civil servants. They were able to go for a bath without being harassed by creditors.

This particular debt collector was a zealot with a capital zzz. He waited for his charge to get up, wash the sweat from his fur, snatch up the tan case and head out of the honey-lit building. Tiger stopped at the exit, handing his rug to a muscle-bound leopard.

'You want to watch that bob over there,' he whispered. 'He don't like your kind. Called you a spotty nose git.' The leopard growled and padded over to deal with the letting agent. Tiger headed for his office, situated in an old, condemned building near Totterdown.

The office was furnished with a desk, a seat cushion and a

goldfish bowl. Tiger dipped a paw into the bowl, scaring the last inhabitant out of its meagre wits. The detective wasn't hungry yet; he'd wait until teatime.

The desk was full of files, records of past glories and recent bills. He placed his tan case on the desktop, tore up late reminders and bank statements. One or two folders fell open, revealing their contents like fleet memories. The Case of the Monkey's Uncle, the Rodeo Pirates, the Married Martinet – that file could never see the light of day again. Into the trash it flew.

A dirty mirror hung above the goldfish bowl. He caught his reflection. The trenchcoat was dishevelled, his whiskers out of place. His fur, grey with concentric black rings, was matted from the day's heat. He felt clapped out.

Back to the files, more rubbish for the tin bin: the Cartoon Conundrum, the Golden Dog, the Living Dustbins, the Goat Train. All mysteries solved by the detective in better times. The police had come to him for answers, and he'd sold them at premium rate. Now all his cash was gone, his brains half daft with too many riddles. His reputation had dissipated with the last generation of quick-witted peelers. His partner had left to study entomology.

Once the last folder had been shovelled into the bucket, Tiger struck a match and dropped it in. The pyre began to crumble, releasing a satisfying sigh. A red glow was mirrored in his lime green eyes. About time the office got some central heating.

'Bored, Mr Straight?' He turned with a start. He hadn't heard the female enter, despite keen hearing. She was perched on the edge of the desk, her tail coiled tight, a thin red dress covering her ginger fur. Tiger stood up, offered her the cushion. She was happy on her perch.

'I'm closin' up, ma'am. No fire sale, no retirement do. I'm out of here.'

'Just as soon as you've heard my piece.' The detective tried to keep an eye on the smouldering paper. It was hard with the distraction on his desk. She talked fast, even for a dame – life or death fast, as if he was the only Private Investigator in the book. He settled back to listen, not that he had much choice.

'I know you got a handle on the Totterdown district. You solved more cases than a hundred cops down that way.' Maybe she was older than she looked. 'I know, my mother told me. You know Argyle Street, the way it breaks off into so many tributaries – little arched alleys and crossroads where no good is happy to take place. I know it too, 'cos my four brothers lived there. Cammy, Beast, Grass, Skead. They ran a pest control business. They don't control anything any more.

'These boys were respected; if they were short of beans and the tax was due, the neighbours would help 'em out. Totterdown's like that. They always paid folk back and made an honest living, as honest as can be in this part of town. They had no enemies as I can think on, apart from the wee critters they exterminated. All the same, I was visiting them last week (they were out of milk, and you know how sour a tomcat gets when he ain't got a saucer to sup). I picked up seven pints from the dairy. Came up to their house, a place with stained roof tiles and rot in the walls. I let out a halloo. No answer. Slunk inside – not a breath. I checked the kitchen, the dining room. Nothing.

'Upstairs they were. Upstairs laid in their beds, looking so peaceful. They were dead, Mr Straight. Killed. Some freak'd tied them down, forced them to eat their own poison. The police don't give a hoot, which only leaves me. I heard you were closing down, came here quick. Wondered if you wanted to end your career in a blaze of glory. Find the murderer and mete out some Argyle style justice.'

The detective had been enthralled by the broad's story. So caught up that he'd allowed the flames to spread from the bucket up the side of the desk. Now it singed his tail and made him jump.

'Excuse me!' He raced down the corridor until he found a discarded litter tray. It was full of sand and well used. Barging back past his would-be client, he threw the contents onto the fire. They didn't set it back by much, but created a terrible stench.

'Not mine. Honest.' Tiger yanked the dame out of his office and they made for the street. 'The building was getting old anyway. I wish you'd turned up a week ago, honey. Coulda paid my insurance.'

The broad looked bashful. 'I don't have any dough. I was hoping that blazing end to your career stuff would be enough to –'

'To sucker me in,' sighed Tiger. She nodded. 'Close,' said the detective. 'Bed and board, that's all I need. A floor to sleep on and a bite to eat. No things attached.'

Not every female trusted a tom enough to let him spend the night in her home. Connie Hant knew Tiger's honest rep, and she needed to find a killer. Stowing a PI in the spare room sounded like a great idea.

'You're hired.'

3

ANOTHER DAY, another new hotel.

For the past few years Cole had been sinking money into leisure. It was a growth industry, booming, or so his financial advisors said. So his corporation had funded hotels, casinos, saunas and sunbaths, all in the hope that tourists would take the bait.

They came. They weren't to know that Totterdown had once been the poorest part of the city. There were still some dodgy back streets if you cared to take a walk. Cole aimed to keep his guests in the hotels and their surrounding compounds, eating and gambling there. That way his investments would eventually pay off.

He liked to oversee the building work – the laying of the first keystone, the last roof tile, the final double glazed window. The workers' morale received a boost and he felt that he had done some work.

Truth to tell his business ran itself. He was called upon to make a decision or two – invest here, sell a subsidiary there. He attended board meetings, business lunches (lots of business lunches), press gatherings and functions. Not real work, nothing that stretched his mind. Only detection did that.

Cole Tiddle, grand viveur, debonair cat-about-town, enjoyed nothing better than solving a mystery. He had fallen into the trade, helping clueless employees, tracking down debtors, finding stolen diamonds as effortlessly as he would scratch a fleabite. The papers loved his successes and he quickly buried his failures.

This week he'd retrieved a lost mongoose, unmasked a flasher at a rollercoaster disco and foiled a blood bank robbery. The hotels had still opened on time, and Tiddles Inc. made a constant profit. No sweat.

His hobby wasn't born of boredom or a desire to help the common moggy. He had a skill for intelligent detection, a rare gift that he'd have been churlish to hide. It was a gift to be shared with the police department, the press and a stranger in trouble. He could afford to devote a lot of time to aiding them. If he received praise and good PR in return, then fine. If a couple of professional dicks were put out of work as a result – tough titty.

Although Cole had never known hunger, he kept himself lean and well-toned. He stuck to a tough fitness regime every morning in the gym. He'd had his wine cellar converted in his youth, and although the equipment was now several years old it was still in good working order – tail weights, a whisker stretcher, a tummy rubber. His routine was consistent and repetitive: he'd stretch his limbs, complete several circuits at a run, then climb a wooden column in the centre of the gym. The column sported stubby branches that he would chew and scratch. His body was toughened daily, and he practised martial arts with disciplined aplomb.

Today his muscles ached for action. He'd rushed his dawn routine to get to the building site, offering the builders a superior nod, giving his new hotel a cursory inspection. The Duncan looked sturdy enough, shiny, welcoming. A room there would be costly but the guests who could afford it would be pampered. The reception desk was already polished and primed. An envelope addressed to Cole sat next to the register book.

He opened the note and gave it a sniff. Room 203. One of his many lady belles, without a doubt. Hopping into a lift, he hoped that she'd be one of the young impulsive types, the kind that felt horny at lunchtime.

No floozy in Room 203. All Cole found was a ball of wool, placed tantalisingly on the bed. He sat beside it, pawed it a little. It rolled away. Stilling it with his other paw, he watched the loose end of the yarn. It didn't move. He crushed it between both paws, losing his composure, twisting his hind legs round so that he could use all fours. In his excitement he fell from the bed, rankling the carpet, panting in a tangled heap of wool. Enough. He was a grown tom with responsibilities and a respectable family. Separating himself from the tempting web, he chanced a last anguished look before leaving the room.

So what, Cole thought as he left the hotel compound. *We all let our fur down sometimes. All males are bairns deep down. I was getting in touch with my inner cub.*

As he took his personal tram home Cole knew he'd done wrong. He resolved to restrain himself in future. The resolution made him feel safer and he relaxed for a cross-city nap. His folly had tuckered him out.

4

CONNIE HANT RESIDED in Lavis Lane, a one-bedroom apartment with no mod cons. Bead curtains were draped over the entranceway, offering her scant privacy from the other fifteen families living in her tenement.

Attempting to brighten the gloomy apartment, she'd tried her paw at a spot of DIY. Her brothers had pitched in, painting the lounge a sunflower yellow, the bedroom pink, everywhere else white. She'd stencilled bluebird silhouettes on the kitchen cupboards. The white showed every hair, and she felt embarrassed if friends visited while she was moulting.

She felt strangely comfortable with her new guest – perhaps due to his role as confidant. She was the first to admit that she was a user. When she hadn't been relying on her brothers, she'd been cared for by one of her boyfriends. She never planned on exploiting them, yet it had happened with the last two beaux. She wasn't much good at holding down a job, doing what the boss told her, acting obsequious. She was too much of a free spirit, getting up when she wanted to, working when she had to.

A regular salary was alien to her. The males in her life had always brought home the bacon, indulged her whims. She'd cultivated a helpless manner that turned the blokes to jelly. Their wallets were hers.

Connie would have been quite happy to settle down with one of those partners, but they never stuck around long enough. Her brothers had been overprotective at times, making threats, throwing garbage at passing suitors. She knew they were only kidding, testing the prospective hubby's mettle. The mates she'd dated obviously didn't have a mettle strong enough to withstand the Hant cats' taunts, as they'd soon given her the boot. Now the brothers were gone, perhaps her love-luck would change.

Tiger was the first male to spend the night in her apartment that year. She was pretty, and her assumed ditziness made her all the more desirable. The detective hadn't made a play for her yet and she was beginning to wonder if he'd been newtered. His lack of interest was exasperating; his grizzled good looks certainly held her attention. There was no way she was going to make the first move. Besides, he had no money; unless he won the lottery, he was no good to her.

Tiger had dutifully slept on a pile of cushions in the lounge, woken by sunlight peeking through venetian blinds. He grabbed himself a salmon for breakfast, prowling the streets before Connie was awake. A female of leisure. He liked that. Without her brothers to pay the rent she'd soon be begging for work. He liked that less.

His main aim was to solve his final case in double-quick time. To do that he had to visit the zoo.

Nub City Zoological Park had once been a botanical garden. Visiting cats had stripped the trees clean of bark and chewed on plants till they withered – despite protesting signs. Although the gardens had long since been filled with exotic fauna, a few notices still remained: NO ROLLING ON THE GRASS, DO NOT FEED THE VISITORS, CHORUSES PROHIBITED.

Unfortunately, most of the animals were more edible than the plants they'd replaced. They were carefully separated from the public by a deep moat. The zoo animals could roam free on their own little islands, their food funded by entrance fees. Only one group of inhabitants couldn't be contained this way.

The keeper who tended to these creatures was dedicated, caring, taking on some of their characteristics. That would have been fine if her charge had been a wombat or a walrus. Natasha Lindsay's wee ones were insects.

They lived in a vast conservatory, all tinted glass and humidity. They weren't cooped up for malicious reasons – many of them had been rescued from bogs or tram accidents, nursed back to health. For safety reasons, glass stood between the bugs and cats who would have dearly loved to eat them.

Although it was clear some arachnids were capable of intelligent thought, insects lived a link further down the food chain. The conservatory contained ladybirds, locusts, beetles, midges and many more species besides. Natasha ate none of them, her love of insects was too great. She'd even taken to wearing a pair of deedle-boppers on her head so the insects wouldn't see her as a threat. A daft theory, but she was there to experiment. She was the only entomologist in the city.

Natasha was obsessed enough to earn herself a nickname. Colleagues called her Bug. The name had stuck since her school-days, when she'd spent more time talking to the flies on her desk than listening to Teacher. She didn't care. She could think of worse monikers.

Her current study was an environmental one, encouraging grasshoppers and crickets to live together in a patch of long grass. It was a noisy experiment.

The only visitor to the zoo that morning was Tiger. He was pleased to find Natasha up so early, looking bright and bushy eared. She was crawling past the long grass, examining a roll of dung left by an errant beetle.

'You get more like your bugs every day.' Tiger unbuttoned his trenchcoat, enjoying the greenhouse heat.

'How would you know? You don't see me every day,' Natasha replied, packing away a magnifying glass.

'Only 'cos of the entrance fee. Times are stiff, you know that. I had to close the business.'

'Shame.'

'There's one last crime to fight. I could do with some help.'

Natasha looked at her old boss. He had to be winding her up. She'd resigned and he knew that she'd taken the zoo job to make some cash and revive her career. She'd never made a good PI side-kick. She was Bug.

'You make a great sidekick,' Tiger offered with his most charming grin. 'You see the little things, the tiny details that every-one misses. Look a place over with me, today. That's all I want.'

'Where?' She could have kicked herself. She knew what curiosity could do to a cat.

'Off Argyle Street. It ain't that bad –' Tiger stressed before

Natasha could protest, '– in daylight. Five minutes. It'll do you good to take a break from these creepy crawlies.'

Oh dear. It was never a fine idea to insult Bug's best friends. She kicked Tiger out of the conservatory and got on with her work.

5

CATS AREN'T NATURAL farmers. Ploughing and planting goes against the grain. They're hunters, chasing prey, eating meat. The only thing they like better than hunting is sleeping. Farmers arise early, go to bed late. Not typical feline behaviour.

The stores needed cereal, plants and milk and somebody had to produce them. Unemployment being high, Old Scrumpy Dean had been forced to take their pay and till some land. Supermarkets – pah! He had no time for them except on pay-day.

The work wasn't all bad. He'd salvaged an electric plough with remote control. When the batteries died he pulled the plough himself, or got Nut to do it.

Scrumpy was a big tom, his muscles developed from sowing and reaping. Not many would trifle with him. He left deep marks in the soil as he crossed his largest field, heading for the cowshed.

Scrumpy brooked no nonsense. A plain-speaking animal, he believed in the value of verbal agreements. Once he'd licked his paw and shaken on a deal, it couldn't be broken. He liked to get his farming over fast so that he could go home, spending most afternoons curled up in front of the fire. His hearth rug bore a bald patch where he lay. He had no 'phone and no television. He enjoyed the peace and solitude of the countryside; they were the only things that made his job bearable. Most of his cattle were well-behaved and only one cow needled him every single morning – a maverick named Nut.

Nut was a sassy beggar, always complaining. The only time she didn't moan was when she was being milked. That was because Scrumpy yanked real tight on her udders.

'Easy there darling,' she'd giggle, 'I'm starting to enjoy myself.'

'Shut up, you dumb Friesian. I'd kick your ass, only it's so fat I'd probably lose my boot.' Banter like this helped keep Scrumpy sane. He had a lot of milking to do – a herd of cows, complaining all the time. *Moo when you going to get heating in this barn, moo the strip lights are hurting my eyes, moo I've got a cramp – can you massage my hooves a little?* Nut was the worst, always edging for a better deal.

'I see my insurance premiums have gone up again.'

'Ain't nothing to do with me,' hissed Scrumpy.

'We got a deal, darling. We all know how I'll end up. No use denying it.' Some of the other cows clamped their ears down in annoyance. 'Come winter I'll be a crate load of Yummy Chunks. Only reason I'm going along with this is for the insurance. In the event of my slaughter, the calves will be well provided for.' Nut batted her long eyelashes.

'So what's yer problem?' asked Scrumpy, loading pails of milk onto a pallet.

'These premiums don't level out, I'll be paying loads more than I should for the same end amount.'

'Blame the banks,' Scrumpy spat in one of the buckets, 'blame the darned superstores.'

'There is an alternative. Double indemnity.'

'The game show?'

'No, silly. It's a clause in my insurance. I get murdered, my family gets twice the money. You bludgeon me with a candlestick, lay the blame on some passing hobo...'

Scrumpy's whiskers twitched. A cow desperate for double indemnity. He'd never heard such a thing.

'I couldn't kill nobody,' the farmer replied, 'unless I was hungry.' The herd cleared their throats anxiously. 'That's me done. I'll hear no more of murder.'

Scrumpy heard nothing ever again. As he left his barn a pitchfork swung up to strike his stomach. He bled to death slowly in the hay; penned in as they were, the cows were powerless to help him.

The zoo always got busier in the afternoon. Little ones were done with school, housewives or full time fathers had finished their chores; jobless cats had nowhere much to go. Bug was kept busy. She detailed the lives of her tiny chums, outlined the rules of their mating games, illustrated alien habits.

The heat rose in the glass cage and she washed herself constantly. She enjoyed the taste of her own fur; it reassured her, calmed her. So much so that she jumped when Tiger tapped on the glass. His claws scraped the steamed-up panes.

'What do you want this time?' she asked, loath to let him in.

'I brought a bribe. A present.' Bug felt silly. Passers-by were cocking their ears in her direction. She let Tiger in and he presented her with a matchbox.

'Not much of a bribe.'

'Check inside.' Something scuttled within: a four-winged lapidicolous nut coupler. Natasha's heart melted.

'It's what I've always wanted.' The creature wriggled in a miniature puddle of poop. She picked it up. 'So rare. Where did you find it?'

'I'm a detective. I'm good at finding things.'

'I'll have to put it somewhere safe.' She placed it in a specially air conditioned tank. Once her back was turned, Tiger ate the nut coupler and clamped his teeth together.

'I'll get someone to hold the fort,' said Natasha as she whistled for another keeper. 'You got something on your face.' Tiger shoved the last of the beetle's legs into his mouth.

6

SOMEONE HAD LEFT the tap on in the Hant brothers' kitchen. The plug wasn't in but a cup sat over the hole. The room had flooded, the floor so wet that if you kicked it water would spray from the carpet. The smell of dirty dishes lingered; the tea towels hadn't been washed in weeks. Mugs waited for the sud fairy to come along and spruce them up, scrape the fungus from their bottoms. The elements in the kettle squealed, not enough liquid in the vessel. Steam tried to raise the alarm; no one attended.

Four stools, rickety and worn at the seat, were cold without their masters' rumps. Mouldy teabags and ripped cartons lay in a sad pile on the draining board.

The detective had already visited the house once, taking care not to disturb anything. He crept slowly through the brothers' bedrooms, ensuring that his tail didn't drag in the dust. The lads had slept two to a room, and the impressions of their bodies remained in each mattress. A chemical scent informed the air – the poisonous powder that they'd used to kill pests. The powder that had been fed to them.

Continuing his snoop, the investigator checked through bottles and packets on bedside cabinets.

The police would have taken away any obvious evidence, but Cole Tiddle had learned that the least obvious evidence could turn out to be the most important.

Cole had to hurry. He had a network brunch to attend at eleven. How had the killer managed to tie up any of the brothers before the others rushed to help?

One photograph had been pinned to the wall in the master bedroom. The four lads, back from a successful mission, holding a pack of dead rats by their tails. Cole felt hungry. The lads were accompanied by their sister, looking innocent and content, her fur cropped and curled. Her do and their clothes placed the photo a decade ago; feline fashion is ruthlessly fickle.

Cole felt little for the aggrieved sister. He hadn't climbed the corporate pyramid by being sentimental. His mind raced, developing theories, exploring possibilities. The brothers could have short-changed a client – hardly sufficient motive for something so brutal. He had to find out more about their past, their characters. A visit to the sister was called for. Judging by her photo, the task would be a pleasant one.

Death was common in the cat city; traffic accidents, scraps over territory, gang wars, breed-related incidents. The police rarely investigated a murder. Nevertheless, when a bizarre killing took place and there was a chance that the perp would strike again – the cops were on the case. For Inspector Bix Mortis, a dour ale-guzzler with a dicky ticker, the only rodent on the force, a token gesture made by the Mayor to soothe race relations... it was just another job to do.

The barn was a mess. Scrumpy's blood had streamed into a central channel that traversed the floor. Hay was strewn everywhere and the place stank of fear and death.

'I never thought a fellow could make such a mess with a pitchfork,' Nut exclaimed. The Inspector made pertinent notes in a minuscule black book. 'I mean guts and straw...'

'You saw him?' asked the rodent.

'Who, dear?'

'The killer. Your boss' murderer.'

'Oh no. Couldn't look. We all closed our eyes, didn't we?' Nut's brethren nodded slowly.

'You reckoned a guy did this?' Bix continued to scribble.

'Beg pardon?'

'"I never thought a fellow could make such a mess –"'

'A mere assumption, Inspector. A rather sexist one at that. Chalk it down to cow chauvinism. I'll tell you – it was scary.'

'You heard a cry, saw Scrumpy fall –'

'I was so frightened I almost milked myself.'

'Thank you, Nut.'

A forensics officer was busy taking measurements and snapshots. Doctor Snow, the pathologist, had already been called to the scene.

'He's been stabbed to death with a pitchfork,' the doctor diagnosed in a breathless tone.

'Thank you.' Bix craned his neck to look up at the cat. Like all mice, he despised the feline race for its ignorance. 'Anything helpful you can tell us?'

'Entrance wound from a low angle. Very steep.' Snow was a balding cat with rubbery jowls. 'Whoever did this was either down on his haunches or your size, Inspector.'

'Lovely.' Bix made a sour face. 'Let's wrap this up. This farmyard's got enough pigs without us trampling about.'

The winter days were shrinking. Sensible souls hibernated, giving their hides a rest from the harsh frosts that were approaching fast. Hailstorms were frequent, warm spells less so. The wind was insidious, blowing rain up noses and into the most secure homes. Only citizens with an iron resolve ignored the weather, going about their business as though spring was ready to commence. Tiger wasn't the kind of cat who let a seasonal shift disrupt his work.

It had grown dark by the time he and Bug reached the Hant Brothers' residence. Youngsters hung round outside, nothing better to do than drink alcoshakes and whack each other with foam bats. The adults tried to ignore them. One of the youths coughed a hairball at Tiger as he passed.

'Cubs are so cheeky these days.'

'And you were the essence of good manners when you were their age?' Bug smirked as she found an unlatched window. 'Looks like someone's preceded us.'

'They might still be here.' Tiger clambered through the window after his friend.

'Nah. They're long gone, I reckon. No fresh pawprints.'

'Could've been wearing mittens.' Statisticians believed that 64% of cat burglars wore mittens while breaking and entering. The majority of arrests for the crime involved kittens who'd lost their mittens.

The cats' eyes became black pools as they adjusted to the gloom. For the most part, they used their whiskers to find their way upstairs and into the master bedroom.

'Some geezer's definitely been here today,' sniffed Bug, 'left his scent. Strong. A big bad tom.'

'Keep a hold on yourself, Natasha. We're looking for clues, remember?'

'Yeah. Murder, deceit, the snuffing out of four innocent existences – I've found something.'

'Already?'

Bug showed Tiger her find. It was a long, slender sheath extension, coated with a blood red varnish. Vain females wore them to give their claws an ornate look. Nail biters and factory workers were particularly fond of the accessory. It glinted in the dark room, reflected in Bug's bright green eyes. She flashed a toothy grin, twisting round on her paw. Passing it to her friend, she stretched her back slowly.

'Was I worth two trips to the zoo? That expensive present?'

'You're worth your weight in kitty litter, doll.' Tiger started to feel guilty about eating her present. It'd given him indigestion. 'You think these boys were transvestites?'

'Cross dressing pest controllers?' Bug batted her eyelashes. 'I don't approve of the life these guys led. If you'd told me what they did back at the zoo, I never woulda come here. But nobody should die like – like they died, even if they did get a taste of their own poison. I'll do what I can to help.'

'Cheers.' Tiger headed back downstairs. 'I'm gonna have to find out who made this extension. Some good old legwork.'

'I get mine from a fine lady named Jo,' Bug mused as she followed Tiger out of the house. 'You've got a hairball stuck to your coat.'

He wiped the gooey matt from his sleeve. 'I was always neat and good-natured when I was young,' he mused. 'Did as I was told, pulled my socks up. Didn't rock the khazba. Once folks realised that – they made my life a tragedy. Used me. It took me a long time to change.'

'There was me thinking you were born a rebel.' Bug handed

him the sheath. It glimmered in the cloud-flecked moonlight. 'I still admire you, boss.'

'You going back to the zoo?'

'Have to. Got an afternoon's work to catch up on. Can't think who's to blame.' She gave Tiger a farewell wink.

'Natasha -'

'Yes?'

'I'll be in touch.' He watched as his old partner slunk round a street corner. Today he'd felt younger, energised. Seeing her again had helped. Wondering if a vet could prescribe something similar, he headed off to report to Connie Hant.

7

SOMETIMES CONNIE WASN'T sure whether she'd made the right choice. She was the one who had to live with her decision, day and night. It was the most serious selection she'd ever made – apart from hiring Tiger. Home decorating was an earnest business; she'd had the whole lounge painted bright yellow with furnishings to match. Now that she was alone without a job she couldn't afford to change it. She felt daft as Cole settled himself on a buttercup cushion, gazing at his loud surroundings.

'My favourite colour's yellow,' he admitted.

'Really? We'll get along great, sure.' She knew he was humouring her. Surely a cat as tough and masculine as her visitor would prefer a more virile colour. Red or brown.

'You don't mind me asking about your brothers?'

'No.' Good. He was asking her anyway.

'They ran their business with money borrowed from the bank; their favourite eatery was the Golden Cage, and they doted on you. So far so right. Did they ever fight?'

'Not as far as I know, and I was always visiting them. Mainly to get away from this crazy colour scheme.' Connie smiled. 'They bickered – in a siblingy sort of way. Winding each other up, for a laugh. They were always laughing.'

'Happy in their work.'

'Exactly. There was a lot of love in our family. Mr Tiddle, you're sure I can't offer you a saucer of milk? It's the least I can do.'

'That's very generous of you. This isn't a social call. My client wants this case solved as much as you do.'

'I need to know who your client is.' She drew close to him.

'They wish to remain anonymous. I want to tell you but a detective is like a priest. I don't break wind in public and I don't give out secrets.'

'Maybe this will change things.' Connie rubbed her nose gently against Cole's forehead. He let out a sigh.

'Mate of yours?' asked Tiger, loping into the apartment. The couple broke apart hurriedly. 'You want me to leave?'

'I'm the one who's leaving,' purred Cole, standing up and stretching. 'I have an AGM at four.' He raised his eyes to meet Connie's, smouldering, full of intent. 'You know the number. Call me if you think of anything that might... help.'

Connie had lost all power of speech. She could only watch as the millionaire left her home, his tail wiggling behind him.

'How many guys you putting up?' asked Tiger, replacing Cole on the buttercup cushion. He'd made a point of ignoring the large tom.

'I didn't hire him,' replied his host in a huff, 'someone else did.'

'Who?'

'Dunno. One of my brothers' friends or neighbours. I don't see how they could afford him.' *Whereas I come cheap*, thought Tiger.

'Any news on your clue?'

The detective shook his blunt grey head.

'Not so far. I've seen about every beautician in town. A few more to try.'

Connie settled back on her narcissus couch, her huff deflated. Tiger was making some headway, trying hard; she had faith in him. Next time she saw Cole, she'd tell that smug fellow what she really thought of him.

8

TEN MILES WEST of Nub City lay the coast, rocky and unkind. A small group of cats eked out a living there, supplying fresh fish to urban areas.

A regular train took the food from the fishing village, cod and tuna packed in briny crates and returned empty. Today the water was choppy, white foam mingling with grey waves. Cole stepped from the train, licking his lips. He'd helped himself on the buffet car and no one had complained.

Sometimes the fishercats tolerated visits from wealthy executives, looking for a respite from the office. For a fat fee a boat could be hired, and the vacationer could join a fishing expedition.

Fishing was a tricky business for cats, wary of water. If they could overcome their fear of getting wet and prevent themselves from scoffing the catch, they had a secure job that would see them through all nine lives.

It took a certain kind of animal to work on the sea. There were no gender or age distinctions – the village couldn't afford to be selective. Those who took the job were rugged, wind-scarred, stank of stale salt. City folk called them mercats, they spent so much time at sea. Extra help was always welcomed, even when it was provided by a pampered puss like Cole.

Deep sea fishing was an intricate art, usually involving two boats. Between them a cat's cradle of rope was stretched, each length of hemp barbed with old claws and sticky with seaweed. Every so often, the mercats would trawl the net and raise it to grab as many fish as possible.

The net wasn't the only way to fish – they'd also scoop food from the water with their bare paws. The catch was dumped in a squared-off area in the middle of the boat. On a long run, the cats would eat some of the raw fish to keep their bellies satisfied.

The mercats usually sensed an impending weather change. They knew a gale was brewing. With Cole in attendance they decided to ignore it, sure that a rough time would shake up the businessman and give them a giggle. Cole watched the waves rise as he helped lower the cat's cradle, feeling a bit sick.

The number of fish in this part of the sea was dwindling. Sewage from the city flowed through pipes into rivers and streams that leaked into the sea. The once clear water was now brown with pollution. Consumers were still eager to eat fresh fish, so the mercats continued their daily trawls. They knew that the life of their village was nearing its end. Some of their stubborn colleagues would move up the coast, seeking an untainted area where they could continue to fish. Most of the villagers would go to the city, find work in a factory or office block. They'd miss the breeze, the lifestyle, the freedom of deep sea fishing. Missing it wouldn't bring back what was lost for good.

For now they were remorseless, increasing their catches against all likelihood, rising earlier, coming home later. The food would all be bad or dead soon. They would make the most of what they had.

Lona was never going back. She'd had enough of her mother's nagging, telling her what to do, treating her like a new-born kitten. She was old enough to go to school now, ready to be responsible. Running away from home was the next stage in her development. She had to find her own way – with her mum's money, make up and jewellery. She'd tarted herself up to look as old as possible, stowed away in a boxcar to reach Nub City. She sat on a crate of herring, relaxed by the train's steady rattle. Her parents would be sorry. They'd start to miss her eventually, worrying about her. She'd show them.

Like most young kittens Lona was impatient. After ten minutes in the dull car she stretched her legs and took a peek outside. She had to be close to the city by now. The world rushed by outside, harsh sunlight hurting her eyes. Through sudden tears she glimpsed the sea.

The train was following the coastline – that couldn't be right. Could trains take a wrong turn? No. It was far more likely that *she'd* taken the wrong turn – heading away from the city instead of towards it. At home she messed up all the time; it seemed as if she couldn't get things right in the real world either. Now she was lost.

Trees and rocks were a blur, whistling past the dirty train. Lona got hungry, sniffed at the crates, tried to open one with her teeth and forepaws. The blurs became large smudges, solidifying into recognisable shapes as the boxcar clanged to a halt. She backed into a corner, waiting for someone to collect the crates. She'd appeal to their better nature, find out where she was, ask them to help her find her way home. She was tired and angry with herself. There was still a lot of growing up to do.

Now that the train had stopped juddering, Lona tuned her keen hearing to another sound. A skritching, hesitant shuffle as if something was trying to keep quiet, hold its breath. It was coming from a shadowy corner of the boxcar. She was not alone. There was a creature in there with her, trying its best not to announce its presence.

Lona's folks had warned her of the animals that ate naughty little cubs, of the dogs and rats and goats that couldn't wait to get their teeth into her if she misbehaved. She hadn't believed their cautionary tales; she was too practical for that. Now she had second thoughts.

Anything benign would have announced its presence when she embarked. There was no way a kindly traveller would make such a sinister sound. Whatever was making the noise couldn't see her in the darkness, and couldn't guess that she'd detected its presence. So she backed towards the corner, ready to spin round at the last moment and confront it.

As she moved carefully backwards, her forepaws outstretched, she detected a smell as black as the skritching. The musty, wheat odour of an animal that hadn't had a bath for months. The fish had obscured the stink until now, but it scared Lona more than the noises.

A small, craggy paw grabbed her shoulder and overbalanced her. Five or six paws grabbed and scratched her, teeth snapping at her windpipe. Mewling, she fainted dead away.

Spray matted Cole's fur and dripped from his whiskers. He hardly noticed. He was distracted by the thought of a package that had appeared in his desk drawer earlier in the week. A sealed manila envelope, no address, no postmark. Twenty-four shots of a male caught in a clinch. Twenty-four frantic, crazed, blissful moments. He was the subject and he had wool on his face.

As he'd lost his head in that hotel room, snared in a trap that shouldn't have caught a new-born cub... someone had watched. A concealed camera had captured evidence capable of destroying his empire. If the public – worse, his shareholders – saw him with his guard down, they would lose all faith in him. Investors would pull out, demanding money that had already been spent on failed projects. That couldn't be allowed to happen.

He trawled his net through the water once more. His serene features showed little trace of concern. His companions had no way of knowing that the envelope had also contained a note. The snapper wanted Cole to solve a crime. If the Hant murderer was not found he would soon be kissing goodbye to Tiddles Inc.

Lona's world was moving again. A different motion this time, an uncertain seesaw. She heard the swirl of waves, smelled the sea, realised she was on a boat. She tried to stand up but her head spun and the vessel rocked. She squatted in the cargo hold where she'd been dumped, washed herself thoroughly. Although she was bedraggled, her mum's jacket and jewellery made her feel presentable. She found her sealegs, banged on the hatch above her and discovered that it had been left unbolted.

She let out a querulous mew as she stepped onto the deck. The white hot sun was high in the sky now, warming her face. Her confidence grew as she failed to spot anybody. She was out of sight of the coastline, there was nothing on the horizon. Large waves crashed against the boat's barnacled hull. In the cabin, the wheel had been strapped still. Padding to the bow, she looked down at the swirling water, recalled the scaly paws that had grabbed her.

Lona hissed as she was lifted bodily off the deck, hanging off the bow. Reaching behind her she found that she was dangling from a boathook, the sharp point digging into her flesh. A thin chuckle reached her on a current of wind, then the boat hook dipped and she entered the water. Lona missed her mother dread-fully. The sea was too cold to think anymore. It was easier to give in to the deep freeze and sleep for a while.

Warming himself by the fireplace, Cole paid a young female to clean his fur. She complied without a word, no doubt dreaming of how she'd spend the cash. The grooming relaxed him as he lapped at a bowl of milk. He emptied the bowl – a day on the ocean had made him mighty thirsty.

As he felt his cockles warm, thoughts drifted back to the case he had to solve. Tomorrow he would meet with Bowyer, the Chief of Police. With the aid of the authorities, the murders would be solved in no time.

Dunbar bay was not the prettiest part of Cambor. It smelled bad. Way back before trains and mass angling expeditions, a feeble sea wall had been built to save a huddle of houses from the water. The mercats had used the bay to moor their boats, swearing blind in the local tavern that they had discovered the most efficient mode of transport in the world.

As the fishing expeditions had grown into an industry, more homes had been built. Struggling for space the area had become increasingly built up, low level shacks with high prices. Territorial disputes were common, with the loser giving up his property to the victor. The sea didn't care about mortgages or lease agreements. It battered the wall and the stone began to crumble. The locals had been too busy scrapping and scraping a living to notice until one year when the water had risen, demolishing half the houses on the front. The cats took to their boats or moved inland. The sea was an unkind host; you didn't mess with it or take it for granted. You tried not to sink.

Now Dunbar Bay was cluttered with trash and dead fish. The water was still here, stuffed with scum. The remaining houses looked onto each other in a protective square, centring on a tiny courtyard where clothes could be hung out to dry. The younger people spent their earnings on luxurious, waterproof furniture – in case their dwellings flooded. The older folk sat upstairs, gazing from their bedroom windows at the craggy coast west of the bay. They twitched their net curtains, assured everyone who cared to listen that the sea level had risen that week, and cultivated a condescending attitude towards the trains – a noisier and far less efficient form of travel than boats.

A couple of houses lay derelict, blinded with bricks through the windows, a haven for sex-hungry toms who left their scent for all to find. No one would buy the old red buildings, aged with salty rain. They were used as a toilet and a nookie parlour. Their front gardens were flowered with wood and plastic, rubbish thrown from passing ships. The air was dominated by smells of sewage and stagnant pools of water, but today there was another taint.

A young couple found its source. Their parents were strict, didn't like them necking. The female was on heat and her partner was excitable. They tripped along the sea wall, the lass gazing at the moon, her partner examining the trash for trinkets.

'This is for you,' said the tom tenderly, offering his mate a silver bracelet. Her eyes grew wide with wonder.

'You shouldn't have!' She gave the bracelet a close examination, finding silt and grit in the links. 'You didn't, did you? Where did you find it?'

The tom pointed guiltily at a mound that had piled against the wall. He apologised for his lack of finesse.

'Don't worry about it, there might be more jewellery down there!'

The couple found more jewellery, modelled by the lifeless form of a kitten. The necklace and earrings made her look younger, not older; a slick-furred tailor's mannequin long out of fashion.

9

GERRY HAD EVERYTHING he could possibly want. He lived on his boat, moored in Cambor harbour beside the mercats he considered to be good neighbours. In the summer afternoons when the sun was game, he'd lie stretched out on the deck and drink in the hot rays. They would make sparkled patterns on the water, surprising him with a different colour for each day of week. He needed the warmth and the rest – his mornings were spent gathering food from the bountiful sea. He caught enough to eat, and passed a couple of fish to the authorities in lieu of mooring fees. He would have been content, had he not possessed a miserable mien.

Gerry never shared a joke in the local tavern, or bought anyone a drink. He wouldn't purr at a passing beauty, or give his priest a courteous nod. He was grumpy to his sister and grumpy to the fish that circled his boat. He supposed that they were taunting him; in fact, they were curious.

Gerry's misery stemmed from his furless physical state. He smelled weird and he'd been devoid of hair since birth, often cold as a result. His ancestors had come from a desert climate, and he still bore the trademarks of their exotic breed – a pointy head and a long, tapering tail. He'd never seen or heard anyone make fun of him, pointing him out as a freak. He knew that was because they did it behind his back, round street corners, out of earshot. They made fun of him and over the years, because of his testy temper, he'd become the naked furless butt of countless Cambor jokes.

Gerry had decided to spend as much time as possible at sea, a recluse in his boat. Once out of sight of the mainland he could show off his kitelike ears, his skinny torso exposed to the brisk elements. It made him shiver and he'd caught a chill a couple of times, yet it felt good to flaunt his bod without fear of derision. Unless he counted the pesky fish.

The monks hadn't laughed at him when they asked to hire the boat. They'd been extremely quiet as monks were wont to be. They'd carried no calling cards: their robes and their tranquil composures had provided proof enough of their identities. They were obviously not seafarers, so Gerry hadn't been sure whether to trust them with his proudest possession.

He'd no idea why they wanted his boat in particular. It had the usual trimmings, stout masts, a deep hold for his catch, brown paint flaking from its hull. There were dozens of vessels like his in the harbour, many of them for hire. He wasn't in the habit of lending out his boat to strangers. He had everything he could possibly want.

He'd refused the monks' generous offer with no good grace. He'd told them where to stick their payment, ready to send them away. They'd negotiated a better deal. Gerry supposed that monks had a lot of time to practice their negotiation skills. Meditation and arbitration. That's what monks did. The offer had been so tempting that he'd lent them his boat for a day. To his relief they'd returned it intact, nice and early so he still had time to take the boat out, hoping to score some herring before the light failed. He stood upright in his cabin, not caring if anyone saw him. He had no reason to care now.

If the fishercat had taken a close look at his boat he'd have noticed a couple of bloodspots down in the hold. They belonged to Lona. He would also have spotted scratch marks on the hull, as the kitten had tried to claw her way to safety before the current swept her away. The grooves were faint; after a few weeks at sea, they would be invisible.

Gusts of wind tickled Gerry's skin. For the first time he could remember, he was happy. He gave the fish round his boat a cheerful greeting, chuckled as he hauled them in and bit a mackerel's head off. When he got back to harbour he would pay a friendly visit to his sister, spend an hour in the tavern, tell a joke or two. He'd been saving them up. For now he headed for the horizon, in full view of any mercats who were barmy enough to be fishing so late in the day. They wouldn't have recognised Gerry if they had passed him, because his figure was obscured by baggy monk's robes, complete with cowl. They kept him warm and dry, and when he wore them he didn't feel ridiculous. He was sure that no one would laugh at him again.

Cole stumbled into Connie's apartment, sharing a joke with her. Tiger was waiting for the couple, greeting them with a scowl.

'I'm trying to solve a mystery here, if you don't mind,' Tiger huffed.

'You haven't cracked the case yet?' asked Cole with a sneer. 'How far have you got?'

'Wouldn't you like to know.'

'Any clues?' Cole removed his opera cloak. He'd taken Connie to see a performance of the Cats' Fugue at the Garden Wall open air theatre.

'One or two,' Tiger assured him. He found himself hanging up his rival's cloak. Cole had a knack for making others feel inferior.

'Lads, lads,' Connie interrupted, 'can you not work together?' Tiger wouldn't speak to her. He'd begged her not to go out with the tycoon, worried that an excursion could leave her open to an attack. Connie was the kind of lady who always did the opposite of what she was told. If her actions made Tiger jealous, all the better.

'You gonna spend the night?' he asked, squinting at his rival. Cole scratched his chin with a manicured claw.

'That's up to Ms Hant,' he purred. She bade him goodnight and rubbed up against him on his way out.

'Don't say a word,' she said to Tiger, strutting into the bathroom. The down-at-heel detective's head spun. He had to arrange new accommodation before Connie did something that he would regret.

10

FELINES AREN'T THE easiest folk to analyse. They're a solitary bunch, don't like to share their feelings unless there's something in it for them. Fortunately Doctor Mildrew was adept at drawing the most insular patients out of their shells. He would listen to them carefully, help them to answer their own questions and make life choices. At the end of each expensive session, he would remind them of the faults that had been revealed. Patients often left the office more depressed than when they went in, but Mildrew believed that the means justified the end: mental fitness.

The working classes wouldn't have dreamed of visiting Mildrew. His books were filled with professional couples, upper class nits and tits, members of the aristocracy and even a few cats with genuine emotional problems. Most of his cases involved overeating disorders, narcissism, young cubs who would chew grass then throw up, nip addicts, males convinced that their paws were too small demanding surgery (he tried to dissuade them), vegans, compulsive washers and sufferers of cupboard love syndrome. He treated them all with equal care and tact. He was their friend and helper. Almost all of them looked forward to coming.

However, some were forced to attend. Inspector Mortis' sessions were funded by the police department. They believed that his unique situation could cause emotional distress, and his thoughts and feelings should be monitored. They'd hired the best psychologist in Nub City to see him once a week. When the psychologist had suffered a mental breakdown, refusing to see the Inspector again, Mildrew had taken over. He considered the sessions a waste of time, although a couple of childhood traumas had been unearthed during his time with Bix. Today he had better places to be.

'I was sure your secretary licked her lips on my way in,' said the mouse as soon as he arrived. 'Seems like everyone sees me as a starter course on their daily menu.'

'Ms Torrancu has just finished her lunch. Full as an egg, she can't possibly have been after you.'

'You've told me to look at every angle, Doc.' Bix hopped onto a firm black couch.

'There's a fine line between being open minded and being paranoid.'

'If you were me wouldn't you be paranoid? I'm small, edible, my legs're only little. I have to have my wits about me every second. My employers are as likely to gobble me up as they are to pay me.'

'Perhaps this explains why you don't have a personal life.'

'Then I'd let my guard down. At work I deal with perverts, murderers and pencil necks. I don't relax; that would be the worst thing to do.'

'You've never spoken of your family.'

'Nothing to speak. Don't know them. I've always fended for myself. I never sought them out, sent a postcard to anyone. Folks tolerate me, barely. They don't care for me.' The Inspector descended from the couch and brushed a crumb from his faun jacket. 'I've got a case to solve.'

'Our hour isn't up yet,' the doctor protested.

'Credit me a few minutes. I'll return, don't you worry.'

As Bix stomped out of the office, Mildrew gave a sage nod. The cop would be back with more whys and woes. He couldn't wait.

'A rum business all round,' Bowyer admitted. His nose twitched with anticipation. 'Bad for our rep. Bad for morale.' The Chief was a tall cat in wellies and a matching green jacket. He stood on the vast lawn that stretched behind his country manor. The grass was kept daintily manicured by slave wage sheep. Nobody asked where the money that funded his lifestyle came from; it was assumed that he'd inherited a healthy income from a dotty aunt. In fact, Bowyer was as corrupt as he was influential. Cole knew this but accompanied the Chief anyway. He needed information and he was getting it.

A hundred yards from the pair sat a catapult, set by a cub. On the scoop lay a small pigeon, its wings clipped. More birds queued up beside the cub.

'We still don't understand who murdered those exterminators,' Bowyer whined, his teeth chattering, 'or why.'

'I wouldn't have thought you'd care. Argyle Street isn't exactly an exclusive area.'

'Quite. Whoever killed the Hant boys is obviously insane. We can't have loonies running about the place, can we? Pull!' The bird on the scoop was flung into the air and Bowyer opened his jaws wide. With a hop he snatched the pigeon from the air and spat feathers from the side of his mouth.

'Next we lose a farmer in a nasty fashion,' said the Chief when he'd finished the bird. 'More work for us.'

'There's been another incident?' Cole asked. 'Pull!' Another bird sailed through the sky. The tycoon caught it and began to pluck it clean.

'Two. The farmer gets forked. Something worse happens this morning in a fishing village not far from here.'

'Cambor.'

'Yes.'

'I was just there.'

'I know. You'll be familiar with a small bay there, a graveyard for flotsam and jetsam. It wasn't trash that washed up there today. It was a drowned kitten.' Bowyer's eyes narrowed. 'Someone had dangled her overboard on a boathook, dropped her in. I'd like to think she never felt the cold water filling her lungs, the helplessness, the chest pains – you're a suspect.'

'I'm not a murderer,' growled Cole. 'I build things, I don't destroy them.'

'I know you're innocent. No one else does. Not so easy to keep out the papers.'

'You're looking for a donation to your retirement fund.' Cole wasn't surprised.

'What do you take me for?' Bowyer hissed. 'I'm the Chief of Police, not some one-bit bent bobby. Your interest in this case has created waves. If your interest ebbs – to the level of, say, nothing – I won't have you hauled in.'

'Got it.' Cole stroked his chin.

'Pull!' Two birds shot from the catapult and Bowyer leaped, grabbing one with his forepaws and the other with his teeth. He snacked on both of them.

'One more question before I leave,' said Cole. Bowyer looked up from his meal. 'Who's on the case?'

'One of our most efficient and smallest officers.' A stray feather tickled the Chief's nose. 'Inspector Bix Mortis.'

II

Wisest of dumb animals
Runs from rats and cannibals
Tatty ear and kinky tail
Following the bad guys' trail

He's the squirt who puts out fires
Catches miscreants 'n' liars
Hides out in a rubbish dump
Scary villains make him jump

Doesn't charge a grinding fee
Offers services for free
As long as he's home for tea
With She-Cat and Wonder Flea

Teaches kittens wrong from right
Saves his hide with hiss or bite
Costume is a tad too tight
Scared of mice, mad as a kite

Heroes are so scarce today
He's the saviour here to stay
Whether we like it or not
Wonder Cat's the best we've got.

'WONDER CAT' THEME

THE FACTORY WAS always cold. The draught froze the crew despite their fur coats. Long since stripped of its machinery, the building was a dusty husk with no insulation, no soul. Wind, rain and pigeons flew in through holes in the roof. Windows were cracked and shutters warped. It made the perfect location for a TV show.

Each floor held a workspace the size of a football pitch, surrounded by smaller rooms that had once been offices. Now only spiders enjoyed the benefits of the air vents, spinning their traps in desk drawers. Metal pins jutted from the concrete, spiking in all directions like cave formations. The machines that they had once supported had produced Harman's Biscuits, before some boffin had suggested that the product might be bad for consumers.* The place duly closed, hundreds of workers lost their jobs and their supply of crunchy perks.

Now the red husk was up for sale – four million to the first real estate developer that came along. Before that, there was an interim function for the factory to perform. Some of the rooms had been transformed into sets, and several film crews had hired it out for a month or two.

Cats love going to the movies. They enjoy sitting in a dark, warm room with a like-minded audience, plenty of food and drink handy in cardboard maxicartons. Anyone whose mobile phone rings in the middle of a film gets their eyes scratched out. Cinemas make their money not from tickets but from marked-up popcorn, milk and pieces of string. The audience has a very short attention span – anything longer than a one-reeler begs intolerance.

Number one at the box office was a yarn starring Scratch and Sniff, a popular cat-and-mouse combo. They'd enjoyed many adventures together, chasing each other across locations around

---

* The biscuits have been found to contain a gelatine substance which may be proved to be harmful when ingested, especially during pregnancy. While no firm evidence can be provided at this time – such proof would only appear after years of research – the negative effects cannot be satisfactorily disproved either. In the meantime, we cannot recommend the vending of said items.
(MAYORAL SURGEON'S REPORT, CENTRAL CITY RECORDS)

the globe. The stories were always the same but the filmmakers took the opportunity to visit exotic locations and generally enjoy themselves. The audiences kept paying to see the movies, no matter how slipshod their quality.

Whatever scrapes they got into, the characters would always survive for another encounter. Scratch the Cat would be charged by his boss with the capture of the notorious rodent, Sniff. Either that or Scratch would be minding his own business, Sniff would come along and tease him until the chase began. Or vice versa. Scratch always won in the end, of course, but Sniff gained small victories in the course of the narrative. An adaptation for the theatre (The Cat Trap) had recently completed the longest run in showbiz history with patrons coming back repeatedly, even though they knew the ending.

Softly Softly Catchee Mousy, the latest Sniff movie, was in the can. The factory was clear for a TV crew to set up, ready to shoot an equally successful series for the small screen.

Hairy Bancroft was hungry. He loved getting fanmail, and he adored the fact that he got more than any of his co-stars. There wasn't a TV personality as worshipped as he. Meowed at in the street, given preferential treatment in public lavatories, he only had one foe: the producers of his programme.

Joel Venet wasn't a mean or petulant guy. He was perpetually stressed, and had no time to molly-coddle his star. He threatened to cut the actor's ample wages, shouted at him when a line was skipped; worst of all, he'd put Hairy on a diet.

A dirty word in the cat dictionary, dieting was the worst thing that could be forced upon them. Burning at the stake, being eaten alive by goats, a gherkin up the nose – all fates were preferable to the Big D. Hairy was powerless to complain; there was a clause in his contract. It was written in print so small that the typist had required a special set of midget keys to set it out. Those wee words, so unassuming in size, insisted that the star of *Wonder Cat* remain under a certain weight. But with the stresses of fame and wealth Hairy continued to balloon.

He looked different in every episode, fat one week, starving the next. His costume had been taken in and out more times than a hokey cokey dancer's leg. He ate boring food, walked from his winnebago to each location, exercised his eyebrows every morning. None of this seemed to suffice; he was gross. Watching the crew stuff their faces every five minutes made things tougher.

Even though he'd signed away his fun, Hairy was a trouper. For years he'd entertained the masses with his deeds of derring-do. He still remembered the audition with awful clarity, although he'd tried hard to erase it from his mind. It hadn't been his first kettle run, but he was still nervous. His agent had told him it was some kind of presenting job, and he'd turned up in a black velvet suit.

He'd soon learned that the producers were looking for something completely different, an athletic type. His background was in modelling; he was known as the Super Chunks Hunk. Their background was in double-dealing, brown-nosing and grabbing as many freebies as possible. He'd read for them ('truth, justice and get out of my way!') unable to glance up from the script, a video camera catching his every grimace.

Back then he'd been shy, wiry and handsome as a crooner. He lacked experience and talent. The producers saw past these deficiencies – never imperatives for a TV star – and saw a greenhorn they could mould, exploit. He would thank them for it. As the show became a success, ratings increased and Hairy's head swelled, he learned some big words: contractual dispute. Moral copyright. Repeat fees. With an efficient lawyer and a series of hypnotherapy sessions with Doctor Matt Mildrew to help him recall his lines, he'd established himself as a major pain-in-the-ass star.

Four wives, six children, twelve agents and one salad later he was knackered. He still provided entertainment for nationwide audiences, who tuned in every week to follow the adventures of a loveable, overweight superhero.

Wonder Cat lived in the fictional suburb of Pickles. He worked with other feisty champions (Wonder Dog, Captain Cow; Super Skunk worked alone) battling colourful villains and getting into scrapes. Hairy's portrayal of an ignorant naïf had been lauded by critics until everyone had realised that he wasn't acting. He was ignorant and innocent. Now he was a national treasure, loved by grannies, admired for his candour in a world of deceit and solicitors. Every year he asked for a raise; every year Joel begged him to lose a stone. Neither cat got quite what they wanted, but the friction helped to keep the set vibrant.

This week's vibrancy was provided by shivering crewmembers, freezing their pads in the draughty factory. Gaffers and sound recordists stood around, shuffling their paws; Hairy was taking too long in make-up.

Jo Madrigal was a voluptuous birman who specialised in deception. She rejuvenated the old, disguised the most notorious of stars and even managed to give Hairy's sagging face some sparkle. He was the first to admit that he'd lost his good looks; his jowls drooped like unset jelly, the bags beneath his eyes had their own matching luggage, his chins flapped and his fur had started to grey. No wonder he spent so much time in make-up. With all the magic of show business at his disposal, he was determined to use every single spell to fix his face.

Jo was his favourite make up artist, best at disguising his furrows. She had a long silky coat and ruff, a round face, full body, her tail long but shaggy, her deft paws white as granulated sugar. She took time and care over each fold, adding foundation and concealer with the deft brushstrokes of an Old Master. She'd also fix the fur on top of his head, which was cursed with a wayward tuft that tickled his right ear.

'What you doing today, Hairy?' asked Jo, making conversation. She was a congenial hostess, warm and sympathetic to everyone's problems.

'No idea, sweetie.' The actor glanced at his script, his chin nudged upright by Jo's firm paw. 'They keep changing the shooting order all around the place. Have to wing it as usual.'

'I wouldn't blame the director,' Jo laughed, 'he's doing the best he can. I think we're already over budget. This is my own make-up kit, you know. The production company ran out of blusher. If I hadn't used my initiative, She-Cat's cheeks would be sallow.'

'Has it started raining again?' Hairy wasn't interested in Jo's woes. 'I'm not leaving this trailer without a brolly.'

The actor admired himself in the mirror while Jo popped her head outside. When it rained in Nub City, it rained darkly. Black clouds raged above the factory, unleashing a steady shower. She whistled for a runner, who sauntered up to the make-up trailer.

'Lord Muck insists on an umbrella,' she explained to the lackey. Rolling his eyes, he disappeared to fetch a brolly. The costume and continuity people would be pleased to see that Hairy's superhero outfit would stay dry, but Jo took exception to the star's insistence that someone hold the umbrella for him. A perk of the job, he called it. She saw it as a petty display of elitism, intended to make the rest of the cast jealous. It worked.

The factory was the least glamorous location the director could find. As Hairy was escorted from the make-up trailer, he passed scrap and junk piled up in the yard before entering a rear passage that was dank and leaking. There wasn't room for the umbrella so the runner held a copy of the script over Hairy's head.

Rain-sodden flags steam-dried beside hot halogens; dry ice was spread round the set by runners waving pieces of cardboard. Extras kipped in an anteroom, ready to spring into inaction in an instant. The director ignored the script and made shots up as he went along; the continuity cat noted all mangled dialogue and miss-takes; gaffers leaned on a console, smoking, breaking wind. Sound recordists gossiped like spider monkeys. The PA ensured everyone was on their mark at the right time; the actors mumbled to themselves, sipping coffee, scoffing biscuits. The producer oversaw everything, the general, the grand magician, holding the purse strings. The producer was a nervous wreck.

The scene in production was a simple one. Wonder Cat would discuss a murder with his mate and partner in crime busting, She-Cat. Joel had made sure that Hairy's lines would be few and simple.

The victim had no enemies. He was bothered by a phone pest? We've a killer to catch.

The words didn't quite come out like that.

SHE-CAT: We've run a trace on the corpse, the family, close friends – they don't know how the killer got into – into – (actress looks for prompt, stifles a giggle, Take 2) – the museum. All his colleagues have alibis.

WONDER CAT: The victim had no enemas.

SHE-CAT: Except for the obscene calls.

WONDER CAT: He was bothered by a pone fest?

Cut.

The third attempt was an improvement, although Hairy was still having trouble with the 'pone fest' line. By the fourth take the director had settled for 'problem caller.' The cause of recurring sound difficulties was tracked to the main actor's stomach, which kept rumbling.

'Could we break for lunch, please?' asked Hairy innocently. The director nodded ruefully, sure that his star acted up on purpose. The crew moved back to first positions, then raced to the chuck wagon for a quick cup of milk. The producer snuck off to satisfy his own vice.

The only thing that kept Joel sane during production was veiled from the rest of the crew. Only once had a Second AD caught him with a speck of white on his nose, and Joel had passed it off as spilt milk.

Sneaking into the gallery, a narrow booth filled with monitors displaying each camera's POV, he began to relax. Tranquillity. No one to ask him daft questions, shout at him, beg him to stretch the budget in their direction. Easing open a console drawer, he rummaged inside until he found a saucer. Pulling it out, he placed it on top of a DAT player.

Joel didn't hate Hairy; he found him endearing. The actor was a creative type, a drama darling. He didn't appreciate the finite budgets, filming costs, and the money it took to keep his saucer full.

Listening out for his colleagues, he leaned over his saucer and opened his mouth. Lowering his flat pink tongue, he curled it into a spoon shape and lapped up scoops of full fat double cream from the saucer. As he swallowed the nectar a cool, delightful feeling slid down his chest, into his stomach.

'Keeping busy, Joel?' The producer looked up, hiding the saucer behind his back. He offered a relieved smile to his colleague, who whacked him in the face with an Apollo stand. Joel fell backwards, banging his head on a console. Before he could pick himself up, his attacker was on top of him, a wire clutched in each forepaw. The producer struggled as the two bare ends of the wires were placed in his ears. The attacker backed off. From the corner of his eye Joel could see a switch being flicked.

12

'YOU'RE COMING WITH me, whether you like it or not.' Tiger sweated in the hothouse, watching a school of greenfly settle on a plant.

Bug couldn't argue with her friend; he had already grasped her by the shoulder and was dragging her from her pedipalps. 'Where's the fire?'

'In the old biscuit factory. They're filming a TV show there. Someone's copped it. Heard it on the police band.'

'You want me to have a look?'

'I want us to examine the crime scene before the cops hop their clods all over the place. You know I wouldn't interrupt your... important research if this weren't a matter –'

'– Of life and death, I know. I could lose my job because of you, pal.' They'd reached the zoo exit. 'I'm supposed to give notice before I take a break. In writing. In triplicate. They're very strict.'

'If they say anything, I'll have a word and explain the severity of the situation. Whatever it takes to smooth things over.'

Bug gave Tiger a smile. She'd enjoyed her visit to the Hant house, had been itching for a new adventure until her old boss had rushed in to grab her.

The 3C had been upholstered by an official with no imagination. He'd tried to please everyone with grey seats and cushions; no one enjoyed the result. Fine lines of blue, red, yellow and green ran across the back of each seat. The floor and windows were trimmed with black rubber. Netting hung from above, ready to bear passengers' parcels and messages. Beside each seat was a Request Stop bell, which could be rung with a flick of a paw or tail. The windows were stickered: NO HISSING, NO DROOLING. The tram got mucky enough as it was, covered in paw prints.

'What's in this for you, exactly? You fancy this Connie dame or something?' Bug curled up on a seat, tucking her tail round her belly.

'I have a mystery to solve. Why do you always think there's

lust involved in these cases?' Tiger took a good look at his friend. She looked cosy.

'These dames are bad for you. Always get you flustered, make you miss things. Side-track you. Why else would you wanna move in with dizzy Ms Hant?'

'She needs looking after. She's in mourning.'

'She's leading you on,' sighed Bug, 'using you. Got you running round chasing after nothing. You gonna tell me where we're headed?'

'It ain't nothing, I'll tell you that much.'

Reaching their destination, Tiger and Natasha hopped off the tram, sniffing at the thick-smogged air. The factory loomed, a stout red tower at the centre. The detective strolled towards it, his assistant at his heels trying to look reluctant. Tiger stopped and pointed.

A group of cats in baggy suits were marching purposefully up the street. At their head, bellowing orders and running to keep up, was a mouse.

'Police,' Tiger explained. 'We've got to beat them to the body.' He hurtled down a side alley, followed closely by Natasha. The pair scattered trashcans, bin bags, cardboard boxes in their wake. Drainpipes arched above them, a skyful of lead-lined tubing. The ground was icy and Tiger skated on frozen puddles of rain and urine. Light at the other end of the alleyway led them to their destination.

Dashing under a security gate and into the monstrous building, they ascended three flights of stairs and reached the set. The police were right behind them.

'I'm Detective Straight, this is my colleague,' Tiger harangued the key grip. 'Where's the body?' Marching pawsteps echoed behind him. 'There are some guys on their way, posing as policemen. Fake ID. Stall 'em.' The grip indicated the gallery; the investigators went in, scanning the room for clues.

'Cream fan.' Tiger placed a paw in Joel's saucer, took a lick. 'A drop of the rich stuff. Looks like he was interrupted mid-meal.'

'This is no time for eating,' Natasha panted.

'There's *always* time for eating. Bastet on a bicycle. The poor geezer's roasted.' The wires still hung from Joel's ears. He was slumped against a swivel chair, a silly grin on his blackened face.

Natasha had already extracted her magnifying glass, giving the corpse a once-over, not the least bit squeamish. Tiger could hear voices arguing outside.

'Take a look at this,' he said, drawing Natasha's attention to the wire trailing from Joel's left ear. Bringing her tool to bear, the assistant found a scrage of red on the insulation.

'Blood?'

'Polish. The same kind that coated that claw extension.'

'Let me guess,' interrupted Inspector Mortis, 'you're two hams rehearsing the next episode. There's been a murder and someone's got to pay?'

'Not bad, Inspector,' said Tiger, towering over the rodent. 'Are you a late lunch?'

'Don't test me, laddie. You're messing with due procedure.' Natasha was ready to leave. She gave her partner a wary look. 'If you've disturbed anything,' the mouse continued, 'I'll have your collars felt.'

'We're not messing with anything. We're leaving.'

'Nobody's leaving until I say so.'

'Nice one, chief,' Natasha glowered. Tiger gave her a shrug. He showed Mortis his card with an impressive flourish.

'You think this will get you special treatment?' piped the Inspector. 'I've heard of you. Thought you'd retired.'

'I wish. My bones ache and my kidneys are kaput. But I still got incisors that are good and sharp.' He proved it by chattering his teeth together. 'My taste buds are tip top... little mousy.'

The Inspector clapped his paws together. The sound was barely audible in the factory, but his underlings hung on his every movement. Two constables pushed Tiger and Natasha onto canvas chairs beside the set.

'How long you gonna be?' asked the detective.

'As long as I like.' Tiger had never seen a mouse wield so much power. The implications were frightening.

With the slow sureness that only a police officer can have, Bix interviewed the crewmembers. The gaffers hated Joel because he was a public school toffee, and he ignored them except when they made a mistake. They hadn't seen anything. No wires or cables were missing.

The sound recordist had always found the producer annoying because Joel would make mysterious slurping noises during a take. The director argued with him about shots and the script supervisor was sick of disputes over dialogue. They were all glad to see the back of him, though they didn't approve of the way he'd died.

Hairy's turn came.

'You can't interrogate me. I'm an icon. I represent something that television viewers nationwide aspire to. Heroism. Masculinity. Swift intelligence. Stoicism in the face of danger.' He prostrated himself in front of Mortis. 'I'm a lively soul. Magazine readers want to know what I eat, what I inhale. I don't want them reading about police harassment, their best-loved pin up grilled by a rodent. They'll march on City Hall and demand the instant dissolution of your police force. If they don't get it (proving once and for all that our democracy is a sham) they'll gobble you up, notebook and pencil.'

'A few questions, Mr Bancroft. That's all.' Mortis was the stoic one, with the panicked actor towering over him. 'I don't watch TV and I don't read magazines. I'm too busy earning my cheese, although I do hear that glossy periodicals make good bedding when shredded. Don't look glum, I have heard of you. You're a liability to your channel. You're a party favour, a fop, a brute who can't remember a line of script. You're a numbskull, a fluff merchant, a blooper and a bloomer. I don't think in terms of repercussions, Hairy. I deal with the here and now. I ask simple questions; I expect them to be answered simply. In your case, I don't think that'll be trouble.'

'My agent knows more solicitors than –'

'The longer you procrastinate, the more suspicious my colleagues become. You want your fans to read about your night in the nick? Your trial? Your sentence?'

Hairy shook his head.

'Did you kill Joel Venet?'

'No,' Hairy sniffled.

'Thank you. Go on home.'

'Is it our turn yet?' asked Tiger, feeling flippant.

'It's your turn when I say it is,' Bix twittered, scratching notes in his tiny book. 'It's your turn.'

'Great. Where do we start? You want to hear about our day in general?' Bug gave the Inspector a wink, but she felt worried. It was a bad idea to rile an official, even one who happened to be a rodent.

'Don't bother with all that nonsense. Stick to the plain truth.'

'That's all you're interested in?' Tiger started playing with one of the cameras, positioning it so that it faced another. Feedback screeched from a monitor; the sound recordist hurriedly turned the volume down. 'No conjecture, or intelligent analysis of the situation, or jokes about frying tonight?'

'Tell me what happened.'

'We heard this guy was dead. We came for a sniff. Held our noses. Ready to leave when you turned up and pooped our party.' Tiger watched the howlaround on the monitor, as the two cameras bounced images off each other. Jigsaw shapes fluctuated on the screen.

'What's your interest in this case?' Mortis asked wearily. He liked to look his suspects in the eye, even if it meant they had to stoop down to him. All the better in fact – they were more likely to crack with a sore back.

'We solve murders.' Tiger still refused to make eye contact with his interrogator.

'I know you've been out of work for a while, Mr Straight. When a person loses their home, their office, their friends – they get desperate.' That got the cat's attention.

'You can't pin this on me, bub.'

'Desperate enough to kill. Job creation?'

'I don't work that way. I've got a sound record. Always kept my whiskers clean.'

'I'm fully conversant with your record.' An aside to Bug: 'It's not as spot-free as he makes out. I don't want to see you at the scenes of any more crimes. I've no time for private dicks.'

'Can we go now?' asked Natasha.

'I suppose so,' said Mortis with a dismissive wave of his paw, 'but I'm sure I don't have to tell you –'

'– Not to leave town. No. We've got lots to keep us busy round here.' Tiger led his friend away from the set. 'Detention's over,' he muttered, 'let's go.' On his way out of the building, Tiger bumped into Jo, the beautiful birman.

'Nice claws,' said Tiger to the makeup artist, 'do them yourself?' Jo's talons gleamed with ripe red varnish – the same shade they'd seen on the extension. Natasha's ears pricked up.

'I do everyone's claws. It's part of my job.'

The detectives introduced themselves.

'I'm Jo.' She gave Tiger a faint curtsey. 'You know who did this terrible thing? 'Cos I'd like to kick his back.'

'You were a good friend of the producer?'

'Nah. The production will be suspended. Until they find another whiskerless wonder to finish the job, I'm out on my ear. No point taking another post in the meantime – this show's so popular, so long running, it's the closest they got to a secure contract in this industry.'

'I don't suppose this accident'll hurt *Wonder Cat*'s success any.'

'That's a morbid thought.' Jo's eyes narrowed.

'I might have to get in touch with you again, miss. Ask you a few questions.'

'Sure.' Jo gave him her card, watched the pair leave, examined her claws carefully. The police were interrogating the director. She wasn't getting home in time for tea.

'It's over,' Bug purred. 'The case is solved. We know who dunnit. The cops will do the dirty work for us. She'll be in jail by nightfall.'

Tiger stayed silent, deep in thought.

'Whassamatter? I got your tongue?' Bug ran round till she was in front of her partner, slowing him down. He gave her a stern look.

'You haven't!' Bug giggled.

Tiger broke his silence. 'Haven't what?'

'Fallen for her.'

'I don't believe this case is as simple as it seems. It has hidden depths. Jo's a suspect, sure, but she's not the only doll who wears red varnish.'

'You're besotted with her. The cops'll put two and two together –'

'They won't make four.' Tiger showed Bug his hankie; it was smeared blood red. 'I tampered with the evidence.'

'Why?'

'I need to do more investigating. Can't have Inspector Mortis diluting the solution.'

'You saw Jo's claws before you checked out the gallery?'

'I took a course in resourceful. Heck, I wrote the training manual.'

'Pleased with yourself?'

'Enthused like you – don't deny it. You know this is serious. Connie's in danger, so are we. Innocent lives.'

'We're not innocent.'

'We're on the right side.'

'So what do the good guys do next? From what you're saying, that varnish we found could be more of a red herring than a clue.'

'Red herring?'

'Aye.'

'We do what any self-respecting cat should do at this time of day. We eat.' There was a café in the zoo. Natasha suggested that they snack there; she could apologise for leaving her glasshouse post. When they got there, her employers didn't want to know.

'Leave this to me,' said Natasha, storming towards the head zookeeper's office. 'I'll meet you in the caf.'

The office sported an eclectic mix of wood floorboards, columns pink as a newborn pup, silver desks and chairs and a heater shaped like a beach umbrella. The walls were yellow and grey with small, circular lights beaming from discreet alcoves. The ceiling was turquoise; another row of inset lights spread starsplashes of yellow overhead. Brent Motter, head of Nub City Zoo, was sniffing Bug's personal file.

'What's going on? Someone else running my area, scaring my subjects?' Her sacred ground had been defiled and her tail bristled at the thought.

'Your subjects are intended for public display,' said Motter, calm but firm. 'We've tolerated your experiments and secrecy up till now. Your papers and reports have been immaculate.'

'Then what's your point?'

'My point is there is no point.' There was a sadness in his eyes. 'People are interested in bugs as a source of food, not of scientific research. You might as well study mince and tatties. We can't fund your work any more.'

'No one can look after the insects like I can. They're my friends.'

'That's why we're having to let you go. You scare the cubs.'

Natasha slammed a paw on the desk, which gave a hollow metallic ring. 'This is entomological discrimination. I shall complain to the Board of Governors.'

'Your methods are too unorthodox to interest any board of study. Putting different classes together, hoping they'll get along. What kind of research is that? We'll give you good references and a week's pay in lieu.'

Natasha was already on her way out of the office.

'Hell mend you, Brent. For all your "we" crap, you're the one who's firing me. I won't forget it.'

The café was a vast, high-tech building with murals depicting edible fauna. Visitors took their mealtimes seriously. Tiger had ordered a chicken, a bowl of milk, beef on the bone, a lucky rabbit's foot and a plate of marshmallows. The starter had arrived when Natasha collared the PI.

'We're leaving.'

'I'm eating!'

'You can't patronise this establishment.'

'The rabbit's foot is a nice touch.'

'They've let me go. I seem to be a liability.' A serving lynx protested. 'Bill me,' Natasha snorted as they hurried away.

13

NUT CROSSED HER legs. She needed the bathroom again.

Since the murder, the barn had become a spookier place to be. Dust rained from the rafters and carpeted the floor. The straw had a mottled taste. Strange echoes and ugly thuds interrupted her sleep. Shadows lost their form, oozed. She wasn't sure what cast them anymore.

There was something about a shadow, a half-glimpsed memory that refused to surface. She would have kicked herself but that was impossible with crossed legs. She unfolded them and went to find the loo.

The sun had set in spades, there was no light to see by. Walking on the tips of her hooves, taking care not to wake her neighbours, Nut manoeuvred past stalls and hay bales. Her eyes refused to adjust to the dark so she kept walking until her nose bumped into something. It was warm and breathing heavily. She gave a shudder, clamping her eyes tight shut.

A blunt object struck her under the chin, knocking her onto the floor. Before she could utter a sound, a second blow to the head whacked her silly. She knew this was the end; as consciousness slipped away she thought of her calves, and a fat cheque from the insurance company.

14

Who needs exercise and runs?
I'm a fan of toasted buns
Low fat cheese, low fat spread
Never were my daily bread
Stop the presses, hold the 'phones
I'm in love with herringbones
Cooler than ten ice cream cones
Frozen in the snow

Hunger ain't my cup of char
Starving doesn't get me far
Who wants to be skin and ribs
When we can be wearing bibs?
With your breath of dover sole
You're my tuna casserole
Now I'm on a jelly roll
I can see my belly loll.

Watch your weight don't watch me wait
My fridge door is heaven's gate
Heading for pasteurides new
So many cakes to get through.
Veg and salad's not for me
Not all life can be fat free
One tum ain't as good as four
Ban diets – stay on the floor.

'DOVER SOUL' LYRICS BY DOCTOR FAT

'CAN YOU HELP me fix my fur? I can't do a thing with it.' Jo hoped that Tiger was joking. He proved her right when he cracked a grin. He'd visited her house with the express intention of grilling her for information. He hadn't got round to it so far; he was distracted.

'I'm a makeup artist, not a furdresser. You're all windblown.' Jo obligingly stroked his head, the back of his neck, fussing over him maternally. He couldn't recall the last time he'd been stroked, and he had a damned good memory. He stood in her front hall, his eyes closed, enjoying the moment. Then he collected his senses and reminded himself why he was there.

'I've got those questions for you if they're not too much to ask.' Tiger cleared his throat.

Jo snatched her paw away, gave her visitor a strange look. He handed over his business card – she sniffed it, reading the scent that formed his credentials. Nodding slowly, she bade him sit on one of the swanky leather cushions.

'You know where you were when your producer copped it?'

'Reckon so,' Jo shrugged, 'I was on set. Hairy Bancroft – the lummox who plays Wonder Cat – gets precious about his laughter lines, the state of his whiskers. I'm always there to touch him up if necessary. The crew'll vouch for me.'

'You always wear those claw extensions?' Jo was wearing her red-varnished claws again. Manual work would have been impossible with those talons attached; Tiger was surprised that she could make Hairy up without poking his eyes out.

'Once they're adhered it's hell getting them off again. They're my one vanity.' Her fur was tousled and she wore a faded white dress. Nothing fancy. Jo had nothing to accessorise, but she still insisted on wearing her extensions.

'So you don't lose 'em very often?'

'Impossible. I chuck 'em away when they're done, when the varnish starts flaking. Not every day. Why the big interest in my nails?'

'One more question,' Tiger mumbled.

'Query away.'

'Can you come dancing with me tonight? I'd like to spend the evening flattering you mercilessly.'

'If every tom gave me a line like that I'd spend my evenings at home. You're different. Call me a guppy, I'm hooked.'

'Fine. Eight o'clock, the Wu Wu Club?'

'My favourite haybarn. See you there.'

Nut was hanging upside down. Her hooves were numb, blood rushing to her head. Straining to look up, she found herself suspended from a steel wire, stirrups looped round her ankles. Her legs ached.

Inchmeal she took in her surroundings. She could smell blood and dead flesh; on the far side of the icy room she could see carcasses swinging from hooks. Dozens of dead cows stripped of their hides, eyes frosted over. An obscene sight. She was next.

To her right almost level with her head was a metal box on runners. It automatically travelled across the floor, and every now and again a thick bolt would jut from its side. There was a greasy pop whenever this happened. Nut dully realised that the box would soon reach her; the bolt would be in line with her skull. She began to struggle, flicking her tail, writhing in her bonds. They held firm.

I ain't going out like this. Straining her udder muscles, she summoned up every ounce of milk in her system and squooshed it upwards. Warm white liquid jetted from her teats, lubricating the stirrups enough for her to wriggle her forehooves free. Now she dangled precariously, swinging close to the box. Gravity did the rest of the work, wrenching her free so she landed in a heap on the concrete floor. Centimetres from her head, the bolt popped. She offered it a derisory snort, stumbling from the slaughterhouse.

The Wu Wu Club had a strict dress code – no butterfly collars, no platform boots, no clip-on ties or studded leather. It was an up-to-date establishment with a young, hip clientele. It wasn't the most lavish club in the city. It was the best Tiger could afford, and the drinks were cheap. So he took the plunge and queued with his date.

He'd managed to rescue some furniture from his apartment and hock it for a bagful of dough. He needed enough to bribe informants, pay off bad guys, impress Jo and generally buy himself out of trouble. The pawnshop provided a short-term solution. Tiger didn't want to think about the long term.

The pumas at the entrance looked uncomfortable in their tuxes. They were on orders to let only hep cats into the club, and asked each oncomer to prove how cool they were. A couple of lads in zoot suits performed a pathetic polka. They were sent packing, their heads hung low. Tiger and Jo watched as two females in front of them pogoed into the club.

'Let me handle this,' said Jo softly, dancing a five second ballet around the bouncers. She was fantastically graceful, a stranger to gravity, floating back to her date. They were allowed in no problem.

The foyer was decorated with soothing greens and blues. Enticing sounds and smells ushered the clubbers onwards; a vast cloakroom was filled with the vain cats' garments. At the end of the foyer lay the club proper, flanked by bars offering live food and milk pitchers.

On a small stage stood a DJ with two turntables. He was joined by a trio of jazz musicians, including a cat with a fiddle. Together they played repetitive music, easy to dance to, hard to forget. Skittish young clubbers capered on a chequered neon dance floor. More laid back, shy or elderly felines sat on cushions, bopping their heads and shoulders to the tunes in ancient catdancing tradition.

Tiger made a beeline for the bar, where Jo offered to buy the first round. Lactose dependants lazed on stools, their weakness given away by their milk moustaches.

'What'll it be?' asked the bartender. The couple couldn't hear him, deafened by the music, each wall an amplifier.

'Two pints of milk,' shouted Tiger, glancing at his date, 'in the bottles.' The drinks came fresh from the fridge. Jo paid the bar-keep and bopped over to a mound of cushions. Tiger joined her as she supped her white stuff.

'Been here before?' she asked. He shrugged; the band had deafened him, and his paws were tapping involuntarily. He watched the DJ on stage, who'd clambered onto the turntables and was spinning at 45 rpm. Jo put down her bottle and dragged the detective onto the dance floor.

Together they muscled their way past boogying couples and began to dance. Tiger nudged Jo's forehead tenderly with his nose, and they relaxed in each other's paws. His money worries faded as he gazed into her jade eyes. The club's resident singer, Doctor Fat, appeared on stage and sang a ballad. His belly quivered with emotion.

A spotlight picked out various dancers, their hind paws kicking up purple dust, the faint smell of sour dairy products in their nostrils. They swanned or smooched or jiggled their way through Fat's set list, blissful smiles on their faces. The spotlight reached Tiger, tilting up to catch his eyes. The singer recognised him immediately.

No words were exchanged. Fat never spoke – he only sang. It was his trademark. He nodded at the saxophonist, who removed the black sling from round his neck and held out his instrument to Tiger. The detective exchanged a reluctant glance with his partner, then shimmied up to the stage. He shook his head but the musicians were already hauling him up to join them. Tiger took the precious sax and wrapped his lips over the mouthpiece. Fat belted out a soulful song, and the crowd stopped mid-step to hear the saxophone's lilt.

Their ears clamped downwards. Some of them went to the bar for a stiff pint; many left the club altogether. Tiger was oblivious, writhing to his own beat, while the band shook their heads and motioned to their engineer to switch off his PA. Tiger didn't need a mike. He was in solo heaven, his paws gripping the sax, his eyes locked on Jo's. She wore a pained expression, so he finished his toneless tune and made an announcement to the dwindling audience.

'I'd like to dedicate this last piece to the prettiest lady in make-up.' The patrons applauded, grateful that Tiger was finishing up. If they'd known that the piece would consist of twenty minutes of noodling, they wouldn't have been so encouraging.

'You're lucky they're so polite in there,' said Jo after the performance. 'Any place else and you'd have been lynched.'

'It was a bit cheeky of me, taking to the stage like that.' They were taking a moonlight prowl homewards. Tonight Tiger felt invincible. 'I hate to overshadow Doctor Fat. He didn't seem to mind. Recognises talent when he hears it.'

'He packed up and left halfway through your act.'

'Yeah. Said he needed to get out of there fast. Know what he means, that place is stuffy.' The sax hung round his neck, spit dribbling from an open valve. 'Maybe I should enter a new profession.'

'You're a fine detective,' replied Jo hurriedly. 'Stick to what you're best at.' Tiger gave her a funny look.

'What I'm best at is what I love. And what I love is music.' He placed the mouthpiece to his puffed pink lips, took a deep breath – Jo yanked the instrument away.

'I'll take that. It's not yours anyway.'

'But I –'

'There's a lot of families in this neighbourhood, you'll wake the kittens. I'll return this to its rightful owner first thing in the morning.'

'Sorry. I love you, Jo.'

'I thought music was what you loved.'

'I wasn't thinking. I didn't plan on – telling you how I felt about us. It slipped out.' Tiger's timing was lousy as ever. They'd reached Jo's house and without a further word, she went inside. He stood in the street for a long time, the night growing colder. Foolish. He was getting side-tracked. Jo reckoned he was a good detective; it was time to live up to his reputation.

Nut was spending too much time in Bertie's tavern. Her pals were present, she'd met her beau for the first time there. Yet it still wasn't the done thing for a cow to prop up a bar. Since Scrumpy's demise she'd been drowning her sorrows, getting over the fright, waiting for delayed shock. There was some niggling thought at the back of her brain, struggling for attention. Frustrating.

Work continued as if no one had died; the dairy had appointed a new boss, and the interim had seen various tabbies collecting the milk. They had cold pads and a brusque demeanour. So after a shift the cows would visit Bertie's – for a quick one – leaving Nut to spend the evening there. She'd wake up next morning in a pool of drool; she was too heavy for the barkeep to carry home. Back to the daily grind, chewing the cud, queuing up in a field for hours, giving milk on demand. She hadn't seen her calves for days.

Every item of bar gossip was old news, every joke as stale as last month's bread. The latest topics of conversation included the poor work conditions, the draughty shed, the big ears on the cow in stall 3B, hoofache and the latest bovine fashions (mostly involving outrageous headgear).

Nut had been an idiosyncratic cow since her college days. She'd spent little time learning how to chew cud in a refined manner; most of her activities had centred on trying to catch a bull's eye. That bull had become her husband, loyal, full of tact and flatulent. She was delicate and bright, with a big family. She was concerned about two large black spots on her forehead, teased about them since childhood. Apparently all Friesians had the same trouble; she'd been affected worse than most, lying awake worrying about her appearance. Hubby chalked it down to vanity. He hadn't suffered catcalls from the local farmers. He couldn't understand.

After escaping from the abattoir she'd reported her abduction to the police. They hadn't sounded particularly interested; they assumed that this was just another example of cow hysteria.

A mouse walked into the bar. It was the cop who'd interrogated her before, Inspector Mortis. He was too small to mount a stool and no one noticed him except for Nut. He scurried past one of the bar staff, who almost trampled the rodent. Unruffled, the Inspector squeaked at Nut: 'Come with me. You're not safe here.'

'You're going to protect me?' asked the cow. 'Where are we going?'

Bix led her out of the bar. 'Police Headquarters. We need to know exactly what you saw —'

'That might be difficult. I can't remember what my kidnapper looked like. My mind's a complete blank.'

Bix's nose twitched in annoyance. He'd already decided that Nut was a typical cow: all she cared about was chewing the cud.

'We're going to have to unblank that mind of yours,' he told her, 'whatever it takes.'

15

AS SOON AS Tiger got back to Connie's place, he aimed for the fridge. It held one pint of milk, which he carried gingerly into the living room. Sinking his weary buttocks onto a cushion, he popped the cap off the bottle and took a leisurely swig.

'What the hell do you think you're doing?' hissed Connie, looming over the private eye.

'Whatever I can to solve this case. I don't wanna be here any longer than I have to.' The cold drink whet his whistle, left him with a milky nose.

'Since when did sniffing for clues include dating your prime suspect?' Connie's ear fluttered.

'I need to find out a lot of things about Ms Madrigal now. Things she might not tell a stranger.'

'I think it's disgusting. If you're tired of this place you can go.'

'So you'll have more room for Mr Suave? Want plenty of space to roll around with him?'

'That's not what it's like.' Connie shut up, wondering if Tiger was jealous. What tom wouldn't envy the buff Cole Tiddle?

'It's what it looked like. I'll give you some privacy.' Tiger dropped the milk into a bin, picked up his worn case and left the apartment. Connie had lost a friend, and she felt strangely alone.

Tiger lolled through Totterdown, his brain spinning with stress. He feared for Connie's life, yet he couldn't stay in the apartment against her will. His pride was too set to allow him to go back, apologise.

The streets of Totterdown were paved with green-grey slabs, mossed over in places for extra traction. Tiger stopped near a short wrought iron gate, exhaling icy breath in primitive rings. A dirty plastic canopy jutted over the pavement, keeping some of the wind off. There was no way Jo could be involved in the murders; she wasn't the brutal type. In the unlikely event that she could have been responsible, she was far too canny to kill her producer.

No alibi, a high level of risk and electrical savvy to boot. He'd been a detective for longer than he remembered to care. His guts told him she was clean.

He wasn't going to give up the case, not after weeks of work. He certainly wasn't going to leave the job to his rival – he only trusted one guy and that cat played the sax. Cole could be busy double-dealing or (worse) get so horny he'd trip up. Tiger wanted to be there, watch him fall. Right now his only lead was a beautiful female desperate for companionship. Drop the case or pay her a visit? No contest!

Leafless trees jutted skyward like TV antennae. The setting sun silhouetted the branches, and staying out late wasn't the done thing in this quarter. The predators came out, seeking a feast. Even a cat who could take care of himself needed to find shelter. Tiger struck out for Jo's house.

Crime solving is a solitary occupation. You can't ask your missus to spend the night with you if you're on surveillance; she'll get bored and you might miss something while you're snogging. The role calls for love of detail, focus, clarity of thought – all the things a relationship can cloud. Tiger had been celibate for years, and he refused to believe that his music had anything to do with it. It'd been a conscious decision on his part to stay frosty.

Connie's original plea had appealed to his ego, his intellect and his belly. Jo invoked baser instincts. He wondered if Connie was jealous, then discounted the fancy. She was focused herself – on Cole's pecs.

Stone buildings gave way to wooden ones with lacy curtains and gleaming chrome drainpipes. Almost there. Two more blocks and he'd have somewhere warm to spend the night. Twelve minutes later he reached her house, a hundred years old, crumbling at the cornices. The windows were dead dark and his distinctive howl prompted no response. Filming of *Wonder Cat* had been suspended pending an inquest. Jo was probably out on the tiles with a butch beau.

Great. He was miles from home, the only friend he had in this part of town was a makeup artist he'd questioned in the course of an investigation... and she didn't appear to be in. Tiger wanted to make sure before he made the long journey home, so he entered the house and sniffed around. The bedroom was his last port of call. He found Jo on an orthopaedic mattress, her eyes wide open. Her breathing was shallow.

Tiger set down his case and tentatively nudged her, listening for a heartbeat. It was so faint he almost missed it. He breathed into her mouth and nose, his actions becoming more desperate as she refused to respond. Her body was cold and she smelled clammy; he wrapped a sheet round her, staying close to warm her. Growing frustrated with his lack of success, he placed a paw on her exposed tummy and jabbed her with his claws.

Jo stirred, pain showing in her eyes. She looked at Tiger, moving away from him, surprised to find him in her bed.

'You're gonna live,' he told her in relief. 'Try and breathe easy. You hurt anywhere?'

'My chest,' she replied, making sure that the sheet covered her from neck to tail. She didn't let any old tom look at her stomach. 'Feels tight. Hard to breathe.'

'It'll pass. Relax. You've had a minor attack is all.'

Jo soon improved, breathing carefully. The room still seemed to be spinning around her, but Tiger was a constant that she could lock onto. He held her tight until she was well enough to talk.

'This minor attack – they wanted me dead.'

'Who?' Tiger fumed. 'Someone slip you a mickey?'

'Gas. Heard noises on the landing. Thought it was burglars. When I went to investigate, I found a pipe leading up the stairs. It started pumping some foul-smelling smoke in my face. I made it to the bed...'

'I didn't see any burglars. No pipe neither.'

'They must have cleared it away, scarpered before you got here. No evidence. It was the kitty killers, mate. They want me dead, same reason they wanted to kill Joel.'

'Which is?'

'I'm trying to work it out. You're the detective. Maybe they don't like our show. Joel's death was in all the papers – maybe they're making a political statement.'

'Nah. If these deaths are linked... the other deaths didn't make front-page news. They would have hit bigger targets, more prominent cats.'

'You're right. I'm not important enough. They're crazy.'

'Did you see anything? Apart from the disappearing pipe, I mean?' As he spoke, Tiger took a gander at the landing. There was a trail of rust leading down the stairs, and a long groove had been left in the carpet.

'Nothing. I was looking out my bedroom window until I heard –'

'The strange noises. Yeah. What did you see?'

'Outside? Some youths coming home from the workhouse. Three of the neighbourhood toms on their way to the local sauna. Guys queuing for the meat market down the road. Nothing out of the usual.'

'I should make some enquiries,' Tiger mumbled.

'It's too late. Not right now. Stay with me, in case they come back – try to kill me again.'

'We need to find out who "they" are. I'm not going to do that sitting here on your oh-so-comfortable bed.'

'It's a special mattress. I spend a lot of time hunched over people in my line of work, painting their faces, fixing their fur. This helps straighten out my back and tail.'

'Fancy.'

Jo led her friend downstairs and they cooked up several kippers. Her near-death experience had given her an appetite, and Tiger was permanently hungry. He picked daintily at the fish, using his tongue to extract the bones and dribbling them onto his plate. Jo picked her teeth with her claws, making eyes at Tiger.

'I was wondering how long it'd take you to pay me a proper visit. Not on some pretext, I mean.'

'Interrogating you? I've run out of questions.' Tiger felt suddenly bashful.

'You got a mother? A father?'

'You'd like my dad. He's a genuine original. If he was any more down to earth he'd be crawling on his belly. Mum died a long time ago.'

'I lost touch with my parents. It was easier to stay away, I guess.' Most cats had an independent streak knocked into them at an early age. The offspring would often go too far, shunning their family. Jo would close her eyes and imagine her folks looking down on her, blissful with pride. Every day their faces became less distinct; soon she wouldn't be able to remember what they looked like.

'If I have kids I'll stay close to them, let them know I love 'em. Even after they leave home, I'll be there for them.'

'That's pretty much the way I feel.' Tiger felt drowsy, cleaned his plate quick. After supper he returned to the bedroom, Jo offering him her bed. It looked mighty cosy: a thick duvet, pillows that were soft but not too soft, a hot water bottle buried deep within.

'It's your place. You take the bed.' Tiger removed his trenchcoat.

'I'm fine in the airing cupboard. It's warm and cosy, and I'm not proud,' Jo protested. 'You're the guest. Take the bed.'

There was no point standing around arguing all night. Sleeping on a bed where she'd almost died didn't appeal to Jo at that moment. Tiger gave his host a friendly sniff on the neck then dived under the duvet. Bliss!

Nevertheless, the gumshoe found himself unable to sleep. He rolled onto his side, then his stomach, hindpaws entwined in a clean green sheet. He poked his nose out from under the covers, sure it had become colder in the room. He was about to sacrifice his place when a paw slipped under the duvet beside him. Slowly and carefully, trying not to disturb Tiger, Jo climbed into bed and stretched herself out. He breathed in her scent, didn't mind her cold pads and sharp claws on his flanks.

'You shouldn't get me excited, not in your condition.'

'You mean I'll be too weak to resist?'

'I'm the weak one,' said Tiger, turning to embrace her. He didn't get much sleep that night.

Connie entered the pub anxiously. She quickly caught sight of Cole, sitting on a leather seat cushion with small brass studs. His hindpaws barely reached the carpet, patterned with red seashells, interspaced with patches of grey. He had found a polished hardwood table close to the kitchen. On it sat a circular glass ashtray, with indents to rest cigarette butts. Two menus were lacquered and tarted up with a sprig of red ribbon on each spine. The items on the menu were garnished with dreadful gags and puns: 'you'll lap up our soup!' 'milk our shakes for all they're worth,' '*The Lost Keys* – the place to meet for a plate of meat.'

TVs were bracketed to the walls, flashing bright pictures at the patrons, mesmerising them, interrupting conversations with the sound of tinkling bells and squeaks. Posters on the walls were a reminder of past pub glories – epic quizzes, famous visitors.

The landlord's moustache was carefully trimmed and waxed, almost as long as the bar at full stretch. Punters traveled from near and far to see the face fungus. The milk was inexpensive; the pub made most of its money from fruit machines, cigarette dispensers and bar snacks. Their vole au vent was a speciality.

'I was expecting somewhere more... swanky,' said Connie as she joined Cole at the small round table.

'I'll let you into a secret,' whispered Cole, tapping his nose with a carefully extended claw. 'Having more moolah than you could hope to spend in nine lifetimes is boring. Deadly dull. Sometimes I like to escape from the millionaire trappings, slum it a little. A relaxed setting like this makes for a fun date. No formalities.' Connie opened her mouth to respond. 'The mutton with lamb dressing looks rather nice. Oh, don't take it personally,' Cole continued, 'I haven't invited you here because of your upbringing or anything like that. I'm not trying to bring myself down to your level – I don't think I could. I'm indulging myself. If you have any whims I'd be happy to tolerate them for you.'

Connie gave her date a mischievous smile.

'Show me the trappings,' she said.

Cole's house was in a far better neighbourhood than Connie could ever aspire to. Each room was the size of her apartment, carefully furnished, ornately decorated. The minute she entered the dwelling she got depressed, vowing to give up DIY for good. She'd worked hard to create a world in which she'd be comfortable; here was a place where her host would always be satisfied.

'Would you like a rub down?'

'We hardly know each other,' Connie said coquettishly. 'After we...'

'It's not a come-on,' Cole assured her. 'My personal masseur's in the west wing. He's excellent at unstiffening the joints. Fancy it?'

Connie nodded, embarrassed. She'd almost put her paw in it there. She didn't want her host to know that she planned to seduce him, work out who'd hired him. Not yet.

The cats visited a sauna room, languishing in the steamy heat. Connie tried to keep her towel on while Cole showed off his sexy body. It got too hot so she let the towel drop, her modesty preserved by the clouds of steam. Once they were ready to leave the room, the masseur was ready to work them over.

'You're a wonder, Snoke.' Cole sighed as his back received a soothing massage. 'Snoke's adept at acupuncture as well, aren't you?'

'That's right sir,' Snoke replied, digging a claw into Connie's gluteus maximus. She unleashed a happy yelp.

Once the pair had been rubbed up the right way, Cole gave his guest a tour. Labyrinthine hallways led to rooms that Cole seldom had the time to visit. They were kept free of dust by a horde of domestic staff, all provided by Purrtemps, an elite employment agency. The few areas that the millionaire *did* use included the games room, where he could play Catch the Bright Shiny Thing or that most popular of pastimes, Chase the Dangly Thing. He also showed Connie a lounge complete with leather cushions, a double sunbed and a movie screen. The kitchens were a part of the house he only visited when panged with the midnight munchies, grabbing himself a bowl of mice pudding or a packet of go-gos. He enjoyed cooking, though he had little time for it in his busy schedule. He saved his culinary conjuring tricks for special occasions and very special ladies.

A nursery waited for the children that Cole had never had. He hoped to fill the room one day; until then he would look at the cots and toys occasionally, hoping they'd inspire him. The simplicity of a cub's building blocks or the merchandising possibilities of a stuffed toy could send ideas rocketing round his head.

'You could house a whole family in here,' Connie mused, pressing the funnel on a scaled-down safari train. It emitted cheerful chuffs and whistles.

'This is for my family,' Cole rasped, ushering his date out of the room. He rapidly regained his composure. 'I didn't mean to be brusque. I was married once. Penny was barren. No, that's not true. I was the one who couldn't provide her with – couldn't make babies with her. We separated.'

'That can't have been the only reason you married.' This was more like it. Connie was getting under his skin, making him open up. At this rate he'd give her the information she needed before the evening ended.

'It wasn't. We got a divorce for other reasons too.'

'She was a gold digger?'

'I should have seen her shovel coming. Gold, silver and jade, my dear.'

'Nothing like me, then,' said Connie under her breath.

'No. Nothing like you. I still hope to have progeny one day. I've been taking fertility drugs, you know.'

'Any side effects?'

'They instill in me the urge to give my guests an exhaustive tour of my home and bore them to death with talk of past relationships.'

'Don't get you horny, then?'

'No. Life's too short for lust, don't you agree?'

'Whatever you say.'

Connie was particularly impressed with the gym and the hallway, which was dominated by a heavy tapestry. Ancient and beautiful, it depicted a group of cats shattering the bonds of slavery. An ancient race had once kept them as pets, cooped up, under control. No feline could put up with such treatment for long. Above the tableau was a heraldic symbol, Cole's family crest. His noble lineage was rooted in servitude.

Connie looked up at the sumptuous cloth, the woven tableau, thinking naughty thoughts.

'Go ahead,' said Cole softly.

'What?'

'Go on. I know what you want to do. Do it.'

'No, no I couldn't.' Connie became bashful. 'What would you think of me?'

'You're not afraid to live out your fantasies. Get up there.' She didn't need any more coaxing. Jumping as high as she could, she unleashed her claws and hooked them into the tapestry. Using them to hoist herself up, she made a scrambling ascent. Within seconds the cloth was ruined, shredded strips floating to the floor.

From the top of the tapestry Connie could see out the window, across the front lawn. She paused for breath, her purchase shaky. Cole joined her on the tableau, breathing hard. Their makeshift ladder swayed from side to side; the hooks that supported it were half out of the wall.

'I think we should get down from here, don't you?' she said.

'If we can…' Cole grabbed at Connie to support himself. 'Help me,' he said as they started to descend. She didn't want to let go of his paw. Within feet of the floor the hooks gave way and the cats landed, covered by the dusty cloth. Connie sneezed.

'You must think I'm awful clumsy,' laughed Cole. Connie shook her head.

'Look what I've done to your tapestry!' she said in dismay. 'I hope it isn't expensive to repair.'

'It'll cost more than the house,' Cole told her in a nonchalant manner. 'Worth it.' She would have felt nervous, but the tom hadn't relaxed his grip on her. If anything, it seemed to tighten.

'Take a look at this,' said Jo cheerfully, waking Tiger from an exhausted doze. She was staring out the window, her naked form haloed by harsh sunlight.

'Don't you have a nightdress or something?' Tiger squinted. 'Someone might see in.'

'Only the birds.' At Jo's behest, the detective climbed out of bed, wrapping a sheet round his middle. Someone had left breadcrumbs out in the street, scattered along the pavement. Birds wheeled and swooped, excited at their find – sparrows, seagulls, and a couple of evil looking crows. They flew past the bedroom window, mere inches from Tiger and Jo.

It was a wonderful and painful sight. The couple fought the urge to open the window and leap for the birds; the winged taunters could easily glide out of their reach, and there were a fair few feet for the cats to plummet. Instead they stood watching the show together, tails locked in a soft embrace, chirruping softly. Their attempted squawks didn't draw any birds to the window ledge; once all the breadcrumbs were gobbled up the feathered creatures returned to the trees, tantalisingly out of reach.

16

TIGER'S DAY WAS spoiled by an invitation. A couple of official-looking bruisers stopped him in the street and took him to Police Headquarters. Inspector Mortis was waiting for him there.

'What's up, Inspector?' The bruisers left Tiger and Bix alone in the mouse's office. 'You got a stirring in your breastie?'

'I'm not satisfied,' Bix grumbled.

'I understand. Can't find a dame who'll sate your needs. You have my sympathy.'

'You know more about Joel Venet's death than you're letting on. For all I know you could be withholding evidence.'

Tiger grimaced. 'There's a cow going bonkers in the next office,' he said. 'Got a pain in her udders or something. She'll probably bust up the joint.'

Bix looked startled. 'Excuse me.' He scooted from the room; Tiger heard a moo followed by a couple of squeaks. He used the diversion as an excuse to look round the Inspector's office.

On the mouse's desk lay an unmarked folder. Between two sections of brown card were pieces of paper showing the bank account details of some familiar folk. Tiger neatly folded the papers and tucked them under his hat. He took the Inspector's small black notebook too.

Bix popped his head back into the office. 'We're going to have to continue this conversation at a later date,' he whined.

'I can see you have your paws full,' the detective replied, bidding him farewell. He refrained from tipping his hat to the cop, preferring to stroll from the building whistling a blues riff.

Doctor Mildrew had a headache. His ears were abuzz with other people's problems. As soon as they opened their mouths he got a headache. He'd sit behind them so he didn't have to look interested, offered a few reassuring *hmm*s to prove that he was awake. With his head full of their complaints he couldn't find the time to sort himself out.

He had his own difficulties to deal with. The landlord kept raising his office rent and he had to increase his fees accordingly.

Fortunately his patients believed that they'd get what they paid for, sure that the more they spent the higher the quality of service would be. In truth they didn't receive a greater number of *hmm*s than any low-rent quack could offer. One look at the doc's gorgeously decorated office reassured them.

Mildrew owned a leather-bound swivel chair with a high back and padded arms. He had not one desk but two on opposite sides of the room, with drawers full of case notes too dull to ever see daylight. A set of red scales sat on one desk, flanked by two fat 'phones and a mug that proclaimed: 'You don't have to be mad to work here but it helps if you have an oedipal complex.' A mouthful even for a learned professional like Doctor Mildrew, but he'd found the gag funny in the china shop.

Humour was an important part of the therapeutic process, although some patients didn't like having their tails pulled and others didn't respect a therapist who clowned around. He was a father figure, an advocate, a smother superior. His office was a confessional booth and his couch a talk show sofa. Patients dreamed about him and asked him to interpret. Nothing hidden there. Mildrew simply booked more sessions for them, kept his bills at bay.

No one appreciated how the debts could pile up. His furniture was scratched to death by disaffected mogs. Vases or ornaments were jarred and smashed as panthers got in touch with their inner rage. Some of the worst cases underwent hypnotic regression; they were prone to pawing at Mildrew's dangling pocket watch or eating it whole while under the influence. He didn't blame them in the least, but he did get through a lot of pocket watches.

The doctor had a scant social life – he had no idea how or where to pick up broads and they'd always found him too cerebral anyway. He'd get off on thoughts or ideas rather than physical acts or visual stimuli. As a youth he'd written fancy love letters to his sweetheart; she'd lost interest in him when he'd failed to back up his words with deeds. As a grown-up, most of his jollies were derived from *Puss in Boots*, the popular adult magazine.

His failings made him an excellent psychiatrist – he could truly sympathise with the lonely, wretched screwballs on his couch. The female patients swore by him. He always had a kind *mm* for them, even if he did ogle their tails every so often.

Courteous, understanding, lecherous. A male prepared to feel your feelings, something lacking in many husbands. Mildrew would listen intently, or appear to with his well-honed hmming.

His most difficult task was not to appear jaded. He'd seen it all and heard more besides – personal worries, marital fatalities, suicides (not all his fault)... one cat had confided a desire to be swung round a small room; another had a fetish for rattraps. Still another had spent all her time watching a goldfish revolving in a bowl in the corner of her living room; he'd reassured her that there was nothing unnatural about that.

'Gotta sec, Doctor?' The screen slid back with a squeak. Inspector Mortis raised an eyebrow, making sure he had the therapist's full attention.

'I always have a second for you Bix. Come on in.' Mildrew nodded the cop towards the couch.

'I've brought a friend, hope you don't mind.'

'I'm amenable.'

'You're not going to charge double?'

'We can discuss billing at the end of the session. Who's the cow?'

Nut glanced around the office, hooves unsteady. Bix introduced her in gentle tones. The doctor tried to get her resting comfortably on the couch. It didn't work; Nut couldn't relax, her udders trapped between two seat cushions. Mildrew gave up and let her stand.

'I want you to hypnotise this cow,' said Bix. Nut let out a low moo. 'She has important information to impart. I have reason to believe that she witnessed a murder and has mentally blocked the details.'

'I don't want to remember anything. Not that I saw a dicky bird.' Nut shook her head sadly. 'I want to go home. My herd needs me, they look up to me.'

'This is unorthodox,' warned the doctor, leafing through a series of charts. 'Cows are notoriously difficult to regress. Large cranium, small brain.'

'Charming.' Nut flicked her tail, tried to look intelligent.

'Okay, here we go.' Mildrew pinned a monochromed chart to

the wall. 'Look at the centre, don't take your eyes off it. Relax.' Nut began to grind her teeth automatically, although she was cudless. Soon her eyes drooped and the doc had her spellbound.

'It's all dark. I'm blind!'

'Open your eyes.' Bix looked on, intent. His paw hovered over his hip pocket, ready to draw out his notebook if necessary.

'It's still dark.'

'What can you hear?'

'A big thumping. Swishing noises, like a rumbling tummy. A botty burp.'

'You're in the womb.' Mildrew explained to Bix that Nut had regressed a little further than expected. 'I want to take you forward, my dear. Picture the shed where you live. Can you see it?'

'Yes, my calves are there. Stop that! Stop biting Lizzie. Bob's always biting Lizzie. To get attention, you know. Farmer Scrumpy's there too. *Moo-hoo!* He's ignoring me as usual.'

'Something bad happened to Scrumpy.' Bix interjected. 'You were there. What did you see?'

Mildrew held up a paw to silence the rodent. 'This is a delicate operation, Inspector. We must peel away layers of this lady's mind until she is free to share her memory. As yet – she won't tell us anything.'

'Oh!' Nut perked up. 'You won't *believe* what happened to me the other day. I asked for some sort of financial assistance from Scrump – I won't go into the details, deadly dull – when what should happen, but he falls down dead. We thought he'd tripped until the blood began to flow. That wasn't so nice.' Bix unholstered his spare notebook, flipped it open to a crisp blank page, pencil poised.

'Go on.'

'I saw – I saw a shadow. Must have been the killer, whoever it was he had to be big. Tall, broad, with a tail like a hemp rope. Round ears. Glimpsed for an instant. Gone.'

'What sound did it make?'

'I don't know.'

Bix repeated his question but Nut shook her head. A tear teetered from one thick lash. The Doc clapped his paws together and she jerked awake.

'What are you doing?' Bix exploded.

'We'd gone too deep. Too traumatic. Any more and her mind would snap.'

'You don't understand, there's a cat killer out there. I have to stop him – you could be next, for Bastet's sake! Put her back under.'

'More than my job's worth. I'd lose my licence –'

'– To print money. I know. How much do I owe you?'

'Six pigeons. Sort it with the secretary on your way out.'

Nut stumbled along Lough Street, dazed and bemused. Bix kept pace, taking care not to get trodden underhoof.

'What happened back there?' asked Nut in a singsong voice.

'You don't remember?' Bix, surprised, related the afternoon's events. Nut stopped in her tracks.

'How could you do that to me?'

'I didn't do anything. I'm trying to prevent another murder. You can help. You're sticking with me till we've rounded up some suspects.'

'You and me?'

'Yep.' Bix motioned Nut onwards.

'Through thick and thin? Like two buddies in an unlikely partnership?'

'No. You're a witness. You didn't see much. The something you did see is better than nothing. So you're going to help me.'

Nut looked pleased. 'Do I get a baton?'

'Certainly not. I'm not deputising you, I'm keeping an eye on you. No batons.'

Nut shrugged, wondering whether the mouse had a smaller truncheon than his colleagues. Some avenues are best left unexplored and this was one of them.

'What now?'

'We visit an old pal of mine,' Bix harumphed, 'who's helped me on more than one occasion.' Okay, the friend had tried to eat him on more than two occasions but that was an accepted hazard for a mouse living in a cat's world. 'I know he'll have a handle on this case. He's a millionaire, builds things all the time. He likes cows. You'll get along famously.'

17

LIKE ALL REFINED cats Cole was a gourmet. He dug nothing more than pizza topped with rat peelings. He could eat three in one go; his perfect physique required plenty of fuel.

The pizzas were supplemented with regular helpings of spring chicks, pasta and juicy insects. A source in the local zoo smuggled out exotic specimens for a fat fee. The keepers knew nothing about it. He found it amusing that their precious wards were being removed right from under their noses. Cole could afford any delicacy he desired.

He was cooking up a repast for a very special guest.

'Bix!' he cried, ushering the Inspector into his house. He'd given his butler the night off. 'This *is* a surprise.' Nut followed the mouse to Cole's drawing room. 'This is even more of a surprise,' said the tycoon as a bovine aroma permeated his home.

'Hope this is okay,' said Bix, self-consciously rubbing his nose.

'I'm expecting a friend,' Cole replied conspiratorially. 'I'm cooking for her.'

'Then she must be really special.' Bix had gratefully received tip-offs and solutions from Cole in the past; he was the rich cat's contact in the police force. They'd met at some press conference. Bix was a media darling because of his unique status, though he eschewed publicity whenever possible. 'I'll make this quick.' The mouse explained Nut's part in his investigation, asking Cole for assistance.

'An intriguing case,' mused the tycoon coldly.

'Case nothing. This is my life in peril here!' Nut spluttered. 'Cats are dead. We need your help.'

'No need to get hot under the horns. There's nothing I can do. I haven't heard anything, I don't know anything. Now it's time I saw you out; my guest'll be here soon, and the dinner demands my attention.'

'Of course,' said the Inspector with a curt nod. 'Sorry to come

85

unannounced.' Once Bix and Nut had left the mansion, the mouse lost his cool. 'Nice one, you silly moo! That chap could've been very helpful to us. Now I'll have to creep back to him and eat crow.'

'I didn't know he'd get upset,' the cow simpered. 'I don't understand cats. How can they be so cruel?'

The last person the jobless Bug wanted to see was Tiger. She fetched a saucer of milk for him all the same; he had a way about him that convinced people to do things for him. Bug knew she was being used, even when her old partner told her she could start work the next day.

'When I told you I needed a job –'

'This wasn't what you had in mind.'

'I was thinking you'd hire me again. As your assistant, instead of getting me to do it for free and putting me to work in a bank.'

'Take a sniff at these.' Tiger waved a sheaf of printouts under her nose.

'Accounts. Dead people's accounts.'

'It's amazing how easy it is to get hold of the deceased's credit records. There are anomalies in every one of these accounts. Some of these folk have been murdered in very nasty circumstances – the Hant brothers, Joel Venet, Farmer Scrumpy. Some of them suffered an accidental death, so the authorities reckoned. They all had regular sums going to a secret account. The only way I can find out who owns the account –'

'Get a bank teller to look it up. An insider job. Me.'

'You said you could do with the income.'

'This is the most boring job on the planet! Answering 'phones, totting up profits, assessing interest rates, mortgage advice, queues of pawsore customers so irate you need a perspex screen to protect you from them – or is it to stop the staff running away?'

'Think about your paycheque at the end of the month.'

'The *month*!'

'We have to make it look above-board, get you ensconced, friendly with your colleagues before we even think of snooping.'

'Looks like you've been doing plenty of that already,' mewed

Bug, brandishing the printouts. 'What did you have to do to get these? Sucker some other poor gal?'

'Not at all. I stole them from the police.'

'Great.'

'They're on the trail too. Losing this should slow them down a bit.' Tiger seemed intent on obstructing police procedure.

'You got something against mice?'

'No way. I just have to sort things out at my own pace.'

'Seems anti-mouse to me. And selfish. You were the one giving me all that "lives at stake" spiel.'

'The villains could win this one, Natasha. One wrong move and they'll cover their tracks completely. That's why we have to tread softly.'

'Control freak.'

'Your new job starts in the morning, 9 a.m. You mustn't be late.'

'I miss my grasshoppers.'

'If we pull this off you'll be a hero. The zoo will welcome you back with open forelimbs. If that's what you want.'

18

THIS WAS IT. On the trail at last. Cole had followed the one eyed figure down back lanes, alleys and main streets, maintaining a fair distance from his quarry. The cultist never looked back, single-minded, moving rapidly. Cole was starting to enjoy himself.

He'd been ready to give up when the break came. Uncomfortable about giving in to blackmailers, he had reassured himself by pursuing Connie. She was responsive up to a point, but he knew that it would be impossible to truly win her affection until he brought her brothers' killers to justice. He'd watched *Wonder Cat* as a cub, knew the form: the hero defeats the bad guys, gets the gal – at the very end of the episode.

With no end in sight, Cole had despaired of ever finding a lead. Little Lona's funeral had given him the key. He'd dismissed the parents as typical trailer trash tabbies; the father didn't even have a necktie. He'd discounted the hooded, one-eyed cat watching from a discreet distance, supposing that he was one of the local holy yahoos. The next day had proved him wrong.

On a routine inspection of the Duncan Hotel, he'd noticed the same dude in the same gothic get-up, joining a convention for the KKC. No one at reception could tell Cole what the initials stood for, so he poked his intrigued nose through the doors of conference room E. It was full of males in capes and cowls, all sitting in silence, waiting for the meeting to start. Cole took a seat at the back, aware of the eerie silence. Finally the boss had arrived, a creature that Cole couldn't possibly have expected. Yet the cats sat rapt, hanging on this animal's every word.

'Cults have been getting a bad name in recent years,' squeaked the leader. 'I should know. I've been handling this organisation's PR for years. You got sex-crazed cults, suicide cults, vegetable cults. We ain't like that. We don't do orgies and we sure as Henry don't abstain from eatin' meat.' The audience nodded their heads in unanimous approval.

'Why are we here?' the leader continued. 'We're here because a great wrong has been committed. It's been going on for far too long and it's about time it stopped. Cats have subjugated other species since the world began turning. They ain't the master race. Such a thing don't exist. It's time to right the wrong.' The spokesanimal's words were welcomed with polite applause. 'To do that we must fight tooth and claw. Decimate traditional ideology. Educate citizens everywhere, show them that our way is best. Only then can we start afresh.'

'When do we start?' asked a seal point in the front row.

'Soon, my brother. As soon as our recruitment drive is complete.'

'What does the KK stand for?' interjected Cole.

'Now here's someone worth recruiting. We have the hotel owner in our midst!' said the leader, his eyes widening. 'Say hello, my brothers.' Some of the cultists turned and waggled their paws in greeting. The leader gave a nod to the one eyed cat, who left the room in a hurry. The meeting collapsed into a drone of administrative details – funding, accommodation arrangements, identity badges – so Cole loped off to see if he could catch up with the cyclops. He'd be back to question the leader later; with any luck, he'd discover a lot more during a personal interview.

The shady character was easy to find in a crowd of cats in lounge dress. He'd hovered in reception for a while as if waiting for the clock to strike, then left the hotel at quite a lick.

Cole reached a part of the neighbourhood he didn't recognise. It became harder to stay hidden with fewer pedestrians to shroud him. A church dominated the skyline on his left, striplights struggling through the stained glass windows. Scaffolding was propped against the spire; no doubt the local priest would be fleecing his flock for contributions. The bell tower had seen better days, and it would take more than a prayer to fix it.

On the right, blocks of flats stood like sentries on duty, surrounded by fences and patches of grubby grass. The fences had once been white; now they were mucked with soot and most of the paint had flaked away.

Cole followed Cyclops downhill, over a meagre bridge with

warning scents sprayed on the rails. The tycoon paused to watch the river surge below; rain had caused the water to rise and brown with upset mud. A tree stooped away from the bank, bent over the river as if drinking from it. A strange smell wafted towards his nostrils. Blood. There was a slaughterhouse upriver. His stomach rumbled.

His prey too far ahead, Cole increased his pace to catch up. A furdresser's salon was closing for lunch. Next door, a betting shop was full of disappointed yells. A co-op sold milk and fresh meat; the last store in the row was a tobacconist's. The road dipped upwards, leading towards the slaughterhouse. Cole followed Cyclops inside, down a set of steps into darkness. There were no pawsteps now, no signs of the cat he'd been following. Only the thud of a panel being shut and bolted behind him. There had to be another way out.

He searched every inch of the room, looking for an exit. He found neither crack nor seam – he was trapped in a metal box, the floor crunchy with detritus. The blood smell was worse than ever.

A mechanical whirring sound heralded more trouble. Either Cole was growing taller, or the room was getting shorter as the ceiling began to press down on his ears, flattening them against his head. Crouching down, he examined the debris on the floor by touch alone. Fragments, sharp, brittle, sitting on a blanket of powder. The ceiling continued its descent. Bones. He was crouching on a pile of bones, collected in a crusher – the bones nobody wanted, leftovers from cattle once the hides, meat and chewy bits had been removed. He had to escape before his body was ground to dust.

Cole remained calm, thinking the problem through, taking care not to miss a detail. He couldn't stand up straight now, down on all fours, his tail probing upwards, waiting for the ceiling to touch the tip. There was no sense yelling or banging on the walls – he wouldn't be heard over the machinery. He couldn't get out the way he'd come, the bones were too broken and brittle to act as props and slow the descent. The tip of his tail was nudged by the ceiling. He lay flat on his stomach, listening to the clanking cogs that worked the crusher.

He'd escape in the nick of time, of course. He always did. The villain would stop the crusher for a brief gloat and Cole would overpower him. Or agree to join his evil gang, then turn the tables. Or blow everything up. Cole liked blowing everything up, though as a result he'd lost his no claims bonus long ago.

It didn't happen. There was no escape this time, no reprieve, no get out clause. No happy ending. As the last breath was squashed from his body, he felt like a mouse in a trap. Cyclops had been the bait, he was the sucker. He closed his eyes and thought of Connie.

19

CATS PREFER NOT to queue. Nub City Bank was full of waiting customers, all wandering around, sniffing at the potted plants, gazing at their reflections in the polished perspex. Anything other than look like they were waiting in line. There was still a system – the biggest tom in the bank got served first. Some of the smallest ones waited half the day, because larger cats were always popping in. Any protests were met with a growl or a sneaky paw-swipe.

Tellers would be presented with bloody corpses, a proud grin on the customer's face. A chit was exchanged for the prize, endorsed with an inky pawprint. Cheques were easier to handle than rotting birds or voles, and for a small fee the banks handled the messy bullion. Sometimes the deposits would live on, flapping about, causing a kerfuffle; the perspex existed to contain the flying feathers, not the staff as Natasha had suspected.

The rarer the species of bird, the greater the value. Some genera were almost extinct because of this. Poorer cats spent a lot of their time skygazing, twitching, wondering how they could catch the creatures that wheeled so high above. They envied the taunting birds as they envied the upper classes, who could easily snatch a pigeon from the window ledge of their penthouse suite.

Bug didn't want to be rich. She *did* want to be in the black, pay off some of the debts she'd racked up while immersed in her studies.

Her new boss Miss Angold wore bifocals, each lens like the bottom of a milk bottle. Despite her poor sight she constantly watched over her employees – especially Natasha. The bug lover was too intelligent for her own good; Miss Angold didn't expect her to last long in the job. After a week or so Bug began to impress her, working overtime through lunch hours and evenings, asking questions about procedure, taking an interest in the most bland of tasks.

Bug wasn't all that excited about banking; she was itching to get back to her fleas. She also wanted to impress Tiger, prove she was his equal. That meant taking risks, chasing up clues herself.

Once Miss Angold trusted her enough to leave her in the office alone, she would act.

Tiger was concerned for Connie. Far as he knew she was fending for herself, still in mourning for her brothers. She was a prime target for the killer and the detective had left her unprotected. He didn't count Cole – the selfish tycoon would be too preoccupied with his own life to care about Ms Hant's. Tiger visited her apartment to deliver a progress report and check that she was safe. He hoped that she'd forgive his earlier outburst and allow him to keep an eye on her.

The devastated Connie had other things on her mind. She'd received an envelope that morning containing her lover's ground remains.

'I was supposed to meet him last night,' she explained, snuffling on Tiger's shoulder. 'A grubby bar he liked. He enjoyed slumming it every so often. I thought he'd stood me up. Then I got this.'

Tiger pored over the envelope's contents.

'How do you know…?'

'I can smell him. Bits of him. I sense he's not out there any more, Tige. I've lost him. I'm jinxed.'

'No you're not.' The envelope bore no postmark or return address. The detective felt no satisfaction at the loss of his rival. Connie's eyes were devoid of peace or hope.

'You've got to find his murderer. Singular or plural, I don't care. Catch 'em and rip off their balls.'

'Sure, sure. Ears, balls, anything. I need something to go on.'

'He was well known,' Connie sighed, 'respected. Had lots of friends and acquaintances. Someone must have seen him the day he disappeared.'

'Did he say anything? Mention anything the last time you saw him?'

Connie pursed her lips.

'Most of the time he gabbed about his new hotel. Showing off, I suppose.'

'I'd show off if I had what he had,' said Tiger in a tactful monotone.

'His hotel was full of strange guests. He was going to check them out, have any undesirables thrown out. Doesn't have anything to do with my brothers, does it?'

'I suppose not.'

'You think the auld enemy might be involved?' asked Connie abruptly.

'I don't. Dogs are nasty, brutish and subtlety isn't their point. Whoever's behind this has cunning, guile, intelligence.'

'Got to be female.'

'I was thinking in more general terms. I smell a cat.'

'That's impossible. We may squabble, claw at each other for personal space, act with spite and greed. We wouldn't cull members of our own race. We're not stupid.'

'Anyone can make foolish mistakes; even a cat.' Tiger knew this from harsh experience.

'Come on. We can stumble or get caught off guard but we always regain our balance. We wouldn't have conquered the land if we couldn't.'

'I want you to stay with a friend until this case is solved – until I find out what happened to Cole.'

'Who'd put me up? I'll hex 'em before the week's over.'

'A very nice lady who works in a bank. Temporarily, at least. Her name's Natasha. She likes insects.'

'Quite a resume. Must be fun at parties.'

'You'd better believe it. She can take care of herself and anyone else in her presence. Let's pay her a visit.'

After he'd dropped Connie off Tiger returned to Jo's house. He'd be able to relax, put his paws up, examine the case in a peaceful environment. Certain things were bound to happen during the course of the investigation. There would be another corpse along any minute, and that unlucky soul would likely disappear. Tiger would get sapped, struggle with some ugly customers, make some smart remarks. He'd tell the police little and drink a lot. His brain would turn hard getting nowhere until a clue fell into place and inspiration struck. These were the rules of the job with few exceptions. Tiger was determined to play it cool. Why struggle to solve the mystery before all votes were in? He'd be methodical, ask lots of questions, take a long nap... by the time he woke up, the case would have solved itself.

His plans for a quiet evening were shattered when Jo invited him in: she had something to tell him.

'I'm having kittens.'

'I know. Calm down a bit, don't get yourself in a tizz.'

'I don't mean that. I'm not upset. I *am* worried about what's going to happen to my children.'

'I didn't know you were a parent.'

'I'm not. Not yet. Gonna be soon.'

'Does the father know?' asked Tiger bashfully.

'Not yet. I'm scared. Don't know how he'll react.'

'Do you want to tell me who it is?' Tiger wasn't sure whether he wanted to know. He was too young to be a dad – any time before he reached pensionable age would be too soon for him.

'Cole Tiddle. Cole's the father. We only slept together once. He made me dinner. That was enough.'

'How can you be sure?' asked Tiger, aghast.

'The timing's right. The vet gave a rough date. Plus Cole's the only guy I've ever slept with.' Tiger found that hard to believe. The night he'd spent with her came flooding back, a night of cuddles and nuzzling, a caring embrace. Nothing more.

'Do you think he'd be alright? How would he take the news?'

'He never will,' Tiger answered brusquely. 'You've lost your opportunity to tell him. He's dead.'

Jo slumped to the floor, her whiskers drooping. The detective tried to help her up.

'Leave me. Just needed to sit down for a moment. It happens when you're pregnant. You lose your footing.'

'How're you going to raise them, Jo?' Tiger asked, his voice tender now.

'They could still have a dad.' Jo's eyes shone. 'I need help, darling.'

'You certainly do. You expect me to give it to you?'

'I don't expect anything. I do a lotta hoping. We could be together – if you still want that.'

'I don't want anything. I need to solve this case. Beyond that...'

'Beyond that, nothing.'

'So we're both lonely. But you're the one who started acquainting herself with the local stud. Why didn't you tell me before?'

'I didn't know before. Not for sure. When I did I – waited. To talk things over with you.'

'Frighten me. You succeeded.'

'So I *am* good at something.'

'Yeah. Good at turnin' me into a bag of jangling nerves.'

20

THE RECEPTIONIST WAS a louche fellow with big dimples. He knew that the ladies went gaga for his face craters, so he'd crease his cheeks whenever he could. His tail was always upright and he treated guests in the manner that suited their social standing. Business executives staying for a night got top star service; low-rent families on a city trip, excited at visiting Nub, weren't encouraged to return – they got the bum's rush. It was obvious that Tiger, who'd been wearing the same clothes for days, was penniless. The receptionist ignored him for as long as he was able, making sure that everyone else in the foyer was served before the detective got his turn.

'It's about the owner. Mr Tiddle.'

'I'm sure that any business of his would be none of yours,' the receptionist replied, looking down his nose at the investigator.

'This was the last place he was seen before he disappeared. Friday. The last place I know of, anyway. Did you see him?'

The receptionist warmed to Tiger's tone. The snooty cat cast his mind back.

'Difficult. There was a big convention here last week. The KKC, don't ask me what it stands for. Lots of conspicuous souls in hoods. One chap in particular had one eye. Hung round here forever, it seemed.'

'What was this convention about?'

'Some kind of animal rights movement. I dunno. I administrate, I don't eavesdrop.' Tiger nodded. 'Mind you,' the snob continued, 'I did hear a couple of them arguing over something. One was going to make a killing. The other advised caution. I assume they were discussing the stock market.'

'Probably. What happened to the one eyed guy?'

'That's just it. I wouldn't have mentioned him but there he was, loitering without intent until Mister Tiddle arrived in the foyer. As soon as One Eye clocked the boss, he barged out of the hotel and was followed.'

'By Cole?'

'Right. Must've forgotten something, eh? A wallet, a watch. I'm always doing that. Leaving things lying around, losing them. Mister Tiddle always finds them for me. A first class detective.'

'You don't say. Thank you. You've been excellent.'

The concierge squashed his mouth into a smile. 'Don't mention it. Any time you need a room –'

'I'll ask a friend. Can't afford this place. Ciao.'

The concierge sniffed as the riffraff left the building. He hoped that Mister Tiddle would turn up soon. It was almost pay-day.

Tiger placed his battered tan case on Jo's coffee table. He took a sniff round, making himself at home. He scrunched his paws on a salmon red carpet flecked with white, breathed an opaque fog on her bay windows, which were half-dressed in net curtains.

He warmed himself at a fire with fake coals, the mantelpiece holding a candelabra and plastic flowers. A mahogany bookcase opposite held dictionaries and reference books. As the light from the window faded, he lit an oil lamp with a long-stemmed taper. Its shade had trees stencilled on it.

Two pairs of frayed argyle socks sagged over a white radiator; Tiger wondered who they belonged to. The lampshade bounced its patterns off cream walls, peppered with black and white photographs in dark brown frames. He tried out both of Jo's sofas – one leather, one upholstered with saggy cloth. Each would accommodate two or three cats, more if they were prepared to get cosy and pinch up together. Tiger lay on his back, gazed up at the white tiled ceiling. Water ripples had been carved into the plaster. Outside, a set of streetlights fizzed into life. Jo lived on a junction and Tiger could see them through the net curtains.

Jo was prepared to put him up indefinitely, although the situation made Tiger feel like a leech. He had been considering her proposition, wondering whether he could do the right thing. She'd always been kind to him.

Bug was deep under cover and had her paws full looking after Connie, so Tiger had no recourse but to accept Jo's offer of a place to stay. He planned to sleep on the floor that night; it seemed right. At least until their wedding night, if he decided to take the plunge.

It did seem right. He'd bumped into Jo for a reason; she made him happy. Except when she sprang unusual surprises on him. If the babies had been his own – it didn't matter. He was going to be a father. Jo could rely on him to look after her when she was tired and help her cope as she gained strength. He couldn't shower her or the kittens with gifts, but she had his full attention. She was stunning, took his mewl away; the thought of her made him want to purr. Thank the holy one for landing him the catch of nine lifetimes.

They would solve the KK case. They just had to look at it from the right angle.

When Jo returned from her visit to the TV studio, she was fuming. Tiger tried to play it cool, asking her what was wrong. She explained that the makers of *Wonder Cat* had let her go, along with most of the production crew. The channel bosses couldn't afford to pay them while their ratings-grabbing show 'rested', and they couldn't count on more work when shooting recommenced. There were many hungry cats in the city desperate for a job in glamorous TV land. Plenty of them could hold a boom, heft a light or paint a face. They'd work for next to nothing, leaving skilled artists like Jo on the dole.

'You'll find something,' said Tiger, trying to believe it.

'I'm pregnant, I've got no employer, no friends. I've got nothing to get up in the mornings for. I want my kittens to live well, have everything they need. I'm not having no schemie babies.'

'Let's get married. Right now.'

'What are you talking about?'

'The way we feel about each other – the way the world doesn't seem to matter so much when we're together – '

'You're off your heid.'

'Oh dear. You're supposed to say, "Yes darling, where's the ribbon?"'

'What ribbon?'

'I was wondering when you were going to ask.' He delved into a trenchcoat pocket. 'Here. Will you wear it for me?' Jo reached out to touch the soft material. It featured Tiger's family colours, red with a gold hem. She held it to her cheek and her heart melted.

'When?'

'Is that a yes, then?'

Jo handed the cloth back to Tiger.

'It's a question. If we were going to get married, when would it happen?'

'I was thinking right away. Less hoo-ha that way.'

'What about our friends? Your dad, that bug lady?'

'They won't mind. Let's do it now.'

'Next week. That'll give us time to notify our finest and dearest. Nothing fancy.'

'Definitely sounds like a yes to me.' Tiger couldn't stop himself from chuckling.

'Let's have another look at that ribbon.'

Bug pulled a sheaf of papers from her jacket pocket. She'd finally been left alone long enough to compare the figures Tiger had given her with the bank records. She could see that several customers were making payments into a particular account. All fine and dandy, except the customers were dead. Someone at the bank was pulling a fast one, and that made Bug wary.

Shivering in the dingy records room, she listened for the sound of another cat. She used her peripheral vision to scan 280 degrees, her muscles poised for flight. Miss Angold hadn't seemed suspicious – that didn't stop Bug being careful. She'd been shown the vault that morning, a vast tomb sealed with a thick steel hatch. The staff at the bank had begun to trust her. She felt almost guilty for betraying them.

The payments weren't being siphoned into one secret account; they were going into several, with a series of digits that didn't match the other customer numbers. Bug printed them out and stuffed them in her breast pocket, along with Tiger's information. Rushing from the records room, she bumped into Miss Angold.

'Good to see you working late,' the boss purred. 'We reward diligence at this bank. And we penalise those who disappoint us.'

'I was boning up on some of your regulations. Finding things out…'

'I know, I know.' Miss Angold let Bug pass.

There were plenty of sight-impaired blokes in Nub City; not so many of them wore hooded vestments. Tiger visited contacts in the church and the theatre, two professional bodies with a lot in common. They were both obsessed with getting bums on seats, giving their customers a rollicking good show, using guilt and guile to extort every penny from the punters.

The manager of the Totterdown Pavilion was preparing for opening night. Although the theatre had been graced by the work of many great playwrights and actors, winter was a slow time of year. Most theatregoers chose to spend the season in bed, sleeping even more than usual in a state of quasi hibernation. This week the theatre was host to the excesses of a local amateur group, Dramatic Paws. Their tales were tawdry, their acting execrable, but all their friends and relatives paid to see them and packed the house. After a seven day run, the audience realised how bad the play was and receipts fell. Ronald Appleby called it community support. The amateurs thought of it as a 'spectacular showcase' for their talents. There was no hint of this when Tiger popped in to see his friend.

A dress rehearsal was in full swing with the director in the wings. He seemed content as a troupe of dancers bumped into each other; he knew that criticism this late in the day would only upset his cast. Some would leave in a huff, others would get emotional. Better to encourage their antics – a laugh from the audience was guaranteed.

'Don't they realise we open tonight?' Ronald asked the detective. He didn't expect a reply. 'They haven't learned their lines, the choreographer's got his legwarmers in a twist and the lead's still dry behind the ears. Thank goodness they're only here for a week.'

'What's next?'

'Didn't you smell the posters on your way in, Straighty? Panto! *Cat and the Beanstalk*. The cubs love it, though most of the gags are aimed at the grown-ups. The performers enjoy themselves more that way.'

'Your reputation ain't tarnished yet. Not with the great stuff you've had on over the years. That tragic thing with the Swampie McMahon soliloquy last summer…'

'…*Wall Story*.'

'That's right. And that show with the monks?'

Ronald's eyes widened.

'*Monk Story* was a lot more than a mere show, my lad. It was pure theatre. The unabridged version of the play performed as it would have been when first written, generations ago. If only we could have changed the audience.'

'What happened to the costumes? Did they get ditched or what?'

'They were purchased from us by a national organisation. Can't recall the name.' The Amateur Dramatics heroine was singing her solo. She would have had a beautiful voice if not for the stage fright that cracked every note.

'Would you have records?'

'Some sort of anagram.'

'KKC?'

'That was it. How did you know? KKC plc. Before you ask there was no delivery address. A one eyed lad collected the costumes. Bit of a sour puss.'

'Didn't it strike you as strange? This organisation taking a job lot of monks' robes from you.'

Ronald patted a wall affectionately. 'This old dear's seen better days. Her make-up may seem impeccable but take a closer look and you'll see cracks.' He pointed upwards. Tiger saw that the ceiling was flaking. 'The foundations are weak. The upkeep's expensive. People think we take their money, pay off the producers and spend the profits on milk and honey. I put my faith and wages into the Pavilion. I didn't ask any questions of KKC plc. I kept my mouth shut and got the roof retiled.'

'Anything I should look out for in the future?' asked Tiger as Ronald led him out of the auditorium. Scenery crashed down around the starlet.

'We have a prestigious production lined up,' blinked the manager, 'once the panto's done its business. A gung-ho play by Julius Kyle. It's the story of a bricklayer called – '

'– *Bricklayer's Story?*' Tiger guessed.

'How did you know? That was the title we were going to go with, yes. What do you think? Too literal?'

'Not at all,' Tiger bade his farewells, 'it's up to your usual standards.'

Tiger and Jo organised the wedding together – that way they could keep an eye on each other. While *Wonder Cat* was out of production and facing the axe, Tiger wangled his fiancée a post at the Pavilion. The theatre didn't pay as well as the TV company; Jo still had enough to feed them both until she got a meatier job. Between the arrangement of the wedding ceremony and providing makeup for a horde of luvvies, she was kept busy. More than that, Tiger had friends at the theatre who promised to protect her.

It wasn't long before the couple had their first tiff. Tiger wanted to invite some unsavoury guests to the reception, because 'they didn't get out much.' Not a good enough reason for the bride-to-be. She was cagey about her family – long after the majority of invites had gone out, she still hadn't informed any relatives of her relationship with the detective. He thought she was embarrassed about him, his lack of money or social status.

After a day's bickering, they agreed to allow each other to invite who they liked. It was a special day that they wanted to share with friends and acquaintances.

'I won't let you down in front of your folks,' Tiger assured his fiancée. 'I ain't a well-bred pedigree animal. I wouldn't win any fancy club prizes. I *do* love you. If your mother and father have a problem with that, we can talk it over before the wedding. Please let 'em know what's going on. I want to meet them.'

'It's not you I'm worried about,' sighed Jo, 'or their reaction to you. I'm worried that you'll get one look at them and run a mile.'

'They can't be all that bad,' Tiger soothed.

'They're old, strict, gruff, respectable, well mannered. They'd pay for the wedding like a shot. I won't let them.'

Jo was determined to pay for the event. Tiger didn't ask her where she was going to get the money from; he offered to remunerate her as soon as he solved his case. Then he planned to knuckle down, get a proper job ready to provide for the babies who were on their way. If it was a full litter they could have several new mouths to feed. He'd always fancied a career in advertising, writing copy for wealthy corporations. Advertising was so ineffective that it seemed like a scam to him – if the seller was lucky, a third of consumers would notice the ad. The number of cats who actually picked up a product was indefinable. He could be an officially backed grifter.

All his life he'd been screwed. Clients had forgotten to pay him. He'd laboured for free in the hope of follow-up jobs. He'd been exploited and abused. He'd always chalked it up to poor business acumen. He didn't have the drive or the mean streak to succeed in commerce. He could spot a pickpocket at a thousand yards, but corporate fraudsters fooled him every time. He'd hoped to learn something from their dirty deals; he'd fallen foul of them instead.

Tiger had set up his detective agency with nothing. The office, the filing cabinet, even the suit had been on short-term lease. Still young, he'd fooled clients into thinking he knew what he was doing. From such lowly beginnings the business had grown, expanded so that he could hire a secretary (Natasha), buy a telephone, have some cards printed. It hadn't taken him long to realise that his worklife ran in peaks and troughs. He could be wealthy one year and close to bankruptcy the next. This year he'd pushed things too far, lost it all. Usually he would have been ready to build things up again from scratch; now it was too late for that. The unemployable PI would have to become an employee.

He could feel himself growing older by the hour, by the minute. Each morning he would check his face in the bathroom mirror, find a new white hair or a wrinkle on one of his pads. He was twelve years old – he could kick the bucket at any time. His brother had dropped dead at the age of ten. Tiger wondered why cats bothered to build anything when their life was so short. It wasn't fair.

Frank would have told him that after death all true believers joined the goddess Bastet up in the heavens. The bad ones weren't so lucky. No scientist or priest had ever proved the deity's existence; she was something people could or couldn't accept.

Everyone needed something to believe in. Tiger had believed in himself. He thought he could still fight his way out of a wet paper bag, solve a mystery, save a life. The case that Connie had brought to him would prove him right or wreck his world.

The Church of the Benign Bastet was a cold, slate-grey building. Tiger hadn't prayed there since his salad days, putting in overtime as an altar cub. He'd formed a strong bond with Father Frank. If anyone knew where the cyclops had got his robes, it would be Frank. The locals confessed everything to him and he was a terrible gossip.

A few cats knelt in pews, purring softly as they communed with their goddess. The high-vaulted ceiling, richly frescoed with gold and white, gave the impression that you were in a train station.

A female sat at the back of the church breast feeding her six kittens. Each newborn could home in on its own individually scented nipple. Brother Barry, the acolyte, stood and stared at the mother until she felt uncomfortable and moved away.

'Still not getting any, brother?' Tiger made Barry jump.

'Any what, Mr Straight?' Barry was young, his face untarnished by strife or stress. His eyes were like two ripe slices of cucumber, glistening in the half-light of the church.

'Female companionship. Sex. Making the beast with two tails.'

'Don't mock the constricted, Mr Straight. You know I've sworn an oath of celibacy. I haven't see a naked female since –'

'Since that time the cops caught you with that hooker.'

'All charges were dropped.' Barry's eyes were downcast. An uncommon moment of strength had led him to the nearest cathouse. On the pretext of saving souls, he'd sampled the speciality of the house – a talkative dame named Claire with tattooed unmentionables. He'd tried to spread the Good Word in a clinch on a sack of kitty litter. The only convert that day had been him, and his antics had ended ignominiously – in a scandal hushed up by the Bishop.

'You got friends in high places.' Tiger waved a paw skywards.

'They don't come much higher than that. I want you to fetch Father Frank.'

'He won't talk to you –'

'Since I had one of his flock rounded up. I know. I need you to be extra persuasive. Unless you want your police file reopened. The Six O'clock News'd love it; so would the parish magazine.'

Barry scurried to the vestry.

Tiger took a look at the altar, swept away by memories of youthful innocence. His parents had sent him to the church to keep him out of mischief, give him something to do on weekends, give them a break. Frank had been like a second abusive father to him and he'd betrayed the old cat's trust. A year ago, a local parishioner had confessed a murder to the priest. Tiger had inveigled the information out of him and made his report to the police. Tiger had been unable to let a killer wander free, and neither could Frank. There was still bad blood between them.

He heard mewling from the vestry. Barry was doing his weasily best to convince Frank to greet his old friend. The priest refused in a gruff monotone. The churchgoers cocked their ears, eavesdropping on their shepherd.

'I'm not going out there. I'm not dressed.' Two old dears shared a titter. Tiger sniffed at a ceremonial cup. It was brimming with clear, cool water. He lapped at it thoughtfully.

'You can't do that.' He swung round, drops of water suspended from his whiskers.

'Do what?' He was confronted by a grey-striped ocelot.

'Drink the holy water. It's been blessed.'

'I ain't drank nothing.' Tiger shook his head and the ocelot was showered in droplets. 'Anythin' blessed by that charlatan ain't in the least bit holy.'

'How can you say that?' The parishioner was shocked. 'Father Frank went to priest school. Right now, he's in communion with the goddess.'

'He's in his room having a fag. While you simpletons kill your hindlegs kneeling on the floor, he's sitting on a plush cushion laughing his asterisk off.'

'Blasphemy!' Frank exclaimed, bursting into the nave. Barry shadowed him. 'Don't listen to this disciple of Hecate, brother.' The high priest landed a placatory paw on the churchgoer's shoulder. 'He plays devil's advocate, sews the sequins of doubt on all our shirts. Block your ears when he opens his mouth. Go back to your pew.' Frank's words were rewarded; the ocelot left the church. The priest reassured the rest of his flock: 'More prayer, my brethren. Remember to practice humility and discipline. An eternity of damnation awaits if you mess up.' To Tiger he said, 'It's against their nature, all this piety. They'd rather be independent. Nevertheless it gives them something to believe in. It fills a void in their lives.'

'I don't know how they find room for praying, with all that eating and sleeping.'

'You can't spend your whole life mucking about. We all need to be constructive from time to time.'

'I wouldn't call this nonsense constructive. Destructive if anything. It stops these fellers thinking for themselves.'

'Individual thought is highly overrated. Better to switch off, lie back and trust in a higher force. You ever been in a lake, my son?'

'Not on your nelly.'

'Swim out into the water and it buoys you. Lie on its surface and you can float. That is what my faith is like, although I use my tail for a rudder while swimming. Here my heart is my rudder.'

'Why do you pious types always speak in metaphors? Can't you speak plain for once?'

'Yeah. Bit boring though, don't you think?'

'Father Frank is a storyteller, a jokeswapper, a well of information,' Barry explained. 'We draw from that well whenever our faith is lacking.'

'Must do a lot of drawing, eh, Brother Barry?' Tiger nudged the acolyte in the ribs. 'Any faith in there? I don't see none, do you, Frank?'

'Don't you have devotions or duties to attend to?' Frank waved Barry away. The acolyte shuffled out of sight, leaving Frank to pat Tiger paternally on the head.

'Don't worry about the water. I drink it all the time. It's not very holy – unless the local tap water is sacred.'

'I doubt that.' Tiger wiped his chin dry anyway.

'So, if you aren't born again what're you doing here?'

'I came to piss you off. Doesn't seem to be working.'

Frank sank to the floor with a sigh. 'I've changed since you shopped that polecat, Tiger. My fur may be smooth but I'm not a soft touch any more. Saving souls is a big deal. You've got to get wise if you want to keep the faith.'

'I tried getting wise. Faith doesn't fill your belly or keep a roof over your head.'

'I never said it did,' Frank squinted. 'I don't exist to provide excuses for you to be sassy, young sir. I don't throw people out of my church very often; I can make an exception for you. Young Barry may look and act daft. He can also be a hard nut if he has to be. I trained him myself.'

'I wouldn't mess with you or your weans, Frank.'

Frank frowned at Tiger, sizing him up. 'You're a city cat –'

'Bored and bred.'

'– Used to city life, hemmed in. No sense of perspective. No tranquility. Leads to spiritual corruption. I've been doing this all my life. I'm incapable of doing anything else. Can you imagine me delivering mail?'

'Not in that frock. Too windy out.'

Frank touched his cheek with a hind paw in a graceful prayer to his antecedents. His head swayed from side to side. He had no inkling of the origins of the ritual; it had been handed down through generations. He took a deep breath and lapped at the holy drink. Tiger grew impatient.

'I thought you might know something about a local group. A society. Its members wear robes, hoods. Like an order of monks.'

'No robed folk in my parish, my son.' Frank completed his ritual and scratched his head. 'There haven't been any monks in Nub City since – well, since the city was founded. They all got pussed off and moved to the coast. They didn't go for the whole civilised progress shebang. They're extinct now, although occasional sightings are made. Folk chalk the apparitions down to a trick of the light, or a bellyful of sour milk.'

'Ever seen a one eyed character hereabouts?'

'There was a poor fellow who lost an eyeball. Sucked out by a cuckolded husband – at least that's what I heard. He was a regular churchgoer for quite a while, until he went and joined a cult. Don't know what it was called, but they're up to some dodgy stuff. Would that be the group you were asking about? Sorry I can't be more help.'

'You can. Where do I find One Eye?'

'Hangs out in a caf. A greasy spoon in the Craigs. Think he owns part of it.'

'Know his name?'

'Sorry, son. I'm not omniscient. Only one entity knows everything,' Frank raised his eyes heavenwards, 'and she ain't telling.'

'I don't know why you waste your time with all this religion,' scoffed Tiger.

Frank smiled knowingly. 'Ask yourself this question – it's the only one that keeps my beliefs alive. There are so many different breeds of cat in this city. A variety of colours, shapes and temperaments. Surely someone created all these forms of life for a reason?'

'It'd have to be a damn good one.'

'Yes, yes that's right. We all have a purpose. I'm not sure what it is.'

'Gee, thanks Father, you've reminded me why I stopped worshipping here. Cheers for the info.'

'Don't thank me. Thank my gossipy flock.'

'Oh, one other thing –'

'Yes, my son?' Frank never got impatient. He had six days' holiday a week; it didn't hurt too much to be patient on the seventh day.

'Could you marry me?'

21

WHEN TIGER'S DAD found him, a stripper was molesting him. She was already down to her essentials, dressed only in a g-string and six tinselled tassels. Tiger was backing away as she pawed him; he didn't want her to think he was a beast. A few pals had joined him in the after hours bar – detectives, snouts and half the Pavilion Theatre Company.

'Put that animal down!' bellowed Ike Straight, ordering a pint from the bar. He was late for his son's stag do, just off the 4s from the East End. 'Who's responsible for this orgy?'

'I am,' admitted Father Frank. He was the worse for drink, waggling his bottom to the distorted calypso beat that emanated from a wall speaker.

'Dad!' Tiger shouted, not sure where to put his paws.

'Make the most of her, son. This is yer last night of freedom, before –' The stripper gave Ike a wink.

'What kept you?' Tiger slurred.

'Got held up. I overslept. I was taking a nap and... well, you know how it goes.' Every cat in the bar nodded. As Tiger rubbed against the stripper's leg, Ike muscled in. 'Don't you have any respect for yer fiancée? Get yer paws off this poor young lady. She's not interested in a slug like you.'

'What about all that "last night of freedom" garbage?'

'Must be getting old. It's a parent's prerogative to change his mind.' Ike took the stripper to a discreet corner and whispered sweet somethings in her ear. Tiger watched her giggle. His father still had the knack; a grizzled old prune with matted fur, his legs were bandy and his breath could have been better. He was only a year older than his son yet he seemed as ancient as a peat bog. The poor young lady didn't seem to mind.

Father Frank was enjoying himself, getting friendly with a female member of the bar staff, anonymous in the city centre. He still looked like a priest, though – in the way he drank, spoke and danced. He'd insisted on tagging along with Tiger, curious about this tired and tested male tradition.

Some of the guys from the theatre sat at a table near the exit. They weren't impressed with the stripper. Tiger spent most of the night gassing with Ronald Appleby, the manager of the Pavilion. By the time the bar was ready to close, Ronald had convinced his friend to audition for pantomime dame at the end of the year. Ike was long gone, taking the stripper with him.

Across the city, Jo was letting her fur down. She was accompanied by a few select friends from the TV production company that had employed her for several years. Her entourage included a couple of actresses, drawing drop-jaw reactions from passing clubbers. Sibyl Silvers, star of *Wonder Cat*, had heard about an exclusive new club called La Chat. They had to go.

The posse had no trouble getting in, taking seats at the crescent-shaped bar and ordering a round of banana shakes. It took a while for them to catch up on the latest gossip.

'Where'd this surprise spring from, sister?' asked Sibyl. 'I never saw you as a blissful bride.'

'Me neither. It's gonna happen though. You can make it to the reception?'

'Wouldn't miss it if I was dead.' The conversation was brought to a halt as a bunch of half-naked hunks hopped onto a raised dais, tails erect, full of themselves. Punters throughout the bar gave mewls of approval as the hunks began to boogie.

Only Jo frowned. There was something not quite right about the show. Her doubts were confirmed as more toms stepped onto the dais. Some were wearing studded collars; others were led around on leashes.

'This is disgusting!' she spluttered as the tethered males were yanked across the club.

'Outrageous,' Sibyl agreed, savouring every moment.

'Trust you to bring us to an S & M club,' said Jo, shaking her head. 'Cats on leads. It's shameful.'

'I didn't force you to come, sister.' Jo knocked back her milkshake and headed out of the club. Sibyl shrugged, took one last look at the exotic dancers, and followed her friends to a more traditional bar.

Tiger's dad was of mixed lineage and proud of it. He was the alga in the gene pool, the swine among pearls, the throwback of the family. He was old and sincere, still fit, gaining girth, eating all the right food the wrong way. He looked on his son with suspicion and high expectation. Ike had spent a lot of dough on the lad's education, had helped set him up, raised him as a free thinker. Sometimes the effort seemed wasted. Right now, Ike had yet to give his approval of his son's nuptials.

He had made the following observations:

Tiger was desperate.

He'd lost his home and belongings, needed a place to stay.

A wife provided instant security, with a place to roost.

His son had always been a loner. Maybe he'd seen other couples happily united, wanted a slice of the wedding cake. It tasted good but staled fast.

The bride and groom were embroiled in a case. During a murder investigation senses were heightened, situations pressurised; in the heat of an adventure it was a doddle for things to get romantic.

Tiger had always been possessive. If Jo was as cute a ball of fluff as the detective had suggested, he wouldn't want her to fall into enemy paws. Marriage wasn't just a declaration of love these days – it was a demarcation of territory. That went for proprietorial females as well as males.

The wedding was a good excuse for a party, getting together with old mates, catching up on unsolved cases. Ike couldn't wait to meet an old flame of his named Sheba. There would also be pomp, punch and mucho food: a big spread always put a smile on a cat's face. A wedding was never a bad idea, unless the groom forgot to turn up or the couple divorced within the month, in which case the largest of feasts was a waste of time. A break up so soon after the gaiety left a bad taste in the mouth. He always cried at divorce proceedings.

Tiger had never been fickle as a kitten, seeing games through to their end, determined to win, chasing the bullies and snatching tuck thieves. As the wee lad had grown into a tenacious, heavy detective, he'd stuck to his suspects' trails with shoes of gum. If he was as devoted in his relationships as he was to the mysteries he solved, the match would last a century.

Jo looked impressive in white, a veil failing to dowse her beauty, ears stuffed behind a tiara, tail waggling from a slit in her train. She looked like an empress, a distant diva, a pregnant pavlova. Nobody said anything about her condition; some assumed she'd been overeating. Pre-wedding nerves or depression. It didn't hamper her style or dampen Tiger's day.

They'd wanted a swift marriage. Corners had been cut, a ceremony swiftly booked, still an event by Nub City standards. It began with a procession through Stenmuir, Tiger in the lead followed by friends and relatives in their brightest regalia. Traversing half the district, the groom reached the registry office. The veiled bride and maid of honour (Sibyl) were there. Persian kittens carried Jo's train, mewing a wedding march.

Tiger and Jo brushed their heads together lovingly, then led their brethren round the back of the building. A feast awaited them, meat and fish laid out on the ground like offerings to some ravenous god.

Although there was more than enough to go round the cats ate every bite. By the time the ceremony began, they were bloated with eats and ready to burst.

Father Frank had donned his best cassock for the job. He had no qualms about Tiger's lack of religious conviction; Jo would be a sound influence on the lad, dragging him to church, getting into theological arguments as all good Nub citizens should. Bickering never hurt a couple in Frank's book; it strengthened their bond. Survive the strife, add an extra year to your anniversary expectancy.

Frank encouraged his acolytes to beat each other over the head with their hymnbooks to settle a disagreement. This prevented their lives from becoming too sheltered, and prepared them for the rigours of the violent world beyond his church. The acolytes he sent to spread the word were also tough nuts. Refuse one of their pamphlets and you'd be given one anyway, stuffed down your craw. When they paid a visit to a house it would be to collect protection money.

Their tactics had proved highly popular, making the congregation swell. A wedding provided a major event, something to remember for a lifetime, all thanks to Frank.

Aunt Farl wore a black knee-length skirt and floral pink bedsocks. A crimson pullover complemented her rusting gold earrings. Her pads were washing-up wrinkled and whiskers sprouted from places they shouldn't have. She liked to act dithery, trying to entertain the family. Forgot names, came out with crazy sayings, asked inane questions. Her folks found her scatterbrained antics annoying. They hoped that she was assuming her idiotic airs, blaming her religious upbringing. They wouldn't tell her the truth of course; instead they smiled and tried not to stay in the same room with her for too long. They didn't get a chance on the day of the wedding.

Aunt Farl had been invaluable in the run-up to the ceremony, arranging Jo's train, flicking crumbs from Father Frank's cassock, ensuring that everyone sat in the right place – her family on the left side of the church, Jo's entourage on the draughty side. They looked awkward in their formal suits and gowns, yanking at their collars, rubbing their corseted tummies. They were also impatient, with attention spans as short as an unfinished jingle. The two factions glared at each other, ready to jostle for territorial space. Tails lashed and eyelids batted. The congregation spoke in hushed mews.

Two kittens sang choral chords as the bride and groom walked to the altar. Two witnesses were ready to sign the marriage certificate – Sibyl and Bug, disguised with a wig. Frank proceeded with a warm smile.

'Do you, Tiger Straight, take Jo Madrigal as your lawfully wedded wife?'

'I do.'

'Will you share sunpatches with her, hunt for her, and leave a little bit of food in your bowl when you've finished eating in case she wants a bite?'

'I'll try.'

Ike sidled up to the desk, told Frank that Aunt Farl was supposed to be a witness. Jo didn't hear him, saw a tinselled tassel stuck to his tail. She started to giggle.

'Do you, Jo Madrigal, take Tiger Straight as your lawfully wedded husband?'

'Tee hee!' Frank took that as a yes.

'Will you at least pretend to show interest in everything he says, laugh at his jokes and refrain from flicking your tail in an agitated fashion when his habits annoy you?'

There were tears in Jo's eyes by now. She couldn't see to wrap the strip of cloth round Tiger's wrist. He helped her and added his own colours. 'I'm sorry,' she managed at last. She used the ribbon to blow her nose.

'This happens a lot,' the priest reassured her. The bride and groom recited their pledge.

As the couple put their pawmarks to the certificate, countersigned by Sibyl and Bug, Jo tried to explain why she found it all so funny. Tiger brushed it off as mild hysteria. He didn't blame her.

By the time the ceremony ended the light was fading. The guests sat on stalls sheltered by canvas canopies, sucking on hookahs and singing a sour cats' chorus. Old ladies gave the groom sloppy kisses. The males nuzzled the bride until she complained. As the stars came out to take a gander, conversation grew more rude and raucous. The cubs were taken home to bed, and the mouthy members of the family performed limericks in the round. The guest list included a who's who of criminal investigation – Wilton Pirie, the genius jailer; John Hood, the brainstorming barkeep; Inspector Mortis and his talkative witness; Marlon Wakely, the bulimic boffin; Carol Griffin, the deductive dinner lady; Alex Van de Weyer, the crime-solving coach. Sam Spayed made herringbone jackets in his spare time. They all understood that no matter how rife theft and murder were, they should have something to fall back on. All except Bix who had a one track mind, as Nut was beginning to learn.

'I'm not invited to weddings very often,' Nut mooed.

'Can't imagine why not.'

'I *am* sure it ain't polite to give the groom suspicious looks all through the ceremony.' Nut waggled a hoof in the Inspector's face. 'I was surprised when you accepted the invite.'

'You know why we came here,' Bix snapped.

'The free nosh?' Nut's stomach was full of freshly chewed grass with buttercup seasoning.

'No, not the nosh. I'm still sure Straight's keeping something from us. A clue, a piece of evidence. Perhaps he and the make-up artist are colluding. I was hoping that he'd let something slip, it being his wedding day and all. I want you to keep your ears open and your mouth shut.'

'Great!' Nut nudged one of the guests. 'I'm going to be a spy.' She turned back to Bix, who was pretending that he didn't know her. 'I think you're very courageous, Inspector.'

'How so?' the rodent replied resignedly.

'You're the most edible thing here apart from the cake. For the cats I mean – you're safe with me. But in this place, you could end up covered in icing and carved into tender bite-sized slices.'

'I'm an officer of the law,' Bix railed. 'If one of these fatties ate me they'd do time.'

'If a cat's hungry enough, I don't think he cares about the repercussions,' warned Nut sadly. 'Take care, Inspector. I'll watch your back.' Her words were small comfort to the small copper.

'Pirie! I see you're visiting from Bast.' John Hood accosted his colleague.

'How d'you deduce that?' asked Carol Griffin. 'The scent on his fur, the mud on his paws, the stains on his coat?'

'No,' Hood replied coolly, 'I saw him getting off the train.'

Tiger had invited some of his old foes to the reception, folks he'd sent to the caboose long ago: Flax Draxar the crazed inventor, Kisselda, Tanktop and a couple of serial scratchers. The heroes and villains got on famously, with a common point of discussion to start from. Their minds were all cesspits of death, corruption, treason and plot. Some of the bad guys were surprised by how much their nemeses had to think like them to beat them; others saw it as a long time goal to convert the detectives to their way of thinking. Using unorthodox methods to catch their prey, they would eventually become just as bad. All the guests agreed the get-together was a fab idea, and asked to be invited to the first anniversary party, if the marriage lasted that long – crime fighters' relationships are notoriously short-lived.

Tiger got a kick out of seeing old alleypals that he thought he'd never see again: the half-dead, the wanted, the watched and the hunted, all ready for a merry reception. All he had to do was ensure they weren't disappointed. To do that he had Doctor Fat imported from Club Wu Wu, ready to serenade the couple under the moonlight. He also had his tan case ready for action once Fat had finished strutting his stuff.

Within the case sat Tiger's joy, his muse and mouthpiece, a shining collection of brass tubes and keys. The sax was all that mattered when a crime seemed insoluble or the blues tapped his veins. When he played, the instrument became an extension of himself, a parping extra limb, warm metal and reed between his lips, the puck of soft padded keys clamping over hungry holes. Steam left his ears and his hindpaws tapped. His eyes rolled; his elbows twitched. It didn't pay the rent (not that he had rent to pay), bring him fame or a fan base of chicks. It brought him peace, even if the audience couldn't get any until he stopped.

Each detective had brought a sidekick, not all of whom were as intelligent as Bug. Some of them asked stupid questions all the time – wondering where they were, what was going on. Others moaned about the tedium of tagging after their partners. The younger ones didn't know any better, itching for a new adventure.

'I don't know why I put up with him,' moaned Bug. Nut agreed with her.

'They treat you like an object, not a living breathing animal. We're all adults here. Why do you put up with him?'

'Reminds me of the old times. At least I have that excuse. When last I saw him I was younger, more optimistic. Hanging around with him brings back those days.'

'I don't know about that, but attending police investigations makes a change from standing in a shed.'

'I know exactly what you mean,' Bug nodded, brushing cake crumbs from her dress. 'I'm sick of working in the same place every day, seeing the same people. Tiger takes me new places. Admittedly grotty places with dead bodies and violent anti-social types, but it still spices my life up with a bit of variety. I'm invaluable to him. Without me he wouldn't have an inquiry. So how come he acts as if I'm not there sometimes?'

'I don't know,' Nut shrugged, 'it's not as if the Inspector can miss me, I'm so bloody big. Always getting in the way, or so he says. I've only trod on his tail once. As far as I know. He can be awful quiet when he's thinking, never shares anything with me.'

Bug bored Nut with stories of past glories long into the evening, until the lights dimmed and a cleaner swept them out with a hard-bristled broom. Bug headed home and Nut went back to the police station. Bix wasn't in his office; she waited patiently for his return. Getting distraught would not get her home.

'This place is getting demolished next week, did you know that?' Ike picked crumbs from his paper plate. 'Whole street'll be gone before your cubs arrive. A business park instead, with the central office slap bang where the church is.'

'I'm sorry to hear that, pop.' Personally Tiger believed in progress. He was sitting on a step outside the reception hall, staring up at the stars. Urban renewal was transforming the city, brightening buildings, gentrifying the slums. No more flophouses or dirty litter trays in the public conveniences. The future looked fair for his children.

'Too right you should be sorry!' his father harangued him. 'You won't be able to take your sons and daughters out this way, show 'em where you got married.'

'You never showed us nothing like that.'

'Me and your ma never got hitched. You're the peculiar one, tying the knot. Most cats're happy livin' in sin.' Ike licked his lips with a rasp. 'Less complicated that way. Life shouldn't be all that complex, son. You look for puzzles where there ain't none.'

'I like to use my brain.'

'You think too much,' Ike spluttered. 'When you were born I got a steady job. Earned enough to feed my family and pay the mortgage every month. Saved up a nest egg for you and your ma. So I lost it all in a blaze o'drugs and carousing! That was after you'd left home. Where's your job? Where's your mortgage?'

'Ain't got one.' Tiger was glum. 'There're things that I have to sort out first – before I rejoin the catrace.'

'You're a quitter. Your business failed; life got too hard for you. You've changed your personal life. Now you gotta change the rest. Give up this detective stuff, son. Pull yourself together.'

'How's Aunt Farl doin'?' asked Tiger, trying to change the subject.

'Collapsed under a table. She was laughing at some joke, got too much for her. Don't worry, she's okay. Your Great Uncle Boff is with 'er. They're having a wheeze on the floor together.'

'Aunt Farl's looking awful frail these days.' Tiger felt guilty. He hardly ever visited his relatives though they lived in the same city. Stubborn pride had prevented him from asking them for help when he'd lost his possessions. At least a few of them had deigned to attend his wedding.

'Mebbe on the outside. Inside she's stronger than I've ever known her. She's found something to believe in – joined a group. It's called the Kitty Killer Cult, but I guess that's a gag. A lot of the old folks are members. You need something to believe in when you're on your last legs, I suppose.'

'Where's this cult based?'

'The Beggars' Temple on Dempster Street. Got a dome like a lemon squeezer, you can't miss it. They dress up in red robes, with hoods and everything. A load of baloney if you ask me.'

'What do you believe in, pop?'

'I believe in you, Tiger. I know you can be a much better father than I ever was.'

'I've got to find Aunt Farl.'

One of the good guys started it. Made an ill-advised comment to an old lag about his failed attempts to take over the world. After 29 fiendish plans (and several years in prison) wasn't it about time the evil genius retired? That was enough to start a brawl.

The hall resounded with the sound of claws popping, ready for trouble. The lag's bottom waggled, his shoulders hunched, launching himself at the big-mouthed hero. His colleagues rushed to his defence – all except Sam Spayed, who hadn't been very active since his sojourn in hospital, and Tiger. Aunt Farl had been carried home to rest – the day's excitement had proved too much for her. Great Uncle Boff had insisted on accompanying her. Now Tiger was busy dancing with his bride. It was the first chance they'd had to talk with each other that day.

'How'd last night go?' Jo asked, swept off her paws.

'Dad stole the show and the entertainment. He's good at that. You?'

'We went to about three different clubs looking for something that wasn't bizarre and out of the ordinary. Stuffed ourselves silly. It went fine.'

Jo couldn't dance for long. Not because of the excess weight in her belly; she'd kept herself fit with daily exercise. She was famished, twirling the groom past the buffet table as often as possible. Despite the feast she'd enjoyed earlier, the little parasites inside her wanted more. So more was what she gave them at every opportunity.

The scrap escalated as the thugs and lowlifes that Tiger had invited joined in. Flax Draxar bit Wilton Pirie's ear, tearing away the tip. Tanktop raked a hindclaw down Marlon Wakely's back. Kisselda spat in Alex Van de Weyer's eye, disorienting him. The heroes fought by the book, parry and thrust. The villains fought dirty, moving in for the kill.

A wedding fishcake arrived and the greedy cats stopped their squabbling to queue up for a slice. The cake lasted about four minutes. Ike decided to prevent any further fights by giving a long, boring speech. 'Now we've kind of settled our differences, a few words about why we're all here. Love.' The guests nursed their black eyes and bloody heads. 'The love that's brought these two together.'

He raised his saucer in the bride and groom's direction.

'It ain't love that brought 'em together,' came a catcall from one of the less tactful guests. Maybe inviting the baddies hadn't been a good plan. Jo instinctively covered her belly with her forepaws. Surely it didn't show?

Ike continued: 'I've seen Tiger here grow into a fine specimen of an old has-been. He's grabbed this gal quick afore she realises how pug ugly he is. His new missus – my daughter-in-law – works in movies, I'm told. No doubt you can find them on the top shelf in yer local video store. We know what you see in her, son.' Tiger gave a wry grin. 'He's intending to retire from the detection business and become a full-time hen pecked hubby. This is one open and shut case that's well and truly solved. Good luck to you, lad. I wish the two of ye all the happiness you can muster.'

Tiger dragged himself upright to deliver a few words of his own.

'I haven't known the love of my life long.' Whoops from the crowd. 'Long enough to find out what an open, genuine person she is. We didn't meet in the sexiest of circumstances –'

'Over my producer's dead body,' interjected Jo. The villains let rip with their best dirty laughs.

'When our eyes met – I knew I'd have to question her. In private. With the lights out.' Embarrassed silence. 'It's not gonna be easy providing for Jo, raising a family. We're gonna do it. With your support we'll make a damn good start. Dames have always made a lot of trouble for me in the past. Always been after something – the goods, revenge, a place to hide. Jo's different, I know she is. I'll do fine by her. She's beautiful, unique... my wife. I'm confident we'll live happily ever after.'

The guests supped more milk before Jo stood to say her piece.

'Blokes have always caused a lot of trouble for me,' she smiled. The comment raised a titter. 'Including this one beside me. I've never known such a daft, doting, gentle soul. I've never wanted to marry anyone either. Here I am. Sorry for the waterworks earlier. Can't wait for the wedding video. Don't know if we'll live happily ever after. I'd like to think so.' She bowed her head, enjoying the applause, then seated herself and drained her glass.

The guests were getting restless again so Ike suggested his son give them a tune. Tiger unpacked his saxophone and played a soulful yet totally toneless solo. Everybody left. Jo took him home and showed off a new nightie she'd bought for the wedding night. He'd drunk too much milk and felt sick, collapsing on the bed before insisting that he sleep on the floor. Jo let him sleep, wondering how she could scrap his sax and get away with it. Feed it to a goat, drop it under a tram or leave it out for the garbage cats. Whatever measure she took would have to be permanent – he'd offer a reward for its return. She'd managed to trash the instrument he'd taken from Club Wu Wu only to find another one in the case that he defended so readily. The mouthpiece was shaped to his lips, he'd tell her, the sax wouldn't play for anyone else. Jo had decided that even if she did manage to destroy the instrument, there was always the possibility that he'd go out and buy another – once he'd got over the tragic loss – maybe take up the violin. She couldn't win.

22

NUT COULD HANDLE the funny looks she got from the clerks. She didn't belong there, mixing with civilised cats. She got in the way, took up too much room, had eaten every blade of grass on the back lawn and all the shrubbery too. She spent six hours a day eating all the greenery in sight. The cats didn't understand why she was still hanging around. Neither did she.

If it was for her protection, there were safer places to be than the station. Cut throats and scoundrels with more guts than a violin wandered in every day, and that was just the cops. Mouse had left her in his office several times as he followed up lines of enquiry – a drowned kitten, a missing surgeon. She saw how wary he was around cats, scampering past them, nose atwitch. It took big balls to work for the police force whatever species you were. The paperwork was terrifying to behold, mounting up fast.

Despite her ordeal a week before, Nut felt strangely homesick. She missed her workmates, the shed, even her boorish husband. She spent many of the daylight hours wondering who'd replaced Scrumpy. Someone equally cantankerous, she hoped. A farmer who could adequately fill her old boss' wellingtons.

This particular morning she felt bloated, not sure why. Her partner or protector or whatever he was hadn't been in his office for 24 hours. Nut went walkabout, a hefty country girl absorbing the sights and scents of a municipal cop shop.

Activity throughout the building was frenetic pushing for chaotic. The harsh winter weather meant burst water pipes, citizens slipping on ice, longer nights for burglars to do their dirty work. All accidents, incidents and complaints were logged in triplicate by the desk sergeant. He wasn't happy about it.

'Get that cow out of here!' he yelled. He was a square faced manx with bushy cheeks.

'It's the Inspector's witness, Sarge,' a constable piped up, 'the one who didn't witness nothing.' The sergeant grumbled to himself and let Nut pass. Reaching the main office, she could hardly move through the throng of frazzled druggies, booked hookers and jaded pigs.

Someone had broken into a marshmallow factory and licked the coating off a whole batch. A suspect had been found puking in an alley not far away. A nest of nip addicts had been uncovered in the heart of the city; now a dozen junkies were going cold turkey in the jug. A militant leader calling himself 'TC' was believed to be organising a gang of strays to carry out scams. The only known fact about him was that he spoke with the commanding tones of an army officer. A shopkeeper was charged with selling dirty magazines.

When Nut spied the shopkeeper she took a step backwards, banging her rump against a white collar criminal. Making her apologies, she approached the retailer who was being interviewed by a shorthaired sergeant.

'I sell those things to holy guys, psychiatrists, all sorts of respectable gentlemen,' the shopkeeper was explaining. He wore a tie-dye sweatshirt and flared dralons. 'I didn't know it was illegal.'

'*Puss In Boots. Toms Only. Tail Action. Stiff Whiskers.*' The sergeant flapped the mags on his desk. The accused took a look round, embarrassed. No one was looking at him except a cow. What was a cow doing in a police station?

'You can get it in bottles, you know,' he smirked to the sergeant, waggling a paw in Nut's direction.

'Can we help you, miss?' asked the copper.

'I'm looking for Inspector Mortis.'

'You see him at my desk? I don't think so. I'm trying to charge a bad guy here.' To the hippy: 'You could do some serious time for this. When you get out your fur will be grey and your kidneys mush.'

'He did it, Officer,' cried Nut. 'He definitely did it.' The sergeant ignored her.

'I'm providing a service,' the hippy whined. 'These priests, they don't get no loving. They need magazines to help them contemplate and stuff. If you want to lock anyone up, lock up the readers. The publishers. Anyone but me. I can't go back in pokey.'

'You've done time before, Mr Sunray?' Seedpod 'Sonny' Sunray's parents had run a commune until their child had reached puberty. Now they were publishers, but Sonny had kept his remarkable name. He was too laid back to change it by deed poll. Too big a hassle.

'It was a long time ago. I was a student. We were protesting about the use of rodents in medical experiments. I got cold cocked with a baton, next thing I know I'm working on a chain gang. It was a major bummer. I was a martyr.'

'You're gonna get the chance to martyr yourself again. This time I don't think the judge will be so lenient.' The sergeant commanded a constable to lead Sonny to the holding cells.

'Hey! What about my stock?' the hippy yelled above the hubbub.

'Confiscated,' replied the sergeant, placing the magazines in his briefcase, 'as evidence.'

'I know him,' Nut mumbled.

'That third rate scumbag. Doubt if he gets out of his neighbourhood much. Only reason he'd have to visit the countryside would be to pick mushrooms.' The DC offered Nut a gentle smile. 'I'll take you back to the Inspector's office. He's due back any second.'

Jo was always getting into trouble. As a kitten her first step had led her into danger in the form of a hot pie left lying carelessly beside her. She'd burned her paw and learned a lesson. Her first trip to the ice skating rink saw her pads caught under a boot blade and a severed claw. It hadn't stopped her skating. Her first date had been a disaster too, a mad fling with a special effects artist with a thing for foam latex. She'd learned a lot about the opposite sex, or a minority group of them at least.

Now she'd lost her head and her freedom to a tom she barely knew. His power and passion had overwhelmed her for an instant that would change her life. Or had she slept with Cole to spite Tiger, make him jealous, get him to notice her? A strange way to draw attention to herself; now everyone pointed and smiled at her swollen belly. The ladies turned to goo and the males found her condition attractive. She was no threat to them, unless she had a notion to roll over them and squash them in the street.

She'd had pregnant pals before and as their weight increased their public appearances diminished. Feeling frumpy, they spent a lot of time indoors. Jo wasn't that kind of girl. She strutted her stuff until she was all strutted out – round the block was the furthest she could go. She enjoyed the sunlight, the cool breeze on her cheeks, the halloos from her neighbours who got used to seeing her out on the town, out of puff.

A frustrated Bix entered the station. His leads had brought him no closer to solving his case: he wasn't even sure if the murders he'd investigated were connected, the modus operandi were always so different. A kitten had drowned in a small fishing village; what motive could there be for taking a young life in such a sadistic fashion? The Hant brothers, poisoned with their own killer chemical. Another sick act. The TV producer – at least he had enemies. As far as Bix knew, none of the production team hated Venet enough to fry his brains to soot. That would require a heap of hate.

He found Nut in his office, delivering a steaming pat in his wastepaper basket. It wasn't her first deposit of the day.

'I'm sorry,' she said demurely, 'I didn't know where to put it.'

'It's okay. Stay downwind of me. Do you want to open the windows?'

'They are open.'

Bix couldn't see properly. Either Nut's stench was overpowering or he'd been working too hard. He was unable to reach the windows. Many other things in his office constantly reminded him of his titchy stature. He used a miniature stepladder to reach the seat behind his desk.

'There was a cat in the main office,' said Nut.

'Really? Oh my. I'd better run and hide. It might eat me!' Bix was a font of sarcastic wit. 'Of course there was a cat out there. Bloody hundreds of 'em.'

'Yes, but I recognised this one. A citizen. The officer with him said he lived in the city. The only way I'd recognise him –'

'Is if he visited your farm. Do a lot of cats pop into your shed?'

'The only one I ever saw was Scrumpy – until he died.'

'So the only way you'd recognise this bloke...'

'...Is if he was there when my boss was murdered, or when I was kidnapped.'

Bix's beady eyes gleamed.

'I'm sure he wasn't one of Scrump's temporary replacements,' Nut continued. 'I could remember, I'm sure. If you could do something for me.' The tag on her ear rattled.

'Anything. What would help?'

'Milk me.'

'I don't think so.'

'Oh, go on. I haven't been milked in ages. A good yank'd clear the cobwebs.'

'I'm a police inspector,' Bix tutted, 'not a dairy maid.'

'How badly do you want to catch this murderer?' The cop didn't reply. Instead he left his seat and positioned his tiny stepladder beside Nut's udders. Clambering up he began to tease one of her teats.

'Moo.' The cow closed her eyes tight. 'That feels good.'

'Anything yet?' Bix wanted answers.

'Keep going,' giggled Nut, 'harder.' She squirted five gallons of milk from her udders, drenching the Inspector. 'He was there! I'm sure. He wasn't alone – I didn't see the other fellow. I saw him. He didn't really want to be there.'

'Of course, it would take two to lift you,' muttered Bix as he hurriedly cleaned his whiskers.

'He distracted me; the other one battered me over the head. Never saw him again until now.'

'Let's go pay him a visit.'

Sonny languished in a holding tank. He'd sniffed a large quantity of valerian on arrest – it had been on his person for medicinal purposes. Now he was high as a kite and twice as giddy. He greeted Bix and Nut with a lazy cheer. He declined to comment on the milk that dripped from Bix's coat.

'Why'd you do it?' asked the horrified cow. She gazed through thick black bars at the hopped-up hippy.

'The money, lady. I make more offa jazz mags than a windowful of gift shop tack. I got a mouth to feed. It needs constant attention.'

'We're not interested in your tawdry wares,' Bix snapped.

He'd whipped Sonny's rap sheet from the sergeant's desk on his way down.

'I'm startin' to feel hungry now, Mr Mouse,' the shopkeeper drooled. 'Anyone ever tried to smoke a rodent?'

'Why did you try to kill me?' asked Nut.

'I had nothing against you, lady. I was doing a favour for a friend. If I'd known his intentions were – I mean, I thought he was playing a prank.'

At Bix's instruction, a guard released Sonny and slapped a pair of cuffs on him. The guard escorted Bix, Nut and a floating Sonny to the hippy's high street store.

'I don't know what you're hoping to find here, Dude. The cop who arrested me, he took all my dodgy gear. Hey, does that mean I'm off his bum charge?'

'You won't go to prison for trading in black market literature,' Bix squeaked, scouring the floor for evidence. 'You'll be booked with kidnapping and attempted murder.'

Scuttling through the shop Bix tripped over a tail. Its owner apologised and helped the Inspector up; this made him angrier.

'What are you doing here?'

Tiger and Bug tried to look innocent. It wasn't easy as they'd already turned the shop outside in. Stock was scattered over shelves and counters. The bead curtain that concealed a back room swayed noisily.

'The shop was left open. We were browsing.'

'Don't give me that. You're in cahoots with this gent, aren't you?' said Bix, staring up at Tiger. Sonny offered the detectives the peace sign with two of his claws. 'What are you really here for?'

'We're not allowed to shop? It's a fundamental right, you know. There'd be something in the constitution about it if we had one. I don't know this guy.'

'We know of him though,' Bug admitted. 'Got a tip off that he might know something about a –'

'A cheap lava lite,' Tiger interrupted, stamping on Bug's tail to shut her up. 'Here's one, purrfect! That's what I need for the office.'

'You don't have an office,' Bix squeaked.

'I will have. Soon. Need to furnish it. Who's the cow?'

Nut introduced herself, explaining that Sonny had apparently tried to kill her. Everyone admitted that this was a mean thing to do, and that she was the best looking cow they'd ever seen on the high street.

Bix ordered the guard to take Nut, the detectives and the suspect back to the station. The Inspector remained to check the stock room beyond the bead curtain. The room was mostly filled with empty cartons and cardboard boxes, although he made a small, unsettling discovery with the potential to put a whole new spin on his investigation.

'How are things, Bix? Everything running to course, I trust?' Back at the station, Chief Inspector Bowyer was making one of his rare appearances. A large seat had been brought into Bix's office for the Chief. He leaned on the desk, which sagged under his great weight.

'Making headway at last, sir. We have a suspect under lock and chain downstairs, he hasn't confessed to everything yet though we're close to breaking him. He had an accomplice – I have my suspicions who that might be.' Tiger and Bug were being detained in the corridor beyond his office.

'Wonderful.'

'Have you seen a cow round here, sir?'

'A cow? Well bless my soul, I thought she was lunch. Sent her to the kitchens. Nice with some barbecue sauce.'

'She's a witness. Might need her if this thing goes to trial.'

'There won't be a trial. In these kinds of matters justice has to be swift, Bix. Any hesitation and the public could start to worry or your suspect could escape.'

'Whatever you say, sir,' Bix frowned, always a stickler for legal procedure. 'I'll go and rescue the cow.'

'Sure. Rustle up another one for me will you, Inspector? I'm famished.'

'I'll see that the chef's made aware of your pangs,' Bix replied tartly. He didn't like to be treated like a waiter, and left the office without another word.

The Chief sat back on his padded cushion, noted the pool of milk souring on the carpet. Various animals running around made for a disorderly station and he liked nothing less. He wanted things to run smoothly. That meant a harsh reputation and an iron rule. He had no friends – those who did offer him a kind word wanted something (like Cole) or rubbished him behind his back. He had many peers and acquaintances, all helping each other to stay on the top rung of the social ladder. The position was precarious but he was party to riches, conspiracies, political and religious manoeuvres. Information helped him to maintain his position as Chief of Police in Nub City.

Bix had climbed as high as he could in the police hierarchy. It was only his stunning intellect and perfect record that had allowed him to reach the rank of Inspector. Bowyer would make sure that he got no further. Bad for feline morale for the grunts to be bossed around by a buck-toothed pipsqueak. He would move Bix to another division – litter patrol, TV licensing, something of that sort. He was sure that the Inspector would understand; perhaps he'd be glad of a less dangerous post. All these murders could have an effect on the rodent's heart, and mice were ever so weak in the ticker department.

'Excuse me. You seen a mouse about? We're waiting for him!' Tiger had nosed into the office, interrupting Bowyer's ruminations. 'We do have other things to do, my friend and I.' Bug was curled up patiently in the corridor. 'Besides being at the beck and call of that little hairball.'

'I take it you're referring to Inspector Mortis,' Bowyer said.

'Yeah. Has he got lost?'

'Carrying out an order for me. He's efficient. You are –?'

'Tiger Straight, PI. Mortis thinks I'm getting in his way.'

'I see. You're looking into a murder or two. You've crossed paths with the Inspector.'

'Been questioned by him. We had nowt to spill.'

Bowyer fondled his tail thoughtfully. 'The Inspector always gets his cat. Doesn't let anyone stand in his way. He can't afford to.'

'Sure.' Tiger looked bored, examined the insignia shaved into Bowyer's jowls. 'How's he getting on?'

'I'm sure he'll let you know all about it during your interrogation.' The Chief provided his most diplomatic smile. 'Isn't that right, Inspector?' Bix entered the office, brushing past Tiger.

'I can't *wait* for the interrogation.'

'I'm going to do a little questioning of my own with our friend downstairs.' Bowyer stood up slowly. 'Fill in some blanks for myself, okeydokey?'

'Very well, sir. If you really think it necessary.'

'I do. Goodbye, Mr Straight. I'm sure you'll be a big help to us.' Bowyer passed Nut and Bug in the corridor. They shared a bunch of grass, Bug nibbling idly on a blade, Nut chewing heavily. She spent eight hours a day chewing. When she wasn't eating or chewing, she was usually asleep. It didn't leave her a lot of time to assist the Inspector.

They sat for a while, watching a busy stream of feline traffic pass by – a cop barking like a vicious dog; a mean margay with a molester's eyes, chained up and heavily guarded; a plump orange cat eating lasagna; a Captain bawling out two hapless rookies. A tough guy in a scruffy suit sneered at Nut as he stumbled drunkenly for the gents.

'My partner hasn't exactly taken a shine to yours, has he?' Bug gave Nut a friendly sniff.

'I hadn't really noticed,' the cow lowed. 'To be honest I'm trying to get home. That's all.'

'A mouse and a cow,' said Bug thoughtfully. 'How did that happen?'

'Oh, no special reason. Extraordinary circumstances throwing two lonely souls together, forging a bond between them.'

'They say the Inspector's very efficient.'

'Who says?'

'His head honcho. The bell cow. Chief Inspector Bowyer.'

'Bix does have a certain air of authority about him, especially for someone with his disadvantages. Do you think a mouse could feel anything for..?'

'Insects don't have this problem,' Bug sighed, 'no love pangs or peer pressure. The females shag anything that isn't disguised a twig, then bite their partners' heads off afterwards.'

'Sounds efficient.' Nut rubbed her sore hooves. 'He's dragged me halfway across the city looking for clues. Finally I give him the goods, and he acts like I'm invisible. As if my usefulness is at an end. I almost landed up in the cafeteria, you know.'

'Doesn't sound so bad.' Bug licked her lips. It was a while since she'd last had a square meal.

'As the main attraction in the mixed grill? I don't think so.'

'What about these goods you gave him?'

'Some hippy implicated in all this. He could have killed me! I don't think the Inspector has even questioned him properly yet. I've a good mind to go down and talk to him myself. Maybe that'll speed things up.'

'Let's do it then,' said Bug, urging Nut into an upright position and leading her down a flight of stairs.

A lot of time and thought had been spent on the holding tanks. The cells had been given a lick of mint green paint, fancy lanterns suspended from the ceilings. The aisle lights cast dull beams onto the prisoners. One cell was open, allowing Bug and Nut into a small area furnished with cushions and a bowl of grey water. The place smelt of rosehip and disinfectant.

'We're looking for the hippy,' said Nut, barely able to squeeze into the cubicle. The Chief faced her, shaking his head.

'Ain't down here,' he belched, 'think he's done a runner.' Sonny wasn't present, though his flares lay on the floor and the heady smell of valerian lingered in the air. Bug peered through a set of bars at the perp in the adjacent cell.

'You see him?'

'Not a thing,' said a scared looking cat, 'I was workin' at minding my own business. Like you should, darlin'.'

'You think he's escaped?' Nut asked the Chief.

'I don't doubt it.' Bowyer left the cell, rubbing his copious belly.

'He's on the lam with no trousers?' Bug sniffed at the flares, her nose wrinkling.

'In disguise,' Bowyer explained. He tried to usher the two females upstairs. 'This is no place for you.'

'He'll probably get himself arrested again,' Nut mused, 'for decent exposure. We'd better get after him, eh, Chief?'

'I'll sort all that out. There're papers to fill in, APBs to bulletin. I don't want you two getting in the way – only slow things down.'

'We understand,' said Bug as she led Nut up the steps. Deciding that the Chief was embarrassed by the incident, she agreed not to mention what had happened.

Jo took up knitting, purling and darning with her needly claws. It wasn't too physically demanding, something she could focus on for hours at a time. She also tried dressmaking: it was impossible to find decent maternity wear for cats, the high street efforts resembling spud sacks. She designed crosswords for the local school magazine, sniffed at baby books. She wore a sports bra with six hefty cups. Tiger was aghast – this wasn't the adventurous femme he'd married. No more hunting, fishing or lovemaking. She was likely to turn on him and give him a scratch when he wanted a cuddle. He hoped that life would get back to normal after the births, that his wife would revert to her old self as if nothing had happened.

Tiger donned his hat and trenchcoat, buttoning it up tight. Night had fallen and the sky was grim with cloud.

'Where you off to?' asked Jo, resting on her sofa.

'Going to see a cat about an eye. Or his lack thereof. A café on West Street.'

'You're not gonna be too long, are you? In case...anything happens.'

'Nothing will,' Tiger purred, 'you're not ready to pop yet.' Jo was seven weeks pregnant. She had a fortnight still to endure.

'You never know,' the newlywed cried as Tiger left the room, 'the babies could be immature.'

He worried every day that he wouldn't be there when the time came to help her to the hospital. After the attempt on her life Jo had seemed blasé about the experience, rarely raising the subject.

But Tiger kept his wits keen – he wasn't just guarding the lady he loved. He was guarding her unborn babies as well.

It didn't take long to reach the café, tucked at the end of West Street as if hiding from customers, another grey building in a row of drab shops and terraced houses, blinds closed, lights dimmed. A canvas canopy shaded the establishment like the peak on a cap; even the streetlights couldn't illuminate its ageing sign. The canopy had been unrolled to keep the sun off; the proprietor hadn't bothered to put it away again. It jutted, gathering dust and city grime, losing its blue and white stripes.

Tiger's eyes prowled round the café, following his food as it scuttled along the counter. The Greasy Hide was the only place in town where the food ate you.

He'd become a regular customer over a period of two weeks, believing the proprietor to be a member of the Kitty Killer Cult. The Cheshire at the till smiled at the clientele, serving them without complaint. Enough to arouse anyone's suspicions. Every night at ten the Cheshire would close shop, nip round the corner, bone up on his rites and chants, go enjoy a sacrifice or two with his pals and back to the missus before she knew any better. Tiger wanted to interview her, though he doubted she'd be able to shed any light on her mate's activities. Many of the females in these parts turned a blinkered eye to the shenanigans of the males.

Tiger was never the last customer out of the shop. He was far too wily for that, waiting in a shadowed doorway across the street. His trench coat collar was turned up against the cold. When the Cheshire finally placed a closed sign in his window and trudged past the detective, Tiger followed ten yards behind. He was grateful for the dirty mist. He knew it was going to rain. It always did on nights like this; the heat rose and congested to form dark clouds that matched moods.

Tiger followed the suspect through streets shining with the slick damp of old rain, stopping as the Cheshire entered a run-down block of flats. The detective crouched in a bundle of trashcans. His green eyes were mirrored in a front window as he looked inside. He could see a group of cats, dressed casually, trading greetings and rubbing against one another, checking out their individual scents.

There was a smack of lightning as a member of the group turned to face him: a grey-faced ghoul with one eye scarred shut. Julius didn't duck, didn't move – the motion might clue the Cult to his presence. Instead he squeezed his eyes tight shut and hoped the light didn't give him away.

Nothing happened. One Eye turned back to the others. They didn't seem to be breaking any laws, but Tiger wanted to hear what they were saying. After a rapid snoop round the back of the building, he found a small flap leading to the cellar. He squeezed through and crept on all fours towards the front room, ears cocked.

Padding through a hallway, following his nose, he judged that the door opposite would lead to the front room. He placed his head against the door and listened. Silence. He stared through the keyhole; no one was there. Perhaps he had the wrong room. Perhaps his prey had gone.

A screen croaked open with a slight push and he stepped forwards, eyes adjusting to darkness. Instead of rich carpet his paws trod thin air, and he fell into a deep oblong pit.

'You must be the dick.' One Eye had been waiting for his grand entrance.

'Astute.' Tiger brushed down his coat with the fedora. 'I've been hired to –'

'To mess up my life. It's not gonna happen. We're turnin' this place into a bathroom, buddy. You're at the bottom of a deep, deep sand tray.' For the first time Tiger noticed four vents at the top of his pit. They began to spew fresh litter, spilling onto him. The pit slowly began to fill – he would be buried alive in a giant litter trap.

23

ONE EYE'S LAUGHTER faded into the distance as Tiger was left to his fate. The detective gained purchase on a pipe that lined the wall, leaping for one of the vents, hoping to block it with his trench coat. Too high. He landed on the sand-strewn floor, grains jamming between his pads. He was already up to his knees in litter and there was no way to climb back onto the ledge he'd dropped from.

Instinctively he began to wash the back of his paw with his tongue. He swallowed more grit, his throat dust-dry, annoyed that he'd fallen into the trap so easily. Like a sucker.

The sand was up to his waist now and he hacked and coughed to clear his throat. His eyes streamed, lids blinking to clear his sight. He'd learned nothing. One Eye hadn't stopped to gloat or reveal his plans; he'd buggered off, left Tiger to die alone. The detective didn't want to go out that way – he wanted a fair death, a glorious one even.

There was a roar in his ears, the sand rushing past him, stifling his breath. He couldn't see the vents any more. Light from the entranceway danced on the grains, giving them a silver gold lustre. Tiger tried to claw his way out. He sank, losing his footing, dragged downwards into the soft litter. He peed copiously. Even a hero can lose control of his bladder in a stressful situation.

He noticed the damp deposit beneath him had hardened. He raised himself an inch. Shucking his trench coat, he grappled towards the pipe that was bracketed to the wall. It was hard going – he couldn't see and sediment slowed his movement. Reaching the pipe, he popped a claw and rammed it into the tubing. Water jetted from the puncture, soaking the sand around him. It toughened up and he clambered over the sodden clumps, hopping onto the ledge.

No cat likes to take a shower. He had a score to settle with One Eye.

The kittens danced inside Jo's womb. At first it had been a soft-shoe shuffle, barely more than a flutter; now they'd discovered the stomp, the mash potato and the black bottom. She felt focused, angry, tranquil and listless by turns, as if each of her offspring had an effect on her, depending on the day of the week. Some were rowdier than others; she couldn't name them until she knew their sex, so she numbered them One to Four instead. One had the largest paws, Three the sharpest claws, Four was the docile one.

She had developed a craving for marshmallows. As Tiger loved them anyway, he kept her well supplied. Determined not to become a baby bore, she picked up no more than one related item per week. Nevertheless, she'd soon collected a pram, cots, sleepsuits, nappies and a papoose for Tiger to carry the infants.

She was fat as a barn and moody as a storm cloud. Her kittens wouldn't listen to her! She'd place her paws on her stomach, tell them to quiet down yet they never responded. If this was what motherhood would be like she'd be visiting the orphanage.

Tiger had quite a story to tell when he returned. She didn't believe a word of it; she was used to toms telling tales. Film and theatre types made a career of exaggerating their parts in life. So when her husband told her he'd faced death mere hours before, she told him that was nice, could he get her a saucer of milk before he went to bed?

As Tiger trudged upstairs to the bedroom, leaving a trail of sand behind him, she shifted her burgeoning belly across the sofa. It was a major effort to reach over and switch on the radio. She twiddled the knobs on the little red transistor until she found the only channel worth listening to. Her favourite show was about to come on. The show featured a good-natured mouse who was always getting into scrapes; a hobo cat helped rescue him from his own folly. Every listener was aware that the cat was the real hero of the piece. However the mouse would occasionally shine, performing kindly acts that improved public relations for mice in the real world. The show was called *Bless this Mouse*.

Tiger returned from the bedroom. He'd given himself a perfunctory bath, taken a fresh trench coat and hat from the wardrobe.

'Where you off to now, then?' she asked idly, listening to her favourite radio show.

'I'm going to see a dame.'

'You can't,' said Mrs Straight. Tiger's heart beat harder in his chest. He was about to find out who wore the trousers in her house. A chance to put his paw down.

'No can't about it, darlin'.'

'You got a message. You got to meet your assistant. She's got some info for you.'

'Already?' Jo hadn't been chastising her husband after all. Wasn't she the least bit jealous, or curious?

'Outside the Beggars' Temple. Dawn. Sounds frightfully shady. You'll dig it.'

'Thanks. Have to meet this dame first. She's a looker. I hope I can control myself.' No reaction. 'She might know something about the jackanapes who tried to kill me. Take it easy while I'm away.'

'I intend to.' Jo was missing her show. She was glad when her husband had left the house. Peace at last.

Behind the Duncan Hotel stood a large yellow structure, triangular with a curved sidewall. Portals dotted round the building led into a network of offices. The central conference suite formed the nerve centre of the Kitty Killer Cult.

The suite adjoined a smaller room, plush and skilfully decorated. Its colour scheme consisted of relaxing browns and mustard, giving the office a rustic air. Both rooms enjoyed the latest AV toys – video conference screens, intercom systems, computer-based display consoles. A partition could be removed to turn the two rooms into one. Behind a heavy black desk, surrounded by memos and calendars, perched on a swivel chair was Big Cheese. He plotted and schemed for a living and he was the best conspirator in the city.

Big Cheese wore a pinstripe suit with an austere silk tie. His round ears cast a heavy shadow against the wall behind him. His tiny eyes flitted about constantly, bloodshot with paranoia. If he could be colluding against others, they could be colluding against him.

He controlled the city. He hadn't invaded the country, marched in with troops or pulled off a political coup. He dominated Nub through the children, the media and the products citizens consumed. He told them what to think and feel.

The take-over hadn't happened overnight. Big Cheese had spent years building theme parks, setting up clubs, financing movies and radio shows. The people loved the movies – *The Aft Aglay Gang, Scratch 'n' Sniff, Inspector Repuss*. Ads for the shows, their memorabilia, associated merchandise and fairground rides were everywhere.

Controlling the city wasn't enough. His domination had begun as a philanthropic venture; now he was bitter and vengeful. It was almost time for the Kitty Killer Cult to strike.

Wendy was always ready to receive visitors, even when they turned up in the middle of the night. She was a lonely lady with a dull life. The highlight of Wendy's day was a trip to her husband's café; if customers were present, she'd nag him about the chores he'd neglected or the promises he'd broken. If the place was empty she'd flex her claws and start a full-on argument. The couple never bickered over anything consequential and they'd never done time in prison for breaching the peace. They fought in private. They'd recently celebrated their silver wedding anniversary.

Tiger found Wendy too hospitable. She fussed around him as she entered her home, offered to rustle up some vole for him. The house was a two up two down that smelled of cabbage corpses. It had been scrubbed so hard that it sparkled, the living room an obstacle course of furniture that was twenty years out of date. Tiger banged a shin on a glass coffee table, almost knocking the glass from its chrome housing. Wendy said nothing. She was far too magnanimous a host to scold him. Didn't hurt to give him a *do that again and you die* look, though.

Such a look was beloved of mothers throughout the city. Although Wendy had never reproduced – that would have required sex with her idiot husband – she was convinced that all males were little children on the inside, brash and mischievous. They needed guidance.

'Watcha lookin' for, Mr Steak?'

'Straight. Tiger Straight. I'm a regular at your husband's caf, lent some money to a one eyed cove. He's always there.'

'Yup. Owns half the business. My husband reckons he's got the better half. Danny, his name is. Danny Tennant.'

'So it is. I've got a brain like a dog, sorry. Like I say, I lent him money. A lot. I need it back in a hurry. Thought you might know where he's at.'

'I don't get around a heck of a lot,' Wendy flapped her housecoat as a parp escaped from her ample mouth. 'I don't know everyone's address.'

'That's a shame. It would've been a big help if you could – if you'd known where Danny could be.' Tiger left the living room. The cabbage smell lingered in his nostrils.

'I didn't say I didn't know where he is,' Wendy shouted after him. 'Not sure about his address. I ken where he hangs out.'

'Yeah, the café. I already know that.' Tiger didn't want to be rude. Neither did he want to waste any more time than he had to with his burping host.

'You must be good friends with him, to borrow him all that cash.' Wendy stopped the detective in the hallway.

'He's good for it.'

'He spent all his dough on the caf. Buyin' his share. These days he hangs out with his old work buddies.'

'Where did he used to work?'

The cheshire cat belched again. 'Apologies. Gotta bad stomach. The neighbours call me Windy Wendy. That's why I spend a lotta my time indoors – with the windows open. I don't have to hang my washing in the back garden. Just open my cakehole and thar she blows.'

'I wish I could remember where Danny worked,' Tiger muttered, trying not to inhale. The cheshire was crowding him now.

'The abattoir, Mr Stake. That's where he'll be. Chewin' the fat at the abattoir.'

Night was almost over by the time Tiger had escaped the clutches of Windy Wendy. The rain had stopped, rapidly replaced by a shower of sleet. He tugged his hat down over his ears, suppressing a shiver. He needed a sunbath.

The rendezvous point was a narrow lane on the outskirts of the city, where only the rats and lowlifes bred. Tiger was on his guard as he approached. He knew not all the rats around here were little guys with twitchy noses and pink feet. Some of them were big cats willing to do anything for a fast buck, as long as it wasn't anything pleasant. A lantern died overhead, forcing him to move on to the next lamppost. He'd be a sitting target if anyone decided to take a pot shot at him, but he didn't want to miss Bug.

She'd promised information, and Bug was a lady who always delivered. While he waited, Tiger unbuttoned his coat and blew a few baleful notes from his tarnished sax, the sounds rising into the starless sky like angels looking for their boss.

'You were right,' said Bug, still shrouded in darkness.

'Ain't I always?' the detective tucked the sax back under his coat.

'How's married life cheating you?' Bug showed herself. She looked hot in a business suit, her tail wrapped over her left forepaw. She had a name badge tagged to her lapel. 'That wasn't so bad.'

'My playing?' Tiger asked hopefully.

'Getting here. Nobody saw me. Everything's cool at the bank.'

'There's no chance you'll blow your cover. Not if you're careful.'

'Ain't I always?' Bug slicked up to her partner, rubbing her forehead against the brim of his hat. 'Got some interesting folk connected with the cult.'

'That's not being careful. I told you – no snooping until you're settled into the job.'

'I don't want to be settled into the job! They trust me. They're all pussycats, especially my boss Miss Angold. She can hardly see the files. She wouldn't be able to tell if I took 'em all.'

'You didn't.'

'I accessed the relevant databases, memorised some names. That's all. Check these out: Doctor Mopp. Hant Bros. Cole Tiddle.'

'They all got money coming out their accounts?'

'Sure. The KKC are siphoning large sums from a lot of dead cats.'

'You know where it's going?' Tiger wanted to hug his assistant.

'I will do. When I get the chance to get sneaky again. Won't be long. I refuse to spend a month in that creepy place.'

24

THE ABATTOIR WAS deadly quiet by the time Tiger found it. There were signs of recent occupation – carcasses swinging gently from side to side, box lunches open with their contents still fresh. He couldn't understand how anyone could eat with raw flesh rotting beside them. He licked his nose, something he always did when he was close to iffy food.

Red lights helped add to the building's macabre character. Tiger tried a couple of rooms, finding nothing. He reached a corridor, also drenched in scarlet light. He stopped suddenly, his back arched. The hairs on his back stood up like cornstalks.

Half a dozen cats, led by a tall, silent wraith of a tom, waited at the end of the corridor. They wore red robes with hems that brushed the floor, long sleeves that covered their paws, hoods that shielded their faces. They looked like demons, spike-topped goblins. They were the most forbidding security guards he had ever seen. He felt cold in their presence.

There was a glint of white under their long sleeves and their teeth looked impossibly sharp. Tiger ducked into an office, hunched as short as he could behind a bureau. Black eyes swivelled in his direction.

The tall guard approached, hands together, sleeves joining so that the arms looked like one flowing silken tube. He said nothing. The silence shook Tiger far more than any threat. The detective stepped into the open, chin up, defiant.

'You can't kill me. I'm cute.'

The guard did not reply. Slowly, he opened his arms and the sleeves fell open, revealing a set of claws as long as bread knives. Ten daggers clattered together as the guard opened and closed his paws in a languorous stretch.

Tiger started to back away. The other guards shucked their robes, displaying their own cruel talons. They moved in and out of vision like dancing tongues of bright red flame. There was only one way out and he didn't want to end up on those claws.

'He's right.' The guards turned in unison to find Bug dressed in her orange suit, a cheeky grin on her face. 'He's cute as a button and twice as dangerous.'

Tiger piled past the guards, scattering them like fleas off a dead dog's back. He raced for the exit, dragging Bug with him. In the old days he would have stopped and fought the guards alongside his partner. Now he was struggling to survive. The swish of their robes on the well-waxed floor was close behind. One of the goblins sunk glass-sharp teeth into his shoulder, knocking him to the floor. They were surrounded, exit blocked.

'Excuse me!' Bug hollered, struggling to avoid their stiletto claws. 'Lady in need of assistance over here!' Tiger hauled himself free of his attacker, who'd lost a tooth in the private eye's shoulder. Tiger drove him away with a vicious backswing, ripping open the cat's throat.

The detective maintained his claws for such an emergency. He would file them carefully, each claw serving a different purpose. He used a snub-nosed claw to attract the lead cat's attention, drawing him away from Bug. The other two felines lined up behind their vanguard.

'I ain't so cuddly when you get to know me,' Tiger grinned, swiping at the cat. He put all his body strength into the blow, which knocked the attackers off balance. Before they could right themselves, the two investigators raced away.

25

TIGER SLUMPED AT the dining table, exhausted. Bug nudged a bowl of meat nearer to him. He arched back in his seat; the smell of the food seemed to offend him.

'Lost your appetite, Tiger?' asked Bug, hair shrouding her rounded face. 'Nice of Connie to put me up, isn't it?'

'Where is she?'

'Out looking for work. She's had more interviews than you've had hot dinners. Heroes've got to eat too, you know.'

'I'm no hero.'

'Oh yeah. Like all cats spend their mornings rescuing a maiden in distress from six ne'er-do-wells.'

'I don't wanna talk about it.'

'You got three of 'em with one punch! It was incredible... damnedest thing I ever saw.'

'Enough!' Tiger slammed the food across the table, bolting from his chair. A tear dribbled down his left cheek. 'I didn't mean to hurt them.'

'But they deserved it!' Bug insisted. Her partner was already heading for his study.

'I don't want to be disturbed.'

Speechless, Bug shook her head. Maybe he was getting too old for the crime fighting business. He certainly needed to brush up on his social skills. She began to clear up the spilled food.

Back in the dawn of medical history, the authorities had realised that if they put sick people in a building they'd only infect each other. The Nub City Infirmary had been split up into a number of skinny edifices dotted around the centre. One of these was devoted to newborn kittens and expectant mothers.

There were signs for the hospital everywhere, all pointing in different directions. Fine if you had a septic dewclaw or a flea problem, but this was an emergency. Tiger and Jo finally reached a building flanked by pacing tomcats, puffing nervously on cigarettes. Tiger squeezed his wife inside, scratching at the reception desk until someone appeared.

'Take these,' said the receptionist.

'What are they?' Tiger grabbed a sheaf of blue papers.

'Mrs Straight's medical notes. Hang onto them.' A fat nurse helped Jo along a narrow corridor and puffed up a steep flight of stairs. The father-to-be brought up the rear, helpless. He tried to retain a dominant air. Impossible – he reached for Jo's paw to remind her he was there. Before they could connect she was hustled into a cubicle with a gurney and small cupboard. Tiger placed his wife's belongings in the cupboard and curled up beside her, scanning a breastfeeding poster on the wall.

A pair of porters lifted Jo onto the gurney and wheeled her into a lift. Tiger followed, making small talk with the midwife, as they were shown the delivery room on the floor below.

'How long till they arrive?' Tiger wondered.

'When they're ready,' the midwife explained. As if on cue, a series of contractions wracked the pregnant cat. 'Your wife's insisted on a natural birth. We can't induce – ' The midwife turned to one of the porters. 'Where are Mrs Straight's notes? They should be right here.'

'Must still be in her room,' said Tiger. He raced up the stairs, not daring to wait for the lift. In the maternity ward he was accosted by the corpulent nurse.

'A little early aren't you?' she snooted, pointing at the visiting times.

'Need notes,' he wheezed, trying to get by. 'Lady in theatre needs medical notes. Now.' The nurse gave a humph, until the anxious cat popped his claws. She let him pass.

In Jo's cubicle, he piled through the clothes and scrunched linen to find the blue forms. Holding them tight to his chest, he transported them back downstairs to the –

Where was the theatre? All the corridors looked alike. This place was alien to him and the disinfected smells confused him. This was a nightmare! He'd chased and scrapped with feral cats, saved the lives of strangers, but he couldn't help the cat he loved.

Tiger took a gamble, eenie-meenie-minie-moed his way down an eastward passage, hunting for a helpful sign. He recognised a grey room, saw a familiar pair of hindpaws drooping off a gurney – Jo!

'Got… got notes,' he panted. The midwife grinned as a high pitched squeal assailed Tiger's ears.

'You have a son, Mr Straight. He's perfect, got all his bits.' The midwife took the sheets from him. 'Already?' he asked.

'Yes. Next one's due in about thirty minutes.' She made the births sound like a tram timetable. He didn't mind; he was engrossed in his bawling child. Its large forehead was creased into a frown, its mouth pouting, paws curling and uncurling. The midwife helped Jo to wash the newborn, warming and cleaning it, giving its circulation a boost.

The vet sterilised his claws, sharp enough to make a caesarean incision, dainty enough to deliver a kitten. Jo made a meal of the firstborn's placenta, building her strength for the coming ordeal.

Tiger watched as the second baby appeared, squealing red white and blue murder. Jo washed its nose and mouth, ensuring that it could breathe properly. She gnawed through its umbilical cord and ate that as well. One male, one female. What sex would the next one be?

Half an hour later the third newborn appeared, another male. His mother broke away the amniotic sac and the tiny creature entered the world. He mewed softly, stirring Tiger's stoic heart.

The final birth was more difficult – a breach. Staying calm, soothing his wife, Tiger purred slowly. The sound relaxed Jo enough for the vet to perform a caesarean, bringing a second female into the world.

'They all okay?' asked Jo, feeling weary. She'd been in delivery for two hours.

'No. No, lover. The last one didn't make it.'

For a moment, Tiger and Jo shared a common pang. Then the mother was wheeled away with her three surviving kittens, leaving her husband with the stillborn baby.

Bug knew where the regular debits were headed. She'd worked out the bank's code for particular accounts, traced the secret party that was benefiting from the arrangement. There were no lights on in the records room; she didn't dare announce her presence. Bug used her eyes to pierce the gloom, checking that her calculations were correct, removing a file from a dusty filing cabinet. Enough proof to expose the Kitty Killer Cult.

Bug wore a mask that obscured the top half of her head. She figured that any security camera would show a disguised figure lurking round the bank, rather than an itinerant clerk. It was dark blue with antennae on top. She'd made it herself.

Neither the mask nor the darkness could prevent Bug's boss from finding her. 'What do you think you're doing there?'

'Doing, Miss Angold?' Bug replied with a start. 'I'm not doing anything. Lazy, that's me. Please don't take umbrage with that. Whatever umbrage is. Do you know? What an umbrage is? I don't think I've got one, whatever it might be…'

'Stop your gibbering, lassie. I know full well what you're up to. You want my job, don't you?' Miss Angold snatched the file from Bug's hot paws. 'I think we're going to have to take you to see the manager.'

'What's this "we" business? You ain't royalty. Let me go.' Angold had her in a taut grip, a claw poking into the small of her back. She nudged Bug towards the vault, ignoring the snooper's protestations.

At the vault Angold dialled a combination and the massive hatch swung open. Bug expected to be shoved into the vault; instead her boss operated a tiny lever jutting from the wall. A panel in the hatch frame slid upwards, leading to a narrow corridor. Urged into the passageway, Bug had to walk on the tips of her pads to squeeze through. There was no way to turn back if she'd wanted to; she was more interested in finding out where the corridor led, and confronting the manager. Angold was close behind, nudging her bifocals up her nose. The panel and hatch closed behind them.

'I've had a hard day,' Bug whined, 'I'm ready for bed. This ain't gonna take too long, is it?'

Angold silenced her with a nip on the tail. The skinny corridor wound left and right for half a mile, leading to an archway so small that the two cats had to squeeze through on their bellies. The other side was a different matter, however – an opulent, wide-open dining room lit with a chandelier.

'Thought you'd never get here,' said its owner, offering Bug a seat. 'Had a good day's snoop?'

'I don't get it,' Bug stuttered.

'What's there to get?' The host took a seat beside her, taking care to remain out of her reach. 'Your credentials were a little too impeccable, my dear. We didn't know what you were after, though.'

'Give a mouse enough cheese and it'll trap itself,' offered Angold. The host glowered at her.

'What are you going to do with me?'

'Same thing we did to Cole Tiddle. The Hant Brothers. There's no way to break it to you softly, my dear – you're nobbled. I would kill you myself, but someone else has requested the pleasure.' Clearing his throat, the host announced the killer's presence. Appearing from the next room was the last person Bug expected to see.

26

OFFSPRING ARE A mystery, a misery and a miracle. They bring fulfilment and tragedy. They age you and rejuvenate you all at once.

Tiger had never sought fatherhood; it had found him. In his crimefighting days he would act as an idol for cats everywhere, a good (if violent) example to them all. When they saw him hogging headlines or accepting awards, they knew what a good guy was. The closest Straight had got to cubs was a school talk or a treetop rescue. Now he was more likely to be found changing a nappy than making the world a better place.

The female kitten was named Baby. White with a grey tail, she mewed constantly and let nothing get between her and her regular feed. Banjo was also assertive, pushing past his brother to get to his favourite nipple. The last surviving member of the litter, Marthin, was quiet and sleepy. He required the most attention, and Jo spent a lot of time nurturing him. The birth had changed her; there was a sadness in her heart as she mourned the lost kitten. She would never be close to her husband again.

Danny Tennant needed a cup of milk. He was thirsty and only a swallow of that white dairy nectar could quench his need. He tried to press a button on the drinks machine, missed. His depth of vision had been sadly lacking since he'd lost his eye.

Before the accident he'd been another furface in the crowd, Mr Invisible, getting away with all sorts of cheap pranks. He'd stolen tinned food from the supermarket, chased protected bird species, eaten in restaurants and fled without paying the bill. He'd bullied police officers and kidnapped kittens. He'd never been selected during an identity parade; his mugshot had not graced the Sunday papers.

His last job as a professional criminal had been a doozy. Hang around a casino, wait until some big winner came out, swat him on the head and bail. The lucky guy would be drunk on his success. The job would be hassle-free and his plan was simple enough to be foolproof.

Danny had wandered around the establishment for a time, played a couple of low-stakes games. Bash the Rat, Tails It Is, Rodent Roulette. Kept his eyes – *his eyes!* – on a gambler who lost a lot and won even more. Some doll was limpeted to him, fawning like a trouper. That wouldn't stop Danny. She'd run screaming as soon as he pounced.

The night had grown old and Danny kept yawning. The casino overfed its patrons with kippers to keep them content. Following the gambler out of the building – Danny had always been a sneaky stalker – he had clocked his quarry with a hefty wallop.

Instead of running for help, the limpet had turned feral. Before Danny had a chance to think, she'd knocked him flat on his back and bitten a chunk from his face. When the police came looking for him he was easy to find. He was the cat with only one eye.

Now everyone looked at him – passers by, victims and villains. He'd done six months in the jug for his attempted robbery – the lady who'd attacked him had received a pat on the back. Danny would never pass unnoticed again. He'd become a victim, and it wasn't an easy feeling.

In prison he'd learned to appreciate the sanctity of all living things. He'd been drafted into a cult dedicated to the preservation of that sanctity thanks to a black caracal named Callum, doing time for breach of the peace.

Caracals were larger and stronger than average, with long ears that tufted at the tip. They made excellent predators and a sojourn in jail was especially frustrating for them. Callum could leap higher, run faster than his fellow inmates. He took digitalis to strengthen his heart, giving him great stamina when necessary. He never tried to escape, patiently waiting out his sentence. Nobody ever wrote to him or came to visit him and he wouldn't have had time to spare with them if they had. He was busy spreading the word amongst the prisoners. A lot of them preferred to see sense rather than offend the big cat.

Callum hadn't been incarcerated because of his breed or his colour. White, blue, ginger and tortoiseshell cats shared a cell with him. He was there because he'd dared to suggest that eating other intelligent animals was barbaric, that it bordered on cannibalism.

He dared to say it out loud, on street corners and in city hall. The Governing Council of Cats had decided to let him stew for a while, hoping that a harsh sentence would cool his fervour. It hadn't.

'Life is sacred, my one eyed friend,' Callum would say, 'nature forms subtle chains, a pattern for all creatures to follow. A mouse dies when nature intends it to die, when it's exhausted its usefulness in the world. Not when we get hungry for a snashter.' The black cat was quite happy to kill in order to protect himself, preserve his own life. Some of the toughest crims on the cellblock took a crack at him, aiming to prove their mettle against a caracal. They failed; Callum told Danny that Mother Nature had a higher purpose all ready for him. The black cat was indomitable.

Completing his sentence, Danny had gone to an address given to him by his guru. There a group of cultists had given him succour. Today he was a fully-fledged member of the Kitty Killer Cult and the boss wanted to see him.

Danny was full of beans when he visited the West End mansion. The manner in which he'd bumped off the detective still made him giggle. A fittingly gritty demise for the hard-boiled snoop. Callum greeted him as he entered the mansion, pointing him towards a study full of vegetarian cookery books.

The boss greeted him and he hastened to make his report.

'Tiger Straight's finished, sir. He don't tick no more. He's one dead dick.'

'Funny.' The boss wasn't laughing. He wasn't doing much of anything, sitting in an armchair with his legs crossed.

'How so, sir?'

'I have it on extremely good authority that Mr Straight still lives. Callum?'

The caracal appeared behind Danny.

'We've drained the sandpit,' the black cat boomed. 'No sign of a corpse. He got out.'

'I can tell you're disappointed, boss,' Danny whined. 'This guy can't do any damage. He don't know anything. He's asking questions but he ain't getting many answers. I'll knock him off if you gimme another chance.'

The boss said nothing, shaking his head slowly.

'Before you give this job to someone else – let me try. I'm not going to fail you twice, am I?'

The boss smiled. Danny stared warily at his gnarled teeth.

'Time to go, pal.' Callum wrapped a forelimb round Danny's neck. 'You've taken up enough of the boss' life.'

'I don't have to put up with this from someone like you,' Danny shouted at his leader. He was scared now. With his paw locked around Danny's neck, Callum led him out of the study and into an unlit hallway. He continued to apply pressure on the smaller cat's windpipe.

'I thought you believed in the sanctity of life?' Danny gasped.

'Scum don't count.' Callum squeezed the life from his friend and returned to the study.

Hairy Bancroft's career wasn't going to plan. Despite his assumed rule of the airwaves, the death of Joel Venet had cast a dark pall over his TV show. If Hairy had been in charge, he would have replaced the producer, continued making episodes without a hiatus. Those programmes would, of course, be perfectly crafted as a tribute to the murdered cat. Viewers would understand; they'd realise how cut up Joel's colleagues were about the death. They'd enjoy the stories and mourn Joel's passing. They'd also understand that the TV channel had to make money, and episodes of *Wonder Cat* always did that.

Instead the lily-spleened executives had decided that there would be a respite. An indefinite one. They'd axed the programme, believing that audiences would see further production as a callous moneymaking venture. Besides, it was time for fresh product; *Wonder Cat* had been running for long enough, it was getting tired and self-referential. Whoever had killed Joel had also killed the series, and Hairy's livelihood along with it.

There's a fine line between reality and TV fantasy. People in the streets had often mistaken Hairy for the crimebusting hero, offered him a friendly sniff as they passed by, gave him money. He'd been gratified by the attention, enjoyed being a hero instead of a poor actor. The children were especially ready to suspend their disbelief, buying his drinks in the local bar, asking for his autograph. One flick of a switch had stopped all that.

When all had seemed lost, his agent had called with a job opportunity. It wasn't a prime time series or a part in the Totterdown Pavilion's new production, *Bricklayer's Story*. Nevertheless, he took the regular work hungrily, afraid that he'd been out of the limelight for too long.

Now his face was everywhere, on billboards, in magazines, on the sides of trams, all marked with his personal scent. He was the figurehead for the largest advertising campaign the city had ever seen. His likeness was used to sell something that every citizen craved – it wasn't a useless gadget that they didn't require, or a pecuniary policy with no dividend. Every cat needed it and ate it almost every day. All Hairy had to do was pose for a few photos, stand in front of a video camera for a day and spray his scent on a lot of posters. The messages were all along similar lines:

FISH! BUY FISH! EAT OUR FISH! OUR FISH IS BEST! IT'S BETTER THAN THE SCABBY FISH YOU USUALLY BUY! ALL DEBONED WITH ALL THE TASTE! FROM THE CLEAN GREEN WATERS OF DUNBAR BAY! PROTEIN! HAIRY EATS IT ALL THE TIME, HE CAN'T GET ENOUGH OF IT! FISH! FISH! FISH!

There was a subliminal theme in the ads if you read between the lines. It would seep into a consumer's subconscious with the subtlety of a late night dream. For no obvious reason the consumers would find themselves eating a lot, and when they ate they were tucking into fish.

Hairy didn't really eat that particular brand every day. He had eaten it once in front of the cameras, an ad that would be broadcast city-wide. It had tasted okay, nothing to get hyperbolic about. He enjoyed his recharged bout of fame but his ego had landed. Success was no longer a given; he would have to plan for future slumps, look to his physical and spiritual health in order to survive.

Fortunately, his current employers had covered the spiritual aspect. They'd invited him to join a cult that worshipped at the

Beggars' Temple. Hairy had always been suspicious of religious organisations, so he'd asked a detective to accompany him. He wanted nothing to do with the police after his interrogation at the factory; he called Tiger Straight instead.

27

TIGER JUMPED AT the chance to watch Hairy's back, sure that the Kitty Killer Cult had Bug. She hadn't been in touch since he'd spurned her cooking, and he didn't consider her the sulking type. He agreed to trail the actor at a discreet distance, following him into the Beggars' Temple.

Hairy gave the temple guard two voles, an offering to the spirits of long-gone beggars. The guard asked the same of Tiger, who produced a juicy hare. It had been a wedding gift, but the guard insisted on taking it. Hairy had already flounced up a flight of stone steps. The guard put the hare in his mouth, clamped down his molars and smiled.

Hairy had vanished by the time Tiger got inside.

A tall cat stooped under the canted ceiling. He showed Tiger a veiled archway. The detective doubled up to descend into a tunnel; it was poorly lit. Ancient tools and weapons shone above his head. They had been bronzed to the tunnel roof.

He reached an antechamber, tiled brown. On the tiles were obscure scent-messages and hieroglyphs. He looked at the hieroglyphs and attempted to translate them. For the first time –

He understood. He hadn't rumbled a league of keen kidnappers, kennel keyholders or kilted kitchen-fitters. Not a gang of kinky kingpins, kissing kinfolk nor knavish knights. The KKC had a more sinister agenda and he was in their domain.

He passed through a rounded entranceway, found a second tunnel that had been carved in the rock. A slab ground into place behind him, sealing him in. The tunnel descended at a steep gradient, Tiger using his whiskers to find his way in the unlit passage. The smell from the charnelhouse above began to fade. The hairs on the back of his neck went cornstalk-erect. He needed to pee.

His legs had grown tired by the time he heard chanting. He was unable to make out the words. A flicker of torchlight led him out of the tunnel into a vast crypt, cobwebbed with archways and helical supports. A group of cloaked cats formed a circle around a mandala, chanting and raising their forepaws in zeal. On the mandala stood Hairy, entranced.

Tiger kept in the shadows near the tunnel's mouth. On the opposite side of the crypt was a spiral staircase that wound upwards, out of danger. The cats stood between him and freedom.

He recognised one of them. The big guy, he'd seen him at the cop shop. The Chief of Police, big, bold and heading for his nook.

'I smell a cat.' The Chief blinked, his emerald eyes penetrating the gloom. 'A snooper. A nosy parker. A fly off the wall. An inter...' reaching a giant paw into the alcove, scooping Tiger out, '...loper.'

The desperate detective began to struggle. One of the brethren snuck behind him, grabbing the scruff of his neck between jagged teeth. Tiger was immobilised.

'I know you.'

His belly was exposed and vulnerable. He tried to shake his head, couldn't. Managed to mutter: 'I don't think so.'

'The gumshoe. Mortis wanted you locked up. You wanted to eat him.' The Chief chuckled, then punched Tiger in the stomach. 'How did you get in here?'

'I'm looking for my friend. Maybe she wanted to join your group.'

'We select our members. This isn't a health club.'

'Shame. I could do with losing a few pounds. What is it then?' Tiger winced as the teeth in the back of his neck sank deeper.

'Get rid of him. And his friend.'

'Hairy! Help me!' The actor was lying down now, breathing heavily. He'd been drugged. As Tiger moved to see if he was all right, the pain in his neck grew and he joined Hairy in the realms of unconsciousness.

28

TIGER WAS A lone hunter, a primitive seeking prey. Trees stretched into clouds draped with swaying vines. Drops of rain dribbled down the bark, glistening occasionally as light fought through the forest roof. He saw a figure dart behind a tree – a small blur, enough to send him in pursuit.

He padded carefully through sparse undergrowth, noiseless. The hunted animal was not aware of his presence, or had discounted him as a harmless neighbour. Tiger was hungry, needed to retrieve supper for his family. He sniffed at the air, making his stealthy way towards the animal, closing the gap using scent and sound. It wouldn't suspect a threat until it met its fate.

The blur had stopped at a concave rock, stooped over and defenceless. The raindrops had collected in a hollow; Tiger's prey was thirsty. The hunter tensed, his ears tilted, ready to warn of potential interruption. His whiskers twitched. His back end swayed from side to side, his tail a charmed snake dancing a slow waltz. He could taste his last meal bloody on his lips, hear the hunted's heartbeat quick and strong. The creature was still in shadow but he felt like he knew every inch of its furry little form.

Tiger leaped forward, pincering his forepaws round his supper. It dragged itself clear of the razor sharp claws, fleeing for cover. Recovering from his momentary surprise Tiger gave chase, weaving past trees and thorn bushes, every step bringing him closer to the terrified animal. He reached out a paw, took a swipe. The flora took on strange shapes, characters of their own; faces laughed at the hunter, legs tried to trip him. Running out of breath he had time for one more attack. This time he brought all four paws to bear, wrapping his limbs round the catch, digging his teeth into its skull. The animal collapsed under his weight.

The game was over. Craning his head forward, Tiger snapped the animal's neck with a savage bite. The little heart stopped beating and the hunter stood clear, allowing his catch to flop onto its back.

It was Marthin. Tiger had murdered his favourite son.

Whatever sunshine had penetrated the rainforest gave up; he was left in darkness. The dead body disappeared and the plants around him oozed together. Sick colours left the leaves and creepers, entering his head through his nose and ears. He tried to cry, couldn't. Let out a slow mewl. Woke up.

Tiger lay flat on his stomach, face pressed against black marble, legs akimbo. He blinked twice, shaking the ugly dream from his head. Checking himself over he didn't seem too badly damaged. The back of his neck was gory where a pair of jaws had been.

He'd been dumped in the open air, a quiet lane that wasn't all that far from Jo's house. Trees arched over the lane, blocking any light from the moon. A row of lanterns hung from branches at long intervals, casting pools of scarlet onto the ground.

Following the lane, Tiger saw something lying not far ahead. At first it looked like a sack or black bin liner. The artificial light made it difficult for him to tell. He closed in on the drab object.

A small, crumpled body lay in the last pool of light. Its limbs were outstretched like a bather doing the backstroke. Tiger knelt down beside the stiff, his brow furrowed, his mind puzzled. Who would want to kill Bug? Knock her down, razor her throat, rip off her orange-red mask? It had been tossed aside, screwed up, its two antennae limp and ragged. That didn't seem right.

Tiger looked at her dead eyes. He should have expected her to make some rash, dangerous move. Some detective he was.

Her tiny paw gripped a piece of cloth, green checked and grubby. He picked it up, recognising it immediately.

'Bless you, Bug.' An invaluable asset till the end. With the help of her pathetic scrap of evidence, he'd be able to catch a killer. It would be the most difficult bust he'd ever make.

Tiger's wife was waiting for him when he got home. She was wearing a green checked dress, slightly torn at the hem.

'I wondered how long it would take you,' she said as he unsheathed his claws. 'You made me so happy.'

'I don't want to stop. Think about tomorrow, Tiger. Can you

live without me to wash and cook and clean for you? Keep the kids happy? Care for you all when someone falls ill? Do you love me?'

'Yes. Doesn't mean I'm not going to kill you.'

'Go on then. She deserved to die. She wanted you too much and you didn't ever realise it. She was never going to be happy.'

'Why did you take off her mask?'

'I did it before she died. I wasn't there to kill Bug. I'm not one of those damned arch villains you're always chasing after. I wanted to kill Natasha. She was the one who deserved it. Your mud-slinging love slut, not your crime fighting companion.'

'That attempt on your life..?'

'There was no gas. I made a groove in the carpet with my paws. Fooled you, Mr Great Detective.' She unbuttoned her blouse, exposing her soft-furred throat. Tiger raised a deadly claw and he touched the point against her skin. The slightest jab and justice would be done. She didn't dare swallow, ready for him. She stared into his eyes, silently imploring. She wanted him to get it over with.

Life would not be over for her for another decade, which she spent in a municipal jail after being frog-marched to the local cops by her husband. Bix was there, cow in tow.

'Case closed,' Tiger sighed, 'she's the killer.'

'They've had a sweepstake,' said Bix with a wry grimace. 'Betting on how long it would take me to solve the murders. Guess nobody's won.'

'Yeah.' Tiger watched as Jo was led down to the holding cells. 'I didn't really want to eat you, you know.' He stooped down to whisper to the mouse. 'I have a lot of respect for authority. I always knew cops couldn't read or write. I'll help you with your report.' He gave Bix a wink. His evidence put Jo in the slammer for good. Despite the strict penal system, she made the best of her last years. Studied, wove baskets, sang in the choir. She didn't talk much. She lived in the past, tucked up warm with her family. She seemed almost oblivious to her incarceration, did as she was told, served her sentence. By the time she was due for parole, she fell ill. Passed away in her sleep. Tiger still mourns.

29

WITH THE CASE wrapped, Bix took Nut back to her farm. A new cat named Chips had taken over from Scrumpy, equally gruff and indifferent. However, he knew his stuff about herbicides, silage, hydroponics and low crop yields.

As Nut returned to her old stall, she felt sad. She'd miss the naked city, the bustling police station and her reluctant counterpart. The barn was so quiet, so lifeless. Not for long.

Bix bade his farewells to Nut and passed the time of day with two cats dressed in blood red robes. *He's forgotten about me already*, the cow sniffled. Her ears perked up as the robed pair snatched the mouse and shoved him in a sack.

'Oi! That's my partner you've got there!' Nut yelled. The other cows ignored her, used to her nonsense. Before Nut could extricate herself from her stall, the kidnappers were gone.

The kittens continued to explore and develop. Baby was a bitch, a prima donna in full soap opera mode. She walked with shoulder pads foremost, dominating the other kittens in the neighbourhood. Marthin was cool, laid back. A drooper, draping himself over things. Banjo, the larger of the two males, led his siblings on expeditions around the block, scent-marking their territory.

Tiger didn't like to leave them alone for too long. He would always recall the first time they'd been allowed in the back garden; it had been a disaster. He'd been checking through the account details that Bug had brought him. He still didn't know why the cultists had let him go, left him to suffer. There were disparities in the accounts that he couldn't explain. He was loath to close the case for good.

He'd head a yell from out back, excited mews, then silence. Rushing out to help his offspring he'd found them relaxing on a battlefield. There was carnage all round them – a sparrow, three pigeons, a headless vole, two enormous magpies. All dead. The kittens were terminators. Tiger had congratulated them on their culling spree, and kept a close eye on them after that.

The local zoological park had developed a machine that emitted a high-pitched signal. It was designed to deter visitors from killing and eating the resident birds. Tiger had made the mistake of taking his little ones to the park. The bleeping machine had provided them with some initial interest. When they got bored with the sound, they strutted past the machine and nobbled three doves. They hadn't visited the zoo again.

At five months old, they'd shed their milk teeth and were almost ready to fend for themselves. Their father didn't want to let them go; they were all he had to remind him of Jo.

A particular account number bothered Tiger and he ran it by Connie when she offered to babysit. She had been alone since Bug's death, her apartment cold and empty. She'd thrown herself into her first job, a designer with a top firm of interior decorators. Her garish ideas had proved very popular with local citizens.

'This is where all the money was being siphoned off to,' Tiger explained, 'it's what Bug died for. To find this out for me. I can't do anything with it – there's no name, no sequence to the account numbers.'

'What if these numbers don't denote the accounts? There's a pattern to them, Tige.' The figures were split into blocks and rows:

13247 42221	13248 22523	13249 979
13247 52221	13248 52523	13249 979
13247 62221	13248 32523	13249 579
13247 72221	13248 22523	13249 279
13247 42221	13248 72523	13249 879
13247 42221	13248 62523	13249 179
13247 42221	13248 92523	13249 879
13247 82221	13248 42523	13249 179
13247 32221	13248 12523	13249 779
13247 92221		13249 479
		13249 479
		13249 679
	13248 22523	13249 379
	13248 82523	13249 379
	13248 82523	13249 379

'They could be safety deposit boxes, lockers, house numbers…'

'…Or post codes.' Tiger thanked Connie from the bottom of his heart, launching into a furious bout of post decoding:

NC7 4EF	NC8 2BD	NCP 9TR
NC7 5EF	NC8 5BD	NCP 9TR
NC7 6EF	NC8 3BD	NCP 5TR
NC7 7EF	NC8 2BD	NCP 2TR
NC7 4EF	NC8 7BD	NCP 8TR
NC7 4EF	NC8 6BD	NCP 1TR
NC7 4EF	NC8 9BD	NCP 8TR
NC7 8EF	NC8 4BD	NCP 1TR
NC7 3EF	NC8 1BD	NCP 7TR
NC7 9EF		NCP 4TR
		NCP 4TR
		NCP 6TR
	NC8 2BD	NCP 3TR
	NC8 8BD	NCP 3TR
	NC8 8BD	NCP 3TR

The postcodes corresponded with some certain well-known byways – Dempster Street, where the Beggars' Temple could be found; Burdock Road, which Tiger and Bug had visited looking for Danny Tennant. The most prevalent postcode referred to a street in a swanky part of town; one house dominated all its neighbours. It was an expensive townhouse owned by a corporate bigwig. Tiger decided to try there first.

'If I'm not back this time tomorrow, come alooking. Take care though.' Connie nodded anxiously, watching her friend from the window as he raced away. Marthin, Baby and Banjo required attention. She would have to settle them down before she headed after Tiger.

The townhouse wasn't all that far from the bank, Tiger noted as he strode up the front drive. Lead-lined windows didn't give much away, and the grey façade gave the building an imposing air. He nosed round the side and found a trades entrance, open and inviting.

The house was gloomy but Tiger's way was lit by a flickering amber light emanating from one of the many back rooms. He headed for the light, found the room in question and was immediately mesmerised by a large glowing box fixed to the wall.

Red and orange colours danced, generating a heat that soothed him, made him feel sleepy. He drew closer, enjoying the sensation that smothered his body. His fur smelled of autumn leaves, his pads began to sweat. Still he moved closer, trying to absorb as much heat as possible before he scorched his nose. It was gorgeous; he was in paradise.

He couldn't help but lie down in front of the box, stretching himself out as long as he could, letting the heat brush his belly. All thoughts of fear or hunger left him as his stomach was filled with ersatz sunshine. He wriggled a little bit closer, getting drowsy. As he curled up for a quick nap, the aperture swallowed him up. There was nothing left of him in the hall except a few stray strands of fluff.

Tiger couldn't move his legs. He felt cooked to a turn, his head numb and his paws raw. The ground slid by beneath him, uneven. He wanted to throw up though there was nothing in his stomach. His eyes were gummed together; strands of mucus obscured his vision. Snapping his lids wide open, he watched adaze as a base-board passed him. The floor was tiled, dirty yellow squares bordered by red and grey rectangles. Each square grated against his cheek. Looking up, he worked out that he was being dragged. A big black cat was hauling him by the tail.

Tiger was dumped in an air-conditioned office, left to recover his senses. A cork notice board hung on one wall, surrounded by red rectangles similar to the ones beneath him. A few notes were pinned on the board, announcing a ceilidh, a conference and a convention at the Duncan Hotel. He was in the headquarters of the Kitty Killer Cult.

Tiger used a leg to hoist himself into a sitting position. It wasn't his leg. Too cold, too stiff. It belonged to a cream-coloured desk with a black plastic trim and four black seats. The seats were bolted on, covered in ink and crumbs. They looked unfeasibly comfortable to Tiger.

Flumping into one of the seats he decided that the floor was better. He wasn't ready to defend himself when the big cat returned.

'Callum,' the heavy gave a bow, 'pleased to meet you.'

'Do I know you?' asked the detective groggily.

'Kind of. We've met before. I was behind you and wearing a hooded outfit. Down in the crypt.' Callum chattered his teeth together. 'I didn't get the chance to introduce myself before, had a mouth fulla scruff. Thought I'd better do it now since we'll be working together.'

'I don't see that happening. There ain't nothing would convince me to work for you.'

'Never said anything 'bout you working *for* me.' Callum's tail fanned slowly from side to side. Tiger's was standing straight. 'You'll be workin' *with* me.'

The detective pursed his lips together. He didn't have dimples. He didn't know what to say either.

'Still need convincin'?' Callum asked at last. Tiger said nothing, allowed himself to be led down a corridor to a gym.

'You going to exercise me to death?' Tiger broke his silence. The caracal shook his head, moved on to the next room. It housed a grand swimming pool. A mouse languished on a sun lounger, nibbling on a dinky slice of edam. The same mouse had greeted Bug in a house not far away. The same mouse that employed Callum, Miss Angold and Danny.

Tiger wasn't looking at Big Cheese. A net had been suspended over the pool, spinning and writhing as its prisoners tried to chew their way out. They were small yet feisty. The poor beggars. What had they done to deserve such treatment? Tiger moved closer to the pool and realised why Callum was holding him so tight. The net held three little kittens – Baby, Marthin and Banjo. Although they squirmed they were wrapped too tight, the netting was too strong, and every movement they made entwined them further. Tiger struggled more than ever; Callum bit hard, drawing blood. The stricken father forced himself to relax, turning back to Big Cheese. His throat felt dry.

'I didn't think. As soon as I found mouse droppings in that

hippie's shop I suspected; I didn't think a rodent would have the gall, but I'm wrong about practically everything these days. Why are you doing this to me?'

'It's the only way to make you see, Mr Straight. See how my people have suffered. You didn't realise, did you? Didn't know what was going on.'

'Those children are innocent.'

'Shouldn't have left them home alone, dear fellow. That's illegal, you know.'

As Callum relaxed his grip on Tiger's nape, the detective broke free. Instead of attacking the caracal backed off, standing between Tiger and the pool. 'They've done nothing to you,' the detective snarled at the lounging mouse.

'And what are mice so guilty of?' Cheese's whiskers quivered with excitement. 'Are they the fallen? This is their hell, they're the damned. You still don't see, do you?'

'See what?'

'I want you to help Callum here with a small task he has to perform.'

'No way.'

'Do it or your cubs will suffer.'

As Callum approached, Tiger addressed the big cat: 'Why are you taking orders from a mouse? There something wrong with you? He got something on you?'

'We're going to do as we're told,' Callum replied. 'Unless you want those kittens drowned.'

'You'd do it as well, wouldn't you?' Tiger's eyes were locked with Callum's, trying to see past the cold stare.

'Too right. No more dawdling.' The black cat led Tiger outside and onto a train. They were the only passengers on board; the detective couldn't even see a driver. Still, the train set off at full steam.

'Where is it we're going exactly?'

'You'll see.' Callum yanked a map from his combats, sniffed at it intently. Tiger stole a glance at it, made out a vast complex with a perimeter fence. Callum folded it away before he could get a better look.

'I can't wait,' said Tiger sarcastically. 'Anything to eat?'

'Nothing for you. Except this.' The muscular cat handed Tiger a paper packet full of black powder. The detective sniffed at it carefully.

'Not to eat.'

'What is it?' Tiger wrapped the powder up again.

'It's a mixture of potassium nitrate, charcoal and sulphur,' Callum grunted. 'Big Cheese put it together.'

'What does it do?'

'Don't ask me. The boss said to set fire to it if and when we need to. It'll distract the enemy.'

'Who are the enemy?'

Callum ignored the detective, taking digitalis to set his heart thumping. It beat like a piston; he was ready for a fight.

The train bumped over a set of points. There would be only one stop on this journey.

Connie had been lingering outside the townhouse for hours. She'd seen no one go in or leave; the whole street was still. She headed to Jo's house to check on the kittens.

No kittens. At first Connie thought that they'd run away, got lost on some childish investigation. It took her a few minutes to realise the truth. The cultists who had used Jo so efficiently had abducted the three children. Connie decided to try one of the other addresses on Tiger's list – Collier Heights in the service sector. She would check every office on the block if necessary. She wasn't going to let her friend down again.

Big Cheese's private train followed the coast, choppy water on one side, green fields on the other. Tiger tried to gain his bearings as the world rushed by beyond his window. He rarely left the city; the sea unsettled him, too big, too deep. Too many mysteries beneath the surface.

The rusty tracks beneath his paws were used mainly for hoppers, the transport of seafood and minerals. The train passed through an abandoned coastal ward, a short swing gate leading to the village green. Soon it was a blurred memory, the train racing south. Callum said nothing, his eyes hard, steeped in thought.

After an hour's travel they reached a grotty station as lifeless as the village. The train gave a sigh as it came to rest, steam escaping from its sides. Callum climbed out, followed by a watchful Tiger.

'Not much of a holiday destination,' said the detective sourly.

'Keep it down. We gotta be quiet about this.'

'I've never been to the seaside before.' Tiger whispered this time.

'Coast is a mile that way,' Callum pointed with his tail. 'Follow me and stay shtum.' Up a flight of steps, onto a bridge that arced over the train tracks, the cats could see how the land lay. The big cat continued to boss Tiger about, telling him to stoop low. Most of the surrounding area was scrubland and brown earth. A hunch of silos and warehouses were Callum's target. A high wire fence surrounded them, too high for even an accomplished jumper like Callum to scale. Tiger could swear that he heard a dog howl. He trembled, hunching his shoulders against the wind.

'They got guard dogs in there?' he shuddered as they approached the fence.

'Naw. Some good impressionists though.' The few floodlights dotted round the facility pointed inwards, so the two cats got good and close to the wire under cover of darkness. The ground was frosty, and Tiger clenched his teeth as iced grass crunched under his paws.

'What are we doing here?' he begged.

'You'll see, little cat. You'll see.' Callum gripped a section of mesh between his mighty teeth, clamping his jaws down on the cold metal. He gnawed at the wire until it started to rend. Tiger was astounded; he stood back, mouth agape.

'I thought you caracals were great at leaping?'

'I don't fancy getting barbed wire balls. You gonna help me here?' the big cat asked, taking a break from his meal. Nodding, the detective grasped some of the broken wire strands and pulled them clear, enlarging the hole that Callum had made. After more nibbling and pulling, the gap became large enough for Callum to fit his head through.

'Not big enough for me,' he spat, 'but I reckon a titchy thing like you'll be able to get in. Then you can run to the gate and open it up. We need to get the gate unlocked.' He yanked his head from the hole and urged Tiger onwards. Obliging, the smaller cat used his whiskers to judge the size of the gap then pushed forward with his paws. Grasping the wire, he pulled his head and shoulders through. 'Stop!' Callum cried, 'get out of there! Guards!'

Tiger couldn't see anything. He was halfway through and it was a lot easier going forwards than backwards. Cocking an ear, he heard a hefty cat approaching. The guard had a small torch attached to his helmet, enhancing his excellent night vision. As he turned his head from side to side the beam swept along the fence, dangerously close to Tiger's nose. He tried to reverse but he was stuck with his hind legs and tail waggling in the air. Callum tried to yank him free as the security cat approached, shining his torch up the wall of a red-roofed building. Tiger panicked, scrabbling at the wire. The guard was mere feet away.

As the beam swung in his direction once more, he was plucked clear by Callum. The big cat clamped a paw over Tiger's mouth, keeping him low as the sentry passed. When the coast was crystal Callum let the detective up.

'I think the hole needs to be bigger,' he admitted.

'Really?' Tiger replied hoarsely. 'You can climb through next time.' Callum nodded, wrenching at the broken mesh. By the time he'd made a cat-sized gap the guard had completed a lap of the complex, and the two trespassers had to lie low again. By chance or negligence the hole wasn't discovered; as soon as he was able, Callum dived through the fence and opened the gate for Tiger. No alarms sounded and no staff came running to investigate.

'What next?' asked Tiger.

'Not far to go,' the big cat replied, leading his accomplice to the red-roofed building. There were no windows to break or signs to guide them; they broke the lock on a corrugated iron shutter, stepping into a dark chamber.

Tiger wished he'd attacked the guard on patrol outside, if only to steal his helmet. He stood still for a moment so that he could listen out for company. Straw rustled across the chamber; cogs cranked and spun in a distant housing. He opened his mouth to ask a question that was never formed. A switch flicked behind them and bright lights blinded their vision. The shutter was dragged closed with an angry bray.

As their eyes became accustomed to the light, the two cats found themselves surrounded by a band of wee, menacing beasties. The mice sniffed at the interlopers, their noses twitching excitedly. Some sat on bunk beds, dressed in white T-shirts and shorts. Others stood as if to attention, arms folded behind their backs, chiselled chins raised. They wore blue slacks and grey cardigans. The livelier ones were ready for trouble, paws clenched, teeth bared. The biggest mouse wore a navy blue tunic with medals pinned to the right breast. A cap made him seem even taller than he really was.

'Looks like you've caught us red pawed,' he squeaked.

'Who might you be?' challenged Callum.

'Fieldmouse Marshall Monty Montague. That's all you'll get out of me.' Monty turned to the mice perched on their bunks. They were digging into white dishes laden with sunflower seeds. 'May as well give it up, lads. Show 'em what we've been up to.' The mice put down their dishes, shifted their bunks around and revealed a tunnel leading out of the building. 'Another feather in your caps, I suppose. At least we had a damned good try.'

Tiger shook his head. 'We don't care about your tunnel.'

'You don't?' a red-faced mouse named Shuggie piped up. 'You have tae! We spent weeks diggin' that flaming thing.'

'We're not guards. We're on your side. Here to help you escape.' Monty gave the two cats a blank look, trying to digest the news.

'Impossible, I'm afraid.'

'You like it here or something?' asked Tiger.

'We've tried to get out so many times, all to no avail.'

'No Avail ain't much of a place, so we came back here,' joked Shuggie. One look from Monty shut him up. The leader showed the cats an anteroom full of junk.

'Past disgraces,' he admitted, pointing to a trap built out of balsa. 'This one we called the trap attack. A cat-sized mousetrap with us as the bait. A guard comes along and SLAM! He's caught. That was the theory. Lost a lot of good mice to a lot of hungry cats with that one.'

Monty showed Tiger and Callum a Shuggie-shaped coffin. 'This seemed like a good idea at the time. One of the lads would feign death, be taken out of the compound to the cemetery, run away while the pallbearers weren't looking. They weren't taken out in a coffin. They were flushed down the loo.'

Tiger unearthed a half-eaten turnip. Whiskers had been painted on with a splayed brush.

'That went really well in the planning stages. As our chaps escaped, we disguised some turnips to resemble them. So they wouldn't be missed if there was a head count or what have you. Once the escapees got over the fence, they would hide out disguised as turnips. No suspicion aroused, you see.'

'Were these disguises good?' huffed Callum.

'Too good,' sighed Monty. Unbeknownst to us the camp Commandant has a thing for turnips. Not only did he gobble up the escapees – he ate their substitutes as well. Gave him the runs for a week, though. Meagre consolation. This was a much better idea.' Monty showed the cats several strips of cloth, split into sections by wooden splints.

'What're these? Camouflage?' The triangular cloth shapes were black or marsh green.

'Wings,' Shuggie explained proudly. 'We got the idea from our mutant friend over there.' Chocolate was a quiet creature who was suspended from the roof by his feet, fast asleep. Webbed flaps grew from his forelimbs. 'He could glide out of here anytime if he could see where he was going. He's as blind as a – well, a very blind mouse.'

'Where did he get the wings?' Tiger asked, amazed.

'They did it to him. The scientists. Messing with nature. A month ago he was a normal mouse. Now he's a freak.' Chocolate opened his eyes sleepily, swinging slightly from his rafter. Then he went back to sleep.

'Why didn't you use the wings you made, then?' snapped Callum.

'Our intention was to glide over the fence to freedom. We'd have to start from a high place – a roof – and we don't think the wings would keep us aloft for long enough. We'd probably land on this side of the fence, right in the lap of a sentry.'

'We're too heavy,' Shuggie sighed, 'there's not enough wind... We'd be reliant on air currents, y'see. Too risky.'

'Why build the things in the first place?' Callum was exasperated.

'Hope, my feline friend, is the only thing that keeps us ticking. Besides, mice are experts with needle and thread. We have a whole division working on disguises and clothes. It didn't take 'em long to knock up some cloth, attach a few matchstick splints.'

'Why're you prepared to risk so much to leave?' asked Tiger. 'You've got food, warmth, a place to sleep.'

'You don't know what they do to us here?' Monty, surprised, turned to Callum.

'He doesn't know,' the big cat explained with a yawn. His mouth was big enough to engulf Monty in one snap.

'Then we'd better show you,' grumbled Monty. Ordering a bunch of the prisoners to open the shutter, he led the cats to an adjacent building. 'Take a look at this, old bean.'

Tiger clenched a window ledge and hoisted himself up so that he could peek through a lead-lined pane, taking care not to be seen by whoever was inside.

Cats in lab coats wandered round the whitewashed interior, making notes on wadded clipboards. Much of the area was split into cubicles, partitioned with heavy glass and plastic. The technicians passed one compartment after another, back and forth, checking the conditions of the inhabitants.

In the first cubicle a mouse was breakdancing. The floor was plated with heated metal, and the rodent was forced to keep moving in order to avoid serious burns. Next to him, a shabby-looking mouse had been treading a short conveyor belt for hours. Occasionally a technician would throw a lever, increasing the pace of the conveyor belt. The creature within was being jogged to death.

Other mice had been coerced into equally infernal experiments.

One poor soul climbed up and down a set of steps. Others had electrodes connected to their brains, were fed toxic chemicals, or swam desperately in tanks of freezing water. Some of the prisoners had eyes or ears growing out of places they shouldn't have been. Tiger strained to get a better look, sickened yet mesmerised by the goings-on. His world was beginning to make more sense, even though the technicians' work seemed so senseless.

The worst was yet to come. Craning his neck, Tiger saw strange activity in a cell near to his window. A group in Stetsons was being taught a series of steps to a repetitive country and western tune. The sorry bastards looked like they were enjoying themselves. One of the indoctrinated captives was Inspector Bix Mortis.

'We have to get him out of there!' Tiger whispered down to Callum.

'We already have a plan that incorporates your presence,' said Monty happily. Taking the cats back to the red-roofed building, he introduced them to Chocolate, the winged freak.

'Cool name,' said Tiger, weary from the atrocities he'd seen.

'Thanks. My sight may be failing but I'm still the best there is at nabbing the Commandant's sweetie rations. Would you like a bite?' Chocolate offered them a bar, a hairy flap of skin tucked round his forelimb.

'No thanks,' Callum interjected. He preferred mice for his supper, but that particular species was off the menu for the moment. 'We don't have time. We *do* have time for your plan.'

'Oh yes. You can get two of us out if the guards believe you're part of the staff. I don't think you can sneak out as easily as you snuck in. You can get two of us out by placing us between your nose and upper lip. One per cat. What do you think?'

'Mousetaches?' Tiger replied, incredulous. He knew why the captives were desperate to escape but their plans left something to be desired. Perhaps their scaled-down brains had something to do with it – too small to deal with such a big problem.

'I have a better idea. It's simpler and it's been thunk up by Big Cheese himself.'

'The big what?'

'Head honcho of the Kitty Killer Cult. Devoted to giving mice what they deserve – and cats their just desserts.'

'Let's hear it,' Chocolate squeaked.

'We've unlocked the main gate. We walk out. If the guards give us any crap, we knock seven shades of sick out of them.'

'Simple and direct,' Shuggie admitted. 'Let's do it.'

'Who goes?' asked Monty.

'You lot,' Callum replied, leading the mice out of their building towards the fence. They moved in single file, shadowing each other closely, eyes skittering on the lookout for sentries. Despite their urge to escape the lads were scared – if caught mid-flight they would be killed on the spot or sent to the cooler, the camp Commandant's personal fridge, all tupperwared up for his supper.

The caracal crept to the gate, easing it open, gritting his teeth as the hinges squealed. Once there was room for a mouse to get through he beckoned the first volunteer.

Brett, a square-headed mouse in a flying jacket, pushed Chocolate to the fore, helping the shortsighted candy smuggler to the gate. Chocolate bumped his nose against the wire, edged through the gate, ran for the cover of the undergrowth beyond.

'Choc's away!' Monty announced excitedly. Tiger shushed him, passing the next mouse to Callum.

One by one the prisoners disappeared into the darkness on the other side of the fence. About half of them had reached sanctuary before a patrolling guard spotted the remaining creatures.

The massive guard took in the trembling mice and the two cats. Holstering his torch he pounced on Shuggie, snapping the rodent's back with a bite. Two paws swept up a couple of stragglers, still in their underwear. Monty led an honourable retreat, scattering his gang across the compound.

Callum attacked the guard, who let out a dismayed howl. The caracal dug his hindclaws into the sentry, splitting his soft belly. 'Get out of here!' Callum shouted to Tiger, who was heading the wrong way. Somewhere on the other side of the complex an alarm sounded and the spotlights began to shift in their direction.

'I've got to rescue Inspector Mortis and the others,' Tiger yelled, 'I can't leave them in that torture chamber.'

'Of course you can! This is your last chance!' The guard bit a chunk out of Callum's shoulder, but his strength was fading fast. Tiger had disappeared into the maze-like lanes of the compound. The caracal finished his opponent quickly with a hefty headbutt. Brushing through the gate, he slammed it shut behind him. The detective could rot.

As Callum and the escaped mice got all the attention, Tiger hid in a dark alcove. This hideaway smelled bad, as if lazy staff occasionally used it as a latrine. He'd always known that scientific experiments were performed on some dumb species – better than testing intelligent cats – but the research he'd seen appeared pointless and painful. After meeting Inspector Mortis and Big Cheese, he found it difficult to think of rodents as nothing more than food. His fellow dicks all had gimmicks – perhaps he'd found his. Tiger Straight, the card carrying vegetarian detective.

Two females in dayglo orange jackets rushed past, torches held out before them. They were headed for the main gate, missed Tiger completely. After a suitable interval, he left his hidey-hole and made for the labs. He planned to muscle his way in, release as many of the test subjects as he could before he was questioned, then head for the hole in the fence. The guards would surely have spotted it by now but they'd be looking outside the compound – they didn't know that he was still in their midst. Surprise was the only element worth using; he hoped it would serve him well.

He breezed into the labs, opening panels on each glass cell he passed. Mice ran from their traps, nipping to and fro around the building, looking for the exit. Tiger reached Inspector Mortis' cubicle, shared with five other rodents. They continued to repeat their pattern of steps, dancing to a dirge about lost love. The detective slid back a panel, allowing Mortis' five companions to flee. The Inspector, however, was happy in his cage.

'I wanna dance! I wanna dance!' he cried, under the influence of potent drugs. Tiger dragged him towards the exit. The sozzled Inspector was bound to draw unwelcome attention. A technician challenged them as they were about to leave the building.

'It's all part of the Big Experiment,' Tiger explained, offensively charming. 'Commandant's orders.'

'That's alright then,' the technician nodded, allowing the entourage to pass. They weren't so lucky with the second cat they bumped into – Tiger tried the same ploy with him, a khmer in tight black leather.

'I am the camp Commandant,' said the khmer with a swagger.

'I wanna dance,' Bix told him.

'Round up these pipsqueaks,' the Commandant bellowed, bringing a squad of guards rushing to his assistance. Tiger was dragged to the khmer's office, a drab brown room with angular, functional furnishings.

'Who was the other cat with you?' asked the khmer, chewing on a turnip. One whiff of his breath was enough to make Tiger wince.

'Just a guy. Said he wanted to show me something. He got the gate open, let me in.'

'That gate can only be unbolted from the inside,' purred the Commandant.

'Then some of your staff must have helped. How do you hire your guards? It's not the sort of thing you'd place in the recruitment section of the local rag. Is there an agency for louts and blockheads?'

'This facility is run by highly trained individuals,' replied the Commandant. 'I train them myself. Apart from the scientists. They do their own thing.'

'What good are these experiments gonna do anybody?'

'Oh yes. You're one of these animal liberators. The technicians test the endurance, the mental and physical dexterity of the mice. The more we learn about them – the more we learn about ourselves.'

'You got a point there. What you going to do with me?'

'It's not often that we get the chance to experiment on our own kind. You'll make an excellent specimen.'

30

CALLUM RAN THROUGH the undergrowth, making for the old station. The digitalis was wearing off and he needed a rest. He could hear a jet of steam leaving his train, the only sign to guide him. Tagging along were a large group of mice, led by Chocolate and Brett, his square-headed helper. Close behind were a crack squad of security guards, growling for blood. To be tracked by a cat is no laughing matter. Natural hunters, they are swift and silent. Even the laziest of their brethren is capable of stealth and cunning. Their night sight is exemplary, and once they have the scent they will follow it for hours. Only once they have filled their bellies will they cease their pursuit. The mice were petrified; Callum was weary. If the guards caught up with them he would have to face them alone. With the odds so heavy against him his size and strength meant very little.

At last the station could be made out in the ashen moonlight. The old building seemed to sag in the middle, ready to collapse through neglect. Callum sent the prisoners on ahead of him.

'Make for that little station. There's a train on the other side. We're leaving in that.'

'What are you gonna do?' asked Brett.

'Give you a head start. Hurry up – we're on a strict timetable.' Looking back, they could see flashes of green closing fast. Beady, hungry eyes and bright torches. With the mice heading for the train, Callum ducked behind a bush.

A whistle blew impatiently. The guards reached the bush and halted, wary. Callum's thick tail lashed from side to side and he let out a long hiss, doing his best to imitate a snake. The guards took a couple of steps backward. They shone torches in the caracal's direction, watching the hypnotic swish of his tail.

The train left the station with a full complement of passengers. Callum chanced a look back at his escape vehicle and a beam of light met his face. Bristling, he puffed himself up as large as possible, arched his back, bared his teeth. By the time the guards were upon him the train was long gone.

First the Commandant ordered his guards to pluck out Tiger's whiskers, in order to deter any attempted escape. Without his sensitive vibrassae he was crippled and in agony. He still kicked and spat as he was dragged into a cold, mirrored room. He was strapped to a padded bench, his exposed stomach pinned down with a metal bar.

'What's this in aid of?' he bawled as the Commandant gloated over him.

'We call it the weight machine,' the khmer explained softly. 'We gradually apply lead weights to this metal bar.' He tapped the chrome with a ragged claw.

'You expect me to diet?'

'No. We expect you to talk. You give us the identity of your accomplice, and we stop adding the weights.'

'I told you. My "accomplice" was just some geezer.'

'We will continue to add pound after pound until you give us a satisfactory answer,' the Commandant bellowed, 'or the breath is crushed out of you for good.'

A puff-cheeked orderly placed a weight on one side of the bar. Tiger was already finding it difficult to breathe. He began to squirm for all he was worth.

'Give us a name. That's all I need.'

'Do they call you the camp Commandant because you're fey?' Tiger gasped. 'Did your mum dress you up in frocks when you were a kitten? Do you like dollies?' The orderly added more weights as the detective yanked his paws from the straps that bound him. Heaving his forelimbs against the metal bar, he held it up long enough to leave the bench. The weights slammed down on the khmer's tail.

Unlatching his claws, Tiger scratched the orderly's nose. The cat collapsed, holding his face to staunch the flow. The Commandant couldn't follow his prisoner out of the room; his tail was trapped and squashed pancake flat. He watched Tiger in dismay, ordering the bleeding cat to give chase.

The dick didn't aim for the gate – still too busy with guards. Instead he re-entered Monty's building, found the leader debriefing Inspector Mortis. The policeman apologised for messing up Tiger's escape attempt.

'No use crying over mouldy cheese,' Monty soothed.

'I'd eat it anyway,' said a stocky mouse named Grant. 'Where is it?'

'It's a metaphor,' Monty explained. 'Don't mind him, big belly, small brain. At least some of us got out.' The Fieldmouse Marshall looked to Tiger for the next move.

'The rest of you are going to get out an' all,' the detective assured them. 'I have a scheme. It's as barmy as one of Shuggie's masterplans –'

'Anything's worth a try,' said Bix.

'So your dancing days are over, are they, Inspector?' Tiger asked cheekily.

'Get us out of here, you furry old fart.'

'Certainly. We'll need those canvas wings you made. I take it we can get onto the roof?'

'No probs,' replied Monty cheerfully. 'We've been collecting stringy cheese, wrapping it together so it hardens like rope. Pongs a bit. Needs must…'

'Fine.'

'Bring me a mirror!' the Commandant screamed, sending a hireling scuttling. He soon returned with a flat silver tray, passing it to the khmer and backing off fast. Trying to angle it at waist level, the Commandant watched lamplight sparkle off the ornate tray. He continued to tilt it until he caught sight of his stub of a tail. Trapped by his own weight machine, he'd had to coil round and chew off his precious appendage. Flakes of bone and fur were still stuck between his teeth. He tried to swish the stump from side to side; it quivered, pathetic. He wanted revenge.

Throwing the tray to his second-in-command, he summoned his best guards and demanded Tiger's head.

'There's plenty of places he could've secreted himself, Sir. A lot of nooks where they could be prepping an escape, or tunnelling out…' The second swallowed hard. 'This facility was built to keep test subjects in. Beyond that – '

'I know. Send in the goons.'

Art and Walter Mirk had been taking it easy for a while. The last full-on search of the ιε Institute had lasted days, with the nosy team unearthing several hidden rodents. They'd do anything to avoid being experimented upon – build cat traps, wrap themselves in blankets, disguise their scent with garlic. Escape attempts were rife despite the penalties – better to die running than to be dissected in a lab.

The goons prided themselves on their efficiency and application. They knew every inch of their territory, every scent and signpost. They could scoot through with their eyes closed in the dead of night. Art was one of those fortunate creatures who loved what he did and made a good living out of it. He didn't cling to his bed covers every morning, groggy and unwilling to go to work. He was up and at 'em, looking forward to a day's searching and destroying. If combining your job with your hobby was the key to happiness, Art was in paradise. His hobby was tracking down and killing furry animals.

Walter was more sadistic. When he saw a mousehole he was hard-pressed to prevent himself from breaking into it. He would not satisfy himself with trapping and killing an escaped prisoner – he would toy with it first. Once it was too scared to move he'd give it the chance to run away. It couldn't take it – too petrified. With a moment's pause to allow realisation to filter in, Walter would finish them off.

Art had never been impressed by his partner's antics. They were pals, so he didn't get in Walter's way when he played his cruel game. Art hoped that his friend would come round eventually, realise that their prey had feelings too. The sadist's actions were immature and unproductive. Art got his job done as quickly and professionally as possible, and it was he who had earned them their reputations as stone cold ferrets.

Today's search would be easy, especially after their long period of rest. Usually they hunted mice, diminutive and difficult to find, so timorous that they'd find a hiding place and stick to it until they were unearthed. Their latest target was a smelly old cat, already worn out and wounded. There were only so many places for him to hide, and most of those were used by lazy guards as pissoirs. A sentry with a full bladder would be as likely to smoke Tiger out as the goons. Once he was in the open – he'd be easy meat.

Walter was particularly looking forward to catching the cat, an animal that he was seldom lucky enough to fight. There was more to tear into, more intelligence and fear in the eyes. Walter's game would last longer that day.

Grant squeezed past dirt walls and groaning supports, scurrying towards the end of the tunnel. He used his paws to dig upwards, frightened yet excited, hoping that he didn't pop up in front of a sentry. It would take some time to gouge the hard earth away, and there was always the possibility that the tunnellers' calculations had been wrong – he could end up on the wrong side of the fence, still in the compound. Tiger's diversion would be for naught and they'd all end up in the labs.

Grant missed his wife and fifteen children. When last he'd seen them they'd been pink and new, sniffing sleepily, infinitely curious. He'd been working on commission, cold calling potential customers. It wasn't easy – not many mice feel the need for double-glazing. But the thought of his hungry family had driven him on. So many small mouths to feed. He'd worked hard until the day when he'd found an enticing piece of cheese in a side street. It had been a large, bright yellow slab. His mother had always warned him not to eat strange food off the pavement, but here he'd made an exception. It'd been a trap, of course. A taut metal spring had unleashed the snare as he clamped onto the cheese. Next thing he knew he was being bossed about by Monty, organising a tunnel out of the compound.

Grant wondered how his family was coping without him. They thought he was dead, without a doubt; he'd been gone too long. Perhaps his wife had remarried, or taken a job. She'd always wanted to work but he'd never let her. The babies would suffer. The earth overhead felt softer, damper. He was nearly there. He was showered in soil and a dim light hurt his eyes. He popped a paw, then his head, from the tunnel, ready to duck under cover at a second's notice. No guards, no sirens. He was out of the compound.

The smart thing to do would have been to make a break there

and then, return to his family, get back to his job. Grant had never been the smartest jacket on the rack. He couldn't leave his friends behind. Nipping back down into the burrow he'd spent months digging, he hollered for Monty to come have a look.

The leader was busy seeing Tiger off. They'd worked out a schedule for their plan – all actions would have to be well timed to ensure everything went smoothly. By the time the moon had descended so that its circumference met the top of the fence, Tiger would be in position and ready to start his distraction. Monty and some of the lads would be on the roof, awaiting a signal. They'd volunteered to act as decoys while most of the mice scampered through the tunnel.

'Go! Take care!' he said to the departing cat.

'This isn't my idea of taking care,' Tiger retorted, 'making a nuisance of myself. At least the Commandant'll be in too much pain to care about us.' He sidled out into the stark shadows of the complex, relying on his keen eyesight to navigate. Usually he'd use his whiskers to detect air currents, enabling him to wander round in the dark without bumping into anything. Now he found it hard going; it was as if he'd lost an essential sense. He headed for the large grey warehouse, crouching for cover whenever a guard passed by, his ears flattening on top of his head. It was taking too long; the pale moon was plummeting behind him. Monty would be climbing onto the roof of his building by now, and if Tiger wasn't ready in time the mice would be spotted. Images of what he'd seen in the laboratory troubled him once more. He had to get a move on, risk being seen, get inside the warehouse.

No one challenged him as he passed the ENTRY FORBIDDEN sign and entered the depot. The barrels he'd glimpsed before were piled high – there were enough dangerous chemicals stacked up to choke every mouse in the city. Tiger took some of Callum's powder from the pouch he'd been given, sprinkled it in a circle round the barrels and trailed it towards the exit. Still no guards – the chemicals were too toxic for anyone to stick close for long periods of time. He lit a cigarette, taking a quick drag. It eased the pain in his jowls. The Commandant spoiled his reverie.

'Shouldn't have lit that thing,' said the leather-clad khmer through gritted teeth.

'So my doctor tells me.'

'I might not have spotted you here, in the dark.'

'No entourage this time, Commandant?'

'I don't need them to finish you. Besides, you've got them running round like headless hens looking for you and your friends. I didn't think you'd turn up so close to my quarters.'

'Cheek's my middle name.' Tiger took another suck on his cancer stick. 'Speaking of cheeks, how's your rear?'

'You took my tail. I took your whiskers. An exchange of sorts, if not a fair one.'

Thank Bastet for some action at last. Slim Rick had been on sentry duty for five nights on the trot, pulling the most boring detail in the compound. Although the camp was vast he managed to make several circuits in a shift. His only consolation was his standard issue torch, which he would waggle at anything he felt like. Although his eyesight was as good as any other cat's, the light penetrated the deepest of shadows. It made strange patterns as he flicked it against the fence. He would point it upwards, watching the light dissipate amongst the clouds. Sometimes the shadows would play tricks on him. He would see phantom mice crawl along the fence, just beyond the harsh beam of the torch. They weren't real. All prisoners were locked up tight.

Slim made sure he knew as little as possible about what went on in the labs. He didn't want to know; he received food and lodging, he was up for promotion and that was enough to keep him content. The escape attempt that day had been on someone else's shift so his job was secure. However, he stayed more alert than usual – the whole camp was on tenterhooks.

They hadn't expected anyone to be able to break into the installation. This was the first time that cats had caused them any trouble – most citizens minded their own business, weren't aware of the goings-on at the IE Institute. Slim was secretly pleased by the day's events. If any more mice tried to flee, he hoped that it would happen during his patrol. It would relieve the tedium of guard duty, and he would catch the offenders. That would get him promoted for sure.

Someone rattled the gate and Slim approached it cautiously. More troublemakers? A cat on the other side of the fence was shivering in the cold, his hindpaws white with frost. He was dressed in a guard's uniform, so Slim unbolted the gate and bade him enter.

'Been hunting the escaped prisoners,' the guard gasped. 'Caught somethin' much more interesting.' Slim tensed as a big black cat was dragged through the gate, five guards pinning him down, staying well clear of his ragged teeth. All thoughts of bravery or promotion left Slim's lonely mind. Callum smelled of death.

'I think you're sick,' Tiger scowled. 'You gotta be. Otherwise you wouldn't be able to mess with these mice. It's amoral.'

'Please.' To the detective's surprise, the khmer burst out laughing. 'Mice aren't important. They're vermin, statistics at best. Morality doesn't come into it. You throw a pebble into a lake – do you care what happens to it? The ripples on the water are more important than that pebble. It's matter that doesn't matter. Dumb and senseless. We're doing good work here, watching the ripples. Learning.'

'You're right,' Tiger lied. 'You're not such a bad guy. Leather suits you, y'know.'

'I know,' said the khmer proudly. Tiger brushed past him, forepaws raised in surrender. Once he was clear of the warehouse he flicked his dog end towards the barrels. The Commandant started to follow him, pricked his ears at a fizzling sound. Callum's powder was aspark, crackling towards the barrels. He went to have a closer sniff; Tiger was running in the opposite direction, ready to dive for cover once he'd put some distance between himself and the –

The Commandant heard a hiss, as if the chemicals in the barrels were bubbling. The sound of compressed air, containers struggling to hold it. The khmer pinned his ears back and snarled, a last expression of defiance before he was caught in a terrible explosion.

Tiger was thrown into the air by the force of the blast. He

landed on all fours and rolled onto his back, watching an amber mushroom cloud rise into the sky. An unearthly smell reached his nostrils; he tried to hold his breath. The chemicals he'd unleashed made him choke, his eyes streaming. He wanted to lick his fur clean.

The mice received their signal, almost knocked from their perch by the explosion. Monty let out a war cry, leaping from his perch with forelimbs outstretched. The others watched to see if he flew or fell – and cheered as he glided towards the fence. They didn't give themselves the chance to get scared, flinging themselves after their fearless leader.

Grant heard the barrels crack open even though he was deep underground. He led a second group of mice through the winding burrow, telling them to move slowly, breathe easily. It didn't take long to reach the exit. Once again he peeked out into the open. Attention seemed to be centred on the gate fifty yards away, where Callum was using the explosion as an excuse to attack his startled captors. With a happy squeak Grant left the hole and disappeared into the undergrowth. His group followed, glancing from side to side, ready for trouble. Nothing stopped them from following him to safety.

A guard held onto each of Callum's legs, another scratching at his tail. He'd had enough. He'd caused enough chaos to give Tiger time to find out exactly what went on at the venerable Institute. The guards did a double take as the warehouse erupted, so he hefted a paw onto the nearest cat's head. Injecting his claws into the skull, he made the cat let go of him and fall to the ground with a howl. Slim raced towards the warehouse, ignoring the fluttering sounds above him.

The captors decided that it was better to knock Callum off than continue their tiring struggle. The frost-pawed guard opened his jaws wide and slavered over the caracal's throat.

Shuggie had been correct: the mice weren't aerodynamically sound enough to glide over the fence. Monty flew too low to pass it; in fact, he was approaching the wire at an alarming rate. Behind him a mouse shrieked, thrilled to be dozens of feet in the air, buoyed by a winter flurry. Monty looked down, watching the guards attack

Callum. There was no such thing as a good cat as far as the mouse was concerned, not after the things he'd seen. Callum had his own motives for helping the prisoners, but he had put his life in peril on their behalf. Monty circled the melee then swooped down towards the cat at Callum's throat. He landed on the guard's back, surprising him. The caracal broke free.

The guard spun round, twisting his head to nip at the mouse. The other cats looked up as a flock of mice sailed through the open gate. Callum joined them, barging past the security staff. Monty was thrown to the ground and stamped to a pulp, his cap in ribbons; his killers bolted the gate and collapsed, knocked senseless by the chemicals that now clouded the air.

Everyone was too busy worrying about the big bang to bother Tiger. He made it to the gate with his hide intact. The guards lay on their sides, unconscious. There wasn't much left of Monty. Tiger mumbled a quick prayer for the mouse, blundered back to the sleeping quarters. Stringy tendrils of cheese hung from the guttering, brushing against his face.

Inside the bunk beds had been shifted with no attempt to disguise the tunnel mouth. Tiger made for the escape route, squeezing his way down the hole. Although it had been built for mice, there was enough room for him to wriggle through if he held his tummy in and stretched himself lengthways. The tunnel threatened to collapse behind him – every movement put a strain on the supports.

The air above was thick with toxic gas by now. Art and Walter were relieved to find the tunnel – it provided some cover and it meant their search had ended. Diving into the darkness, they used their noses and whiskers to navigate the treacherous burrow. It was a tight fit for them and the tunnel mouth closed behind them. They could only move forward.

Tiger heard the digging behind him, knew that he was being followed. The pursuers were making a lot of noise, too clumsy to be mice. As far as he knew Monty had successfully evacuated his lads. Tiger tried to speed up, breathing heavily. If some of the chemicals had reached the tunnel he could suffocate where he lay.

He jolted as Walter bit his tail. Kicking the goon with a swipe of his hind paw, Tiger moved on. There was no light ahead, only the sound of trickling earth. The roof would give out at any time.

The goons were blooded now. They would dig their way through the tunnel, chew through the cat to get out if necessary. There was no room for their quarry to turn and fight; he didn't stand a chance.

Tiger stopped moving, flattened himself into the cold soil, listening closely. A shower of dirt and stone sounded up ahead. The roof was caving in. A support cracked, earth came tumbling down in front of his nose. He was cornered.

He shoved his aching face forwards, using his nose and forepaws to make a path. The soil was loose enough for him push on, but his pace had slowed so much that the ferrets caught up, nipping at his pads. In a frenzy Art and Walter muscled towards him, trying to climb through the tunnel side by side. Another support gave way, burying them together.

Unable to breathe, Tiger smashed his way through the burrow, dragging himself out into the open. He took a deep breath and promptly coughed it out again, spitting a metallic taste from his mouth. The chemical cloud was rising but he wasn't clear of it yet. Holding a paw over his mouth and nose, he stumbled towards the train station. To his surprise, Callum was waiting there with the steam train, which had returned to pick up any stragglers. With the remaining mice already on board, Callum helped the detective into a carriage and the train whistled on its way.

31

'NOW DO YOU understand?'

'I think I can see where you're coming from.' Tiger stood in the gym, dishevelled and whiskerless, slouching with fatigue. Callum was slightly ruffled, while Big Cheese looked impeccable as ever, flanked by robed bodyguards. He invited the cats to sit down, with bowls of water close by to quench their thirst and platefuls of fish to replenish their strength. Callum tucked into his portion; Tiger abstained.

'Good. Shall I tell you what isn't so good? That wasn't the only facility round here, you know. Last year 1,457,292 mice were experimented on. A few survived. Murdered so that household appliances, food additives, cosmetics, toiletries, tobacco could pass the safety test.'

'What are you hoping to achieve?'

'I lost my brother to lewisite. They shaved his back, rubbed the poison into his skin. He was in agony for a month. They gassed my sister and electrocuted me, leaving me for dead. I rose again, Mr Straight, to avenge my family and set up a Kitty Killer Cult.'

'That doesn't give you the right to destroy my family too. Let 'em go, please. I'll help you.'

'They stay where they are now. I'd like to say they're being looked after; I'm afraid they're in terror for their lives. You understand my motives. I don't think you're going to agree with my methods.'

'How do you get cats to do your dirty work? Rig secret bank accounts? Murder their own kind?' Tiger stalled for time, watching Connie appear from a shadowy hallway.

'They disagree with the research experiments almost as much as I. I have the mental wherewithall to convince them that killing certain community members will help the cause.'

'That little kitten, Lona. How could her death help?' spat Tiger.

'A test of loyalty for my brothers, Mr Straight. I told them that she had to be destroyed and they believed me. Those members of the cult who have qualms about murder – your wife for example – well, I help them along a little.' Big Cheese held up a tiny capsule. 'Marlax. A mixture containing *valeriana officinalis* and acetylsalicylic acid, among other things. A small dose drives cats wild, almost psychotic; an overdose is fatal. A surgeon named Selwyn Mopp helped developed it – before he died. Too much shopping, I understand.'

'You gonna poison all the cats in this city? That's a toxic brew you've got in your paw.' Tiger signalled to Connie with his ears, waggling them in the direction of the swimming pool.

'You should try some of the fish,' Big Cheese sneered. 'It's quite delicious. Isn't it, Callum?'

The caracal didn't reply. Shaking his body from side to side, his eyes bloodshot, he was having a rabid reaction to the fish.

'Don't look like the fish agreed with him.'

'He'll meet a destructive, painful death.' Big Cheese shook his head slowly. 'Got to hurt.'

'Your chemicals are in the fish everyone's eating?'

'Call it an experiment. A marketing project to see how gullible your race are.'

'I don't get it. This'll be a dead city.'

'Select members of the Kitty Killer Cult will be spared. You can survive as well, Mr Straight. Pledge an oath to me and I'll let you live... I'll let your babies live.' A bell rope dangled beside the mouse. He batted it with a free paw.

'Your brethren have already had a few goes at me. Killed my partner. They didn't sink low enough to attack my kids.' Tiger spared a glance at Callum. He was hunkered down, biting so hard on his lower lip that blood was beginning to flow.

'I changed my mind. Saw your true potential. It took a while, but I saw it. I had to order the death of your assistant, however. A show of strength.'

'Join you? I might as well join the Commandant, help him with his experiments, if I could tell the difference between you both.'

Big Cheese pulled on the bell rope. In the distance, the kittens squealed. The mouse addressed his henchcat: 'Get rid of him, Callum.'

The caracal wasn't the sanest animal in the room at this point.

Frenzied and hungry, he loped for the closest food source in the room – a small, succulent mouse. Caught by surprise, Big Cheese let out a squeak as Callum devoured him. Tiger ran for the pool-room, desperate to save his babies; Connie joined him. The mouse's guards jumped onto Callum, ready to avenge their boss. They soon changed their minds. The big cat threw them against the dining table, emitting a deep-throated yowl. The guards backed off fast, running from the room.

Sniffing the air, his mind fuzzy, Callum followed Tiger and Connie in the direction of the swimming pool.

The kitlings fell into the water, mewing in unison. Connie fell into a crouch at the poolside, scanning the water for signs of life. The children were struggling beneath the surface. Overcoming her fear, she rolled into the deep water, stretching out her limbs to scoop up the little ones.

Tiger snatched at the net, using it to fish for the kittens. They were getting weaker, running out of breath. Connie splashed and choked, blinded. Tiger yelled directions to her, watching her tail quiver as she descended. The ripples ceased; Tiger couldn't see. He'd already lost his wife, the kittens' mother – would he lose the rest of his family as well?

A paw yanked at the net, almost unbalancing the detective. He hoisted a tiny figure from the depths. Tiger got as close to the water as he could, claws out, trying to gain a solid purchase. He pulled Banjo clear, Baby wrapped round her brother's tail. Tiger dipped his forepaws into the pool, helped Marthin free. There was no sign of Connie. Making sure that the kittens were breathing, Tiger held his nose and flopped into the pool, eyes stinging as he searched for his friend. By the time he found her, her lungs were full of water.

Placing Connie on her side, Tiger began to wash her rapidly. A shadow loomed over them. Callum still had his claws unsheathed, mouth bloody. The kittens were too weak to run; their father was too busy trying to revive Connie to care if Callum attacked him.

Bending down, the caracal placed a hefty paw on Tiger's shoulder.

'She's dead,' he said gently. Tiger didn't listen, sniffing at Connie's face, desperate for signs of life. A sobered Callum found a piece of canvas, wrapped it round the shivering infants. They revived to find their father weeping for joy over the spluttering form of Connie Hant.

Epilogue

SOON AFTER THE case of the Kitty Killer Cult, Tiger retired to look after his kids. He took small divorce or surveillance cases to supplement his welfare cheque, but stakeouts are tough with a pack of squealing weans in tow.

He loved to watch them grow, let them fend for themselves – yet he was always there for them. He'd amuse them with bedtime stories of old cases, battles with villains like Tommy Thin, the serial kitten drowner. Adventures with Bug, solving mysteries, getting into scrapes.

Rain battered at the windows, begging to come into the house and smother him with damp drops. The panes rattled now and then, craving attention. No Bug to share a meal, no wife to hold him close. His children were his sole joy. Soon they'd be old enough to help with chores, if they didn't bugger off first in a quest for independence.

The house was colder without Jo. She'd kept him warm, held him close, her hot breath on his neck and lips. The bed was half full, the teapot half-empty. Nobody nagged him or wasted his time conjuring foolish chores to keep him busy. His spare time was flat and there was too much milk in the fridge. It went off but Tiger still drank it. His tastebuds were numb and his stomach an unquenchable well.

The cubs would soon be old enough to see their mother, seek their misfortunes, look for jobs and accommodation in Central Nub. He'd tried to teach them as much as possible, using reverse psychology whenever he could. Preaching to them hadn't worked – he'd told them not to follow in his pawsteps and they'd already started playing detective. The other day he'd caught Banjo looking for smugglers in the back garden. He'd changed tack. Drink! Try smoking and eating vegetables! Take a dead end job! They'd learn by their own mistakes instead of his. It would take a little longer but they seemed to want it that way.

Occasionally he'd hear a police whistle or a shop alarm, grab his coat and hat. He never left the house. He was getting too old, and worried that he'd get himself killed. He had aches and buzzing in his ears, felt slower, clumsier. Who would be around to welcome the cubs if he got his fool head knocked off? It was wiser to stay indoors. Read about crime in the papers. Give the authorities a few tips over the phone. That was all he needed to keep content for now.

Thanks to Bix, the Kitty Killer Cult had been disbanded and outlawed. The mouse had taken all the credit for exposing the conspiracy. He was now living with Nut in a coastal commune, where animals didn't judge each other according to their species. The effects of Big Cheese's marlax were mercifully short-lived; the Cambor fish were taken off the market and Gerry the mercat had to sell his red robes to make ends meet. The mice that Tiger had rescued from the research compound had sold their story to a tabloid newspaper. With the money from their exclusive they'd bought the camp and transformed it into a training centre, teaching mice survival techniques with help from Callum and other ex-members of the cult. The centre turned a tidy profit.

Chief Inspector Bowyer had taken early retirement, and no blame for the dastardly murders, despite eating a suspect. Miss Angold was now manager of the Nub City Municipal Bank – her predatory nature had proved highly useful in the financial world. Ike Straight published educational books.

Tiger had taken his sons and daughter to a business park in Stenmuir. He'd tried to explain to them that he'd married their mother there, that he missed her gravely. Marthin, Baby and Banjo were too busy playing round a fledgling willow tree.

As the rain withdrew its siege, Tiger drifted off to sleep. He dreamt of past glories on an underworld battlefield, his sidekick Bug looking up to him, waiting for him to save the day.

Some other books published by **LUATH** PRESS

Milk Treading
Nick Smith
ISBN 1 84282 037 0 PB £6.99

Life isn't easy for Julius Kyle, a jaded crime hack with the *Post*. When he wakes up on a sand barge with his head full of grit he knows things have to change. But how fast they'll change he doesn't guess until his best friend Mick jumps to his death off a fifty foot bridge outside the *Post*'s window. Worst of all, he's a cat. That means keeping himself scrupulously clean, defending his territory and battling an addiction to milk. He lives in Bast, a sprawling city of alleyways and claw-shaped towers... join Julius as he prowls deep into the crooked underworld of Bast, contending with political intrigue, territorial disputes and dog-burglars, murder, mystery and mayhem.

This is certainly the only cat-centred political thriller that I've read and it has a weird charm, not to mention considerable humour...
AL KENNEDY

A trip into a surreal and richly-realised feline-canine world. ELLEN GALFORD

Milk Treading is equal parts Watership Down, Animal Farm, and The Big Sleep. A novel of class struggle, political intrigue and good old-fashioned murder and intrigue. And, oh yeah, all the characters are either cats or dogs. TOD GOLDBERG,
LAS VEGAS MERCURY

Smith writes with wit and energy creating a memorable brood of characters...
ALAN RADCLIFFE, THE LIST

Driftnet
Lin Anderson
ISBN 1 84282 034 6 PB £9.99

Introducing forensic scientist Dr Rhona MacLeod...

A teenager is found strangled and mutilated in a Glasgow flat.

Leaving her warm bed and lover in the middle of the night to take forensic samples from the body, Rhona MacLeod immediately perceives a likeness between herself and the dead boy and is tortured by the thought that he might be the son she gave up for adoption seventeen years before.

Amidst the turmoil of her own love life and consumed by guilt from her past, Rhona sets out to find both the boy's killer and her own son. But the powerful men who use the Internet to trawl for vulnerable boys have nothing to lose and everything to gain by Rhona MacLeod's death.

A strong new player on the crime novel scene, Lin Anderson skilfully interweaves themes of betrayal, violence and guilt. In forensic investigator Rhona MacLeod she has created a complex character who will have readers coming back for more.

Lin Anderson has a rare gift. She is one of the few able to convey urban and rural Scotland with equal truth... Compelling, vivid stuff. I couldn't put it put it down.'
ANNE MACLEOD, AUTHOR OF THE DARK SHIP

But n Ben A-Go-Go
Matthew Fitt
ISBN 1 84282 041 1 PB £6.99

The year is 2090. Global flooding has left most of Scotland under water. The descendants of those who survived God's Flood live in a community of floating island parishes, known collectively as Port. Port's citizens live in mortal fear of Senga, a supervirus whose victims are kept in a giant hospital warehouse in sealed capsules called Kists. Paolo Broon is a low-ranking cyberjanny. His life-partner, Nadia, lies forgotten and alone in Omega Kist 624 in the Rigo Imbeki Medical Center. When he receives an unexpected message from his radge criminal father to meet him at But n Ben A-Go-Go, Paolo's life is changed forever. He must traverse VINE, Port and the Drylands and deal with rebel American tourists and crabbit Dundonian microchips to discover the truth about his family's past in order to free Nadia from the sair grip of the merciless Senga. Set in a distinctly unbonnie future-Scotland, the novel's dangerous atmosphere and psychologically-malkied characters weave a tale that both chills and intrigues. In *But n Ben A-Go-Go* Matthew Fitt takes the allegedly dead language of Scots and energises it with a narrative that crackles and fizzes with life.

I recommend an entertaining and ground-breaking book. EDWIN MORGAN

... if you can't get hold of a copy, mug somebody MARK STEPHEN, SCOTTISH CONNECTION, BBC RADIO SCOTLAND

the last man who tried anything like this was Hugh MacDiarmid MICHAEL FRY, TODAY PROGRAMME, BBC RADIO 4

going where no man has gone before STEPHEN NAYSMITH, SUNDAY HERALD

The Road Dance
John MacKay
ISBN 1 84282 040 0 PB £6.99

Why would a young woman, dreaming of a new life in America, sacrifice all and commit an act so terrible that she severs all hope of happiness again?

Life in the Scottish Hebrides can be harsh – 'The Edge of the World' some call it. For the beautiful Kirsty MacLeod, the love of Murdo and their dream of America promise an escape from the scrape of the land, the repression of the church and the inevitability of the path their lives would take. But the Great War looms and Murdo is conscripted. The village holds a grand Road Dance to send their young men off to battle.

As the dancers swirl and sup, the wheels of tragedy are set in motion.

[MacKay] has captured time, place and atmosphere superbly... a very good debut. MEG HENDERSON

Powerful, shocking, heartbreaking... DAILY MAIL

With a gripping plot that subtly twists and turns, vivid characterisation and a real sense of time and tradition, this is an absorbing, powerful first novel. The impression it made on me will remain for some time. THE SCOTS MAGAZINE

The Great Melnikov

Hugh MacLachlan

ISBN 0 946487 42 1 PB £7.95

 A well crafted, gripping novel, written in a style reminiscent of John Buchan and set in London and the Scottish Highlands during the First World War, *The Great Melnikov* is a dark tale of double-cross and deception.

We first meet Melnikov, one-time star of the German circus, languishing as a down-and-out in Trafalgar Square. He soon finds himself drawn into a tortuous web of intrigue.

He is a complex man whose personal struggle with alcoholism is an inner drama which parallels the tense twists and turns as a spy mystery unfolds.

Melnikov's options are narrowing. The circle of threat is closing.

Will Melnikov outwit the sinister enemy spy network? Can he summon the will and the wit to survive?

Hugh MacLachlan, in his first full length novel, demonstrates an undoubted ability to tell a good story well.

His earlier stories have been broadcast on Radio Scotland, and he has the rare distinction of being shortlisted for the Macallan/Scotland on Sunday Short Story Competition two years in succession.

Short, sharp and to the point... racing along to a suitably cinematic ending, richly descriptive, yet clear and lean. THE SCOTSMAN

The Strange Case of RL Stevenson

Richard Woodhead

ISBN 0 946487 86 3 HB £16.99

 A consultant physician for 22 years with a strong interest in Robert Louis Stevenson's life and work, Richard Woodhead was intrigued by the questions raised by the references to his symptoms. The assumption that he suffered from consumption (tuberculosis) – the diagnosis of the day – is challenged in *The Strange Cast of RL Stevenson*. Dr Woodhead examines how Stevenson's life was affected by his illness and his perception of it. This fictional work puts words into the mouths of five doctors who treated RLS at different periods of his adult life. Though these doctors existed in real-life, little is documented of their private conversations with RLS. However, everything Dr Woodhead postulates could have occurred within the known framework of RLS's life. RLS's writing continues to compel readers today. The fact that he did much of his writing while confined to his sick-bed is fascinating. What illness could have contributed to his creativity?

This pleasantly unassuming book describes the medical history of Robert Louis Stevenson through a series of fictional reminiscences... I thoroughly enjoyed it. This would make a charming gift for any enthusiastic fan of RLS. MEDICAL HISTORY JOURNAL

RLS himself is very much a real figure, as is Fanny, his wife, while his parents are sympathetically and touchingly portrayed. SCOTS MAGAZINE

his factual research is faultless, resulting in a very good and very readable novel written in the spirit of the time... My prescription: take one of the five parts per diem as a lovely Book at Bedtime.' BRIAN DAVIS , TIME OUT

FICTION

Six Black Candles
Des Dillon
ISBN 1 84282 053 2 PB £6.99

Me and My Gal
Des Dillon
ISBN 1 84282 054 0 PB £5.99

The Bannockburn Years
William Scott
ISBN 0 946487 34 0 PB £7.95

Outlandish Affairs: An Anthology of Amorous Encounters
Edited and introduced by Evan Rosenthal and Amanda Robinson
ISBN 1 84282 055 9 PB £9.99

The Fundamentals of New Caledonia
David Nicol
ISBN 0 946487 93 6 HB £16.99

POETRY

Drink the Green Fairy
Brian Whittingham
ISBN 1 84282 045 1 PB £8.99

The Ruba'iyat of Omar Khayyam, in Scots
Rab Wilson
ISBN 1 84282 046 X PB £8.99 (book)
ISBN 1 84282 070 2 £9.99 (audio CD)

Talking with Tongues
Brian Finch
ISBN 1 84282 006 0 PB £8.99

Kate o Shanter's Tale and other poems
Matthew Fitt
ISBN 1 84282 028 1 PB £6.99 (book)
ISBN 1 84282 043 5 £9.99 (audio CD)

Bad Ass Raindrop
Kokumo Rocks
ISBN 1 84282 018 4 PB £6.99

Madame Fi Fi's Farewell and other poems
Gerry Cambridge
ISBN 1 84282 005 2 PB £8.99

Scots Poems to be Read Aloud
Introduced by Stuart McHardy
ISBN 0 946487 81 2 PB £5.00

Picking Brambles and other poems
Des Dillon
ISBN 1 84282 021 4 PB £6.99

Sex, Death & Football
Alistair Findlay
ISBN 1 84282 022 2 PB £6.99

Tartan & Turban
Bashabi Fraser
ISBN 1 84282 044 3 PB £8.99

Immortal Memories: A Compilation of Toasts to the Memory of Burns as delivered at Burns Suppers, 1801-2001
John Cairney
ISBN 1 84282 009 5 HB £20.00

Poems to be Read Aloud
Introduced by Tom Atkinson
ISBN 0 946487 00 6 PB £5.00

Men and Beasts: wild men and tame animals
Valerie Gillies and Rebecca Marr
ISBN 0 946487 92 8 PB £15.00

FOLKLORE

Scotland: Myth, Legend & Folklore
Stuart McHardy
ISBN 0 946487 69 3 PB £7.99

Luath Storyteller: Highland Myths & Legends
George W Macpherson
ISBN 1 84282 064 8 PB £5.00

Tales of the North Coast
Alan Temperley
ISBN 0 946487 18 9 PB £8.99

Tall Tales from an Island
Peter Macnab
ISBN 0 946487 07 3 PB £8.99

The Supernatural Highlands
Francis Thompson
ISBN 0 946487 31 6 PB £8.99

CARTOONS

Broomie Law
Cinders McLeod
ISBN 0 946487 99 5 PB £4.00

THE QUEST FOR

The Quest for Charles Rennie Mackintosh
John Cairney
ISBN 1 84282 058 3 HB £16.99

The Quest for Robert Louis Stevenson
John Cairney
ISBN 0 946487 87 1 HB £16.99

The Quest for the Nine Maidens
Stuart McHardy
ISBN 0 946487 66 9 HB £16.99

The Quest for the Original Horse Whisperers
Russell Lyon
ISBN 1 842820 020 6 HB £16.99

The Quest for the Celtic Key
Karen Ralls-MacLeod and
Ian Robertson
ISBN 0 946487 73 1 HB £18.99
ISBN 1 84282 031 1 PB £8.99

The Quest for Arthur
Stuart McHardy
ISBN 1 842820 12 5 HB £16.99

ON THE TRAIL OF

On the Trail of William Wallace
David R Ross
ISBN 0 946487 47 2 PB £7.99

On the Trail of Robert the Bruce
David R Ross
ISBN 0 946487 52 9 PB £7.99

On the Trail of Mary Queen of Scots
J Keith Cheetham
ISBN 0 946487 50 2 PB £7.99

On the Trail of Bonnie Prince Charlie
David R Ross
ISBN 0 946487 68 5 PB £7.99

On the Trail of Robert Burns
John Cairney
ISBN 0 946487 51 0 PB £7.99

On the Trail of John Muir
Cherry Good
ISBN 0 946487 62 6 PB £7.99

On the Trail of Queen Victoria in the Highlands
Ian R Mitchell
ISBN 0 946487 79 0 PB £7.99

On the Trail of Robert Service
G Wallace Lockhart
ISBN 0 946487 24 3 PB £7.99

On the Trail of the Pilgrim Fathers
J Keith Cheetham
ISBN 0 946487 83 9 PB £7.99

On the Trail of John Wesley
J Keith Cheetham
ISBN 1 84282 023 0 PB £7.99

On the Trail of Scotland's Myths & Legends
Stuart McHardy
ISBN 1 84282 049 4 PB £7.99

LUATH GUIDES TO SCOTLAND

The North West Highlands: Roads to the Isles
Tom Atkinson
ISBN 0 946487 54 5 PB £4.95

Mull and Iona: Highways and Byways
Peter Macnab
ISBN 0 946487 58 8 PB £4.95

The Northern Highlands: The Empty Lands
Tom Atkinson
ISBN 0 946487 55 3 PB £4.95

The West Highlands: The Lonely Lands
Tom Atkinson
ISBN 0 946487 56 1 PB £4.95

HISTORY

Scots in Canada
Jenni Calder
ISBN 1 84282 038 9 PB £7.99

Civil Warrior
Robin Bell
ISBN 1 84282 013 3 HB £10.99

A Passion for Scotland
David R Ross
ISBN 1 84282 019 2 PB £5.99

Reportage Scotland
Louise Yeoman
ISBN 1 84282 051 6 PB £6.99

Blind Harry's Wallace
Hamilton of Gilbertfield
[introduced by Elspeth King]
ISBN 0 946487 33 2 PB £8.99

Plaids & Bandanas: Highland Drover to Wild West Cowboy
Rob Gibson
ISBN 0 946487 88 X PB £7.99

Napiers History of Herbal Healing, Ancient and Modern
Tom Atkinson
ISBN 1 84282 025 7 HB £16.99

POLITICS & CURRENT ISSUES

Scotlands of the Mind
Angus Calder
ISBN 1 84282 008 7 PB £9.99

Trident on Trial: the case for people's disarmament
Angie Zelter
ISBN 1 84282 004 4 PB £9.99

Uncomfortably Numb: A Prison Requiem
Maureen Maguire
ISBN 1 84282 001 X PB £8.99

Scotland: Land & Power – the Agenda for Land Reform
Andy Wightman
ISBN 0 946487 70 7 PB £5.00

Old Scotland New Scotland
Jeff Fallow
ISBN 0 946487 40 5 PB £6.99

Some Assembly Required: Behind the scenes at the Re-birth of the Scottish Parliament
David Shepherd
ISBN 0 946487 84 7 PB £7.99

Notes from the North Incorporating a brief history of the Scots and the English
Emma Wood
ISBN 1 84282 048 6 PB £7.99

Scotlands of the Future: sustainability in a small nation
ed Eurig Scandrett
ISBN 1 84282 035 4 PB £7.99

Eurovision or American Dream? Britain, the Euro and the Future of Europe
David Purdy
ISBN 1 84282 036 2 PB £3.99

NATURAL WORLD

The Hydro Boys: pioneers of renewable energy
Emma Wood
ISBN 1 84282 047 8 PB £8.99

Wild Scotland
James McCarthy
ISBN 0 946487 37 5 PB £8.99

Wild Lives: Otters – On the Swirl of the Tide
Bridget MacCaskill
ISBN 0 946487 67 7 PB £9.99

Wild Lives: Foxes – The Blood is Wild
Bridget MacCaskill
ISBN 0 946487 71 5 PB £9.99

Scotland – Land & People: An Inhabited Solitude
James McCarthy
ISBN 0 946487 57 X PB £7.99

The Highland Geology Trail
John L Roberts
ISBN 0 946487 36 7 PB £5.99

Red Sky at Night
John Barrington
ISBN 0 946487 60 X PB £8.99

Listen to the Trees
Don MacCaskill
ISBN 0 946487 65 0 PB £9.99

WALK WITH LUATH

Skye 360: walking the coastline of Skye
Andrew Dempster
ISBN 0 946487 85 5 PB £8.99

Walks in the Cairngorms
Ernest Cross
ISBN 0 946487 09 X PB £4.95

Short Walks in the Cairngorms
Ernest Cross
ISBN 0 946487 23 5 PB £4.95

The Joy of Hillwalking
Ralph Storer
ISBN 1 84282 069 9 PB £7.50

Scotland's Mountains before the Mountaineers
Ian R Mitchell
ISBN 0 946487 39 1 PB £9.99

Mountain Days and Bothy Nights
Dave Brown and Ian R Mitchell
ISBN 0 946487 15 4 PB £7.50

Mountain Outlaw
Ian R. Mitchell
ISBN 1 84282 027 3 PB £6.50

SPORT

Ski & Snowboard Scotland
Hilary Parke
ISBN 0 946487 35 9 PB £6.99

Over the Top with the Tartan Army
Andy McArthur
ISBN 0 946487 45 6 PB £7.99

SOCIAL HISTORY

Pumpherston: the story of a shale oil village
Sybil Cavanagh
ISBN 1 84282 011 7 HB £17.99
ISBN 1 84282 015 X PB £7.99

Shale Voices
Alistair Findlay
ISBN 0 946487 78 2 HB £17.99
ISBN 0 946487 63 4 PB £10.99

A Word for Scotland
Jack Campbell
ISBN 0 946487 48 0 PB £12.99

TRAVEL & LEISURE

Die Kleine Schottlandfibel [Scotland Guide in German]
Hans-Walter Arends
ISBN 0 946487 89 8 PB £8.99

s Explore Edinburgh Old Town
Anne Bruce English
ISBN 0 946487 98 7 PB £4.99

Let's Explore Berwick Upon Tweed
Anne Bruce English
ISBN 1 84282 029 X PB £4.99

Edinburgh's Historic Mile
Duncan Priddle
ISBN 0 946487 97 9 PB £2.99

Pilgrims in the Rough: St Andrews beyond the 19th hole
Michael Tobert
ISBN 0 946487 74 X PB £7.99

LANGUAGE

Luath Scots Language Learner [Double Audio CD]
L Colin Wilson
ISBN 0 946487 91 X PB £9.99 (book)
ISBN 1 84282 026 5 CD £16.99

FOOD & DRINK

The Whisky Muse: Scotch whisky in poem & song
various, edited and compiled by
Robin Laing
ISBN 1 84282 041 9 PB £7.99

First Foods Fast: how to prepare good simple meals for your baby
Lara Boyd
ISBN 1 84282 002 8 PB £4.99

Edinburgh and Leith Pub Guide
Stuart McHardy
ISBN 0 946487 80 4 PB £4.95

BIOGRAPHY

The Last Lighthouse
Sharma Krauskopf
ISBN 0 946487 96 0 PB £7.99

Tobermory Teuchter
Peter Macnab
ISBN 0 946487 41 3 PB £7.99

Bare Feet and Tackety Boots
Archie Cameron
ISBN 0 946487 17 0 PB £7.95

Come Dungeons Dark
John Taylor Caldwell
ISBN 0 946487 19 7 PB £6.95

GENEALOGY

Scottish Roots: step-by-step guide for ancestor hunters
Alwyn James
ISBN 1 84282 007 9 PB £9.99

WEDDINGS, MUSIC AND DANCE

The Scottish Wedding Book
G Wallace Lockhart
ISBN 1 94282 010 9 PB £12.99

Fiddles and Folk
G Wallace Lockhart
ISBN 0 946487 38 3 PB £7.95

Highland Balls and Village Halls
G Wallace Lockhart
ISBN 0 946487 12 X PB £6.95

Luath Press Limited
committed to publishing well written books worth reading

LUATH PRESS takes its name from Robert Burns, whose little collie Luath (*Gael.*, swift or nimble) tripped up Jean Armour at a wedding and gave him the chance to speak to the woman who was to be his wife and the abiding love of his life. Burns called one of *The Twa Dogs* Luath after Cuchullin's hunting dog in *Ossian's Fingal*. Luath Press was established in 1981 in the heart of Burns country, and is now based a few steps up the road from Burns' first lodgings on Edinburgh's Royal Mile. Luath offers you distinctive writing with a hint of unexpected pleasures.

Most bookshops in the UK, the US, Canada, Australia, New Zealand and parts of Europe either carry our books in stock or can order them for you. To order direct from us, please send a £sterling cheque, postal order, international money order or your credit card details (number, address of cardholder and expiry date) to us at the address below. Please add post and packing as follows: UK – £1.00 per delivery address; overseas surface mail – £2.50 per delivery address; overseas airmail – £3.50 for the first book to each delivery address, plus £1.00 for each additional book by airmail to the same address. If your order is a gift, we will happily enclose your card or message at no extra charge.

Luath Press Limited
543/2 Castlehill
The Royal Mile
Edinburgh EH1 2ND
Scotland
Telephone: 0131 225 4326 (24 hours)
Fax: 0131 225 4324
email: gavin.macdougall@luath.co.uk
Website: www.luath.co.uk